SECRETS
Vicious rumors that mean nothing—
and everything!

"High-tension. Fascinating. Nobody, surely, is better equipped to describe all of this, and Bailey makes the most of it . . . An absorbing story."
—*San Francisco Chronicle*

"Bailey, just as much a spellbinder in print as he is in the courtroom, spins out a melodrama alive with legal intrigue."
—*Publishers Weekly*

"A real humdinger . . . Distinctly superior!"
—*John Barkham Reviews*

"Nice and crisp, especially the cross-examination . . . and the seamy background of the cases—a web of corrupt witnesses, old grudges and criminal mischief—has the gamy reek of the real thing."
—*The New York Times Book Review*

SECRETS

The truth can cheat you
and set the wrong men free!

**Selected by Book-of-the-Month Club,
The Playboy Book Club, and
Lawyer's Literary Guild**

SECRETS

A Novel by
F. Lee Bailey

This low-priced Bantam Book
has been completely reset in a type face
designed for easy reading, and was printed
from new plates. It contains the complete
text of the original hard-cover edition.
NOT ONE WORD HAS BEEN OMITTED.

SECRETS

A Bantam Book / published by arrangement with
Stein and Day, Publishers, Inc.

PRINTING HISTORY

Stein and Day edition published December 1978
4 printings through February 1979
Book-of-the-Month Club edition June 1979
Macmillan Book Club edition February 1979
Preferred Choice Bookplan February 1979
A midwinter selection of the Playboy Book Club
Bantam edition / October 1979
2nd printing

All but six of the characters in this book are fictional crea-
tions, and any resemblance to persons living or dead is
coincidental. The real people are: Helen Dudar, Judge Kevin
Duffy, Arthur Miller, Alfred C. Redfield, Wallace Turner,
and Theo Wilson.

ISBN 0-553-12896-5

Published simultaneously in the United States and Canada

Bantam Books are published by Bantam Books, Inc. Its trademark, consisting of the words "Bantam Books" and the por-
trayal of a bantam, is Registered in U.S. Patent and Trademark
Office and in other countries. Marca Registrada. Bantam
Books, Inc., 666 Fifth Avenue, New York, New York 10019.

This book is dedicated to Judge Gary Somerville, a symbol and a composite of the many superb trial judges—state, federal, and military—that I have been privileged to appear before in more than twenty-five years of trials.

Acknowledgments

My deep gratitude to Dr. Cyril Wecht, pathologist, colleague, and friend who is the coroner of Allegheny County, Pennsylvania for his guidance in the medical section; to Arthur Miller, famed physical oceanographer of the Woods Hole Oceanographic Institute; to Edna Adams, Marsha Marx, Harriet Christeck, and Barbara Burie for their tireless efforts in retyping the manuscript; and to Sol Stein, Patricia Day, and Wallace Exman for patient and excellent editorial advice.

Contents

1

NIGHT WATCH
Thursday, June 8

The wind from the southwest blew at a steady clip, driving the big ketch at eight knots. The night was clear, and the electric autopilot held a course of east by nor'-east. The main, mizzen, and working jib were trimmed to precision, the latter on a traveler so that there would be no sheets to handle when tacking.

Below, in the main cabin, a soft light glowed from the hurricane lamp on the aft bulkhead. The power in the hugh storage batteries was reserved for the autopilot, the Loran navigation radio, and the radar, whose round, black screen was lit only by the azimuth rings, showing clear seas for the next sixteen miles.

The woman put aside her magazine and gazed at the man who snored softly and intermittently on the windward bunk. He had been sleeping heavily since shortly after they had set sail three hours earlier. It was now midnight; she was supposed to awaken him to take the watch. She knew that, exhausted and filled with whiskey, he would never be able to keep his eyes open for thirty minutes even if he could be roused. She would get him up at four. Seven hours was always enough.

She slid her hand under her wool slacks and slowly rubbed her belly. There was an ache in her loins as she looked at him. It would have to wait till morning when they would tie an air mattress to the deck and make love in the sunshine. She rose from her chair, crossed the cabin to the galley, and lit the propane burner under the tea kettle.

Suddenly, above the hiss of the fiberglass hull sliding through the sea, she heard a soft but audible splashing sound, coming and fading. Pulling a windbreaker on over her sweater, she stepped up through the companionway to the center cockpit. She intended only to glance about quickly and did not put on her life jacket or her safety line. If he had been awake, she thought, he would have scolded her severely.

She noticed a bank of cumulus clouds overtaking them from the stern. The moon seemed to duck in and out of the clouds, dappling the faint light on the water. The compass, glowing a dull red, was steady on course. The helm moved jerkily but rhythmically from side to side, answering the commands of the microcomputer in the autopilot. For a moment, she allowed her eyes to adjust to the low illumination. Then she noticed, only fifty yards to the south of the ship, two dark shapes surface and then submerge. That was where the splashing sound was coming from!

She stepped to the windward rail for a better look, grasping a mizzen shroud lightly in her right hand to steady herself. She could make out two medium-sized whales swimming in escort to the ship.

She watched them, marveling to herself at the smooth grace with which their massive bulks cleaved the black water. So rapt was her attention that she did not notice the slackening in the breeze as it dropped to ten knots, then five.

The rattle of the sails she heard too late. As the first cloud passed overhead, the wind veered suddenly and sharply to the northwest. A strong gust seized the mainsail and jibed it hard to starboard.

The outhaul cleat on the end of the boom smashed the base of her skull, fracturing bone, and propelling her headfirst into the sea.

The whales took no notice.

The autopilot trimmed the rudder to hold course on the port tack, and the *Kenyon* rose to eight and one-half knots as the new breeze steadied out slightly stronger than its predecessor.

It was nearly five o'clock when the man awakened to an acrid smell in the cabin. The tea kettle, dry now, was glowing cherry red over the low blue flame of the propane cooking element, burning its life away. He shook his head and felt the stabbing pain of a hangover headache. He looked around the cabin for the woman and thought she might have gone on deck. But no, there were her life jacket and safety harness on the hook next to the chart table. She wouldn't venture topside at night, even in good weather, without proper regard for the rules.

He stumbled aft to the master stateroom, checked the head, then lunged to the forward cabin. Vacant. Could she have fallen asleep in the cockpit? Possibilities flashed through his brain in a jumble when suddenly he realized that they were on a port tack. When had she jibed the ship? He snatched his safety harness from its hook and charged up the ladder to the cockpit. He clipped the shackle to an eye in one of the starboard stanchions, scouring the deck in the graying hint of dawn.

Vacant.

The pain in his skull shrieked at him that she had gone overboard while he slept, and he began to shout "No!" in a rising crescendo as if he could alter the fact by denying it. The pit of his stomach, cold and knotted, wanted to vomit out the horror that was determined to envelop him. He had to wake from the awful nightmare that could only be a dream and find her sitting quietly in her chair below.

When his mind had begun to slowly, agonizingly recover from the shock, a part of him began to think. The training of the subconscious took over mechanically from the conscious, which was jellied, incapable of logical thought. The facts must be pieced together.

The continuous recorded weather broadcast reported that a cold front had passed the eastern shore of Massachusetts at eleven o'clock, moving at a speed of twenty-five knots. Little weather was associated with it, other than brisk northwest winds and cooler temperatures. The ocean water was forty-eight degrees. He computed swiftly. The front would have overtaken the ketch a little after midnight, forty miles to the west. The ship had jibed then, perhaps unexpectedly. The most obvious, classic, sailing accident at sea, a boom slamming across the deck uncontrolled. . . .

The hands were reluctant as they hauled in the main sheet until the boom was nearly centered over the cockpit. The eyes saw the clump of hair caught on the outhaul cleat and the brown stain on the anodized aluminum of the boom. The fingers touched the stain with horror, and a part of it scaled off and blew away on the wind, like dark ashes.

She was dead. There was no hope.

The man stared mindlessly over the stern at the uncaring sea where his love had gone. His body shook with great, shuddering, sorrowful, heaving, lonely, wracking sobs. . . .

2

THE MEETING
Monday, June 26

Walter Barrett's watery blue eyes, sad features above a weak chin, and forlorn expression stared unhappily out of his office window in the back of the old Essex County Superior Courthouse in Salem on the north shore of Boston. His uncle Carl, due to arrive soon, always made Walter feel uncomfortable.

Walter, thirty-five, given lately to a budding softness in the paunch, had lost his father in a plane crash when he was five; his father's brother Carl had acted as surrogate. While showing little or no affection or pride for the boy, he had driven him relentlessly up to and through law school and had then arranged for him to join Carl's influential firm, Barrett, Worcester, and Howe. Walter, try as he might, could muster only an average performance as a lawyer and had grown accustomed to his uncle's frequent grimaces of disdain. Then after Walter had been ten years with the firm, Essex County District Attorney, Kevin Halloran, had accepted an appointment to the Superior Court Bench, and Carl had used his considerable muscle in the Governor's office to get Walter an interim appointment to the vacated post. Walter did not view with great optimism the primary in September or the election in November. A number of more experienced trial lawyers were making noises that they might give him some vigorous opposition at both plateaus. Walter knew, furthermore, that Essex County, while reasonably balanced, was no Republican stronghold. Walter was not personally terribly enthusiastic about the job, but he knew that his uncle intended to see to it that he ran—and ran hard—to keep it. Carl enjoyed having the prosecutor of his county of residence conveniently at the end of his private telephone line.

Carl Barrett waddled into Walter's office unannounced, as he always did, scowling, as he usually was, and plopped into the worn, overstuffed, leather chair next to Walter's desk. He was a homely hulk of a man with a froglike countenance and a rim of gray hair. He wore large, round glasses through which he was in habit of staring, heavy-lidded and impassive, whenever he was discussing a matter of consequence.

"Walter," he began, coming right to the point, "I believe that we may have on our hands perhaps one of the most important homicides in Essex County's history."

Walter, reflecting on the joke about the Lone Ranger and Tonto, resisted an impulse to retort "What's this *we* shit, white man? *I* am the goddam district attorney of this goddam county, not your goddam puppet or your goddam partner." Instead, he cleared his throat. "I, uh, wasn't aware that there had been a homicide. Is this something very recent?"

"Oh indeed," replied the elder Barrett, his eyes lighting up, "Yes, indeed. Earlier this month, perhaps. At this point I should say suspected homicide, but I think careful inquiry into the circumstances will show it to be quite real."

"Who is dead?"

"A single lady named Sarah Hansen. Early to midforties. Quite a handsome creature I'm told. An interior decorator of some talent. Lived alone on Marblehead Neck. Hasn't been seen for almost three weeks." Carl paused, measuring his nephew's reaction.

"I know the woman you're talking about," he said.

"I've seen her a few times at the Boston Yacht Club over in the harbor. Who says she's missing?"

- "An excellent source," replied Barrett. "My good friend Detective Lieutenant Gilardi of the State Police headquarters unit stopped by to visit with me this morning. It seems that Gilardi was listening to a telephone conversation between a man and a woman two days ago in connection with an unrelated investigation. Heard the man say something to the effect that 'Sarah *was* a wonderful woman.' Started checking around for reports of missing persons and came up with this Hansen woman's name. Checked further, and found that no one— neighbors, people at the yacht club, her answering service—has seen hide nor hair of her since the seventh of June. That's nearly three weeks ago."

"Who were the man and woman Gilardi overheard?"

"He couldn't identify the woman," said Carl. "But the male voice, and the owner of the telephone from which the call originated, was Michael Kilrayne."

"Jesus," said Walter, as if he had been kicked sharply in the backside. "Jesus H. Christ!"

At seven-fifteen that same evening, Walter Barrett sat sipping a vodka martini in a booth at LeRoux' Cocktail Lounge in Ipswich, waiting for the arrival of Detective Lieutenant Joseph Gilardi. Carl had thought it best that the initial meeting be unobserved by members of the staff, and particularly by Detective Sergeant Ed Wilson, Walter's regularly assigned chief investigator. His afternoon meeting with Carl had lasted for three hours, and the old man had made it all too clear what he was to do. Go after Kilrayne like a mongoose after a cobra.

There was little doubt that Kilrayne had disposed of the woman as ruthlessly as he demolished witnesses on the stand and abused litigants who were the victims of his rough legal tactics. Good, thorough investigation would show that, and Gilardi was the man to handle it.

The best and smartest on the force, it was said. Carl could arrange his assignment to the case.

More important, Carl had said with undisguised pleasure, Walter needed some increased visibility for the forthcoming election. Too many men in the street would not recognize his name by September.

Although Kilrayne was Boston's top criminal lawyer and enjoyed some degree of popularity, he was viewed as a womanizer and a man of too much cunning by naive folks, Carl believed. Walter's willingness to bring this legal giant to the bar of justice for an infamous crime could win him nothing but a good press and the admiration of the "better class of voters," whatever that was. Walter was a little snowed by the whole idea, and yet he could not suppress a faint buzz of excitement.

Detective Lieutenant Joseph Gilardi shook hands briefly as he slid into the booth across from Walter and ordered himself a Wild Turkey bourbon on the rocks. He was of medium height, forty-eight, swarthy, and heavy set. His lined face was set off by thick, black hair just going to gray, and dark, button-brown eyes that had stared more than one killer into a confession. He was not an unattractive man and had long since foregone the usual detective's affinity for pipe-rack suits and white socks in exchange for a fair measure of sartorial elegance. He could have passed for a successful Italian businessman from Boston's North End. He had in fact been raised in Revere, the eldest of seven children, street-wise before he was a teenager. In twenty-three years as a police officer, he had matured into a tough, shrewd cop, with the indefatigable doggedness of a Columbo. With only a high school education behind him and several men with college degrees in police science on the force, Gilardi had amassed a superior record of success by cutting corners.

Gilardi took a deep draw of his bourbon and smiled pleasantly at Walter.

"I understand your uncle filled you in on our conversation this morning?"

Walter nodded. "He did, but I'm not sure I believe there's much of a case so far. One missing person, no corpse, and a phone conversation which was probably illegally overheard. And the suspect, if you can call him that, knows the homicide game better than I do and probably better than either of us."

Gilardi was somewhat taken aback by the forceful stand of the young prosecutor. Carl had led him to believe that Walter was a fellow of easy persuasion. He suspected, correctly, that more than one vodka martini had been doing some of the talking. He decided to dispense with the pleasantries and meet fire with fire.

"We have quite a bit more than that," he replied softly but heavily. "First, we have my gut feeling that Kilrayne knocked this woman off. You won't like this, but when you've been in the business a while you'll learn to trust the gut of an experienced detective, particularly in homicide cases. Second, I've established that Kilrayne represented this Hansen woman twelve years ago for driving while intoxicated, so he knew her. Third, I've checked her house—not a thorough search, I'll do that tomorrow, just a quick look-see. There's a sterling silver, table-type, cigarette lighter on the mantelpiece in the living room. Inscribed on the underside in very tiny characters—so tiny I had to use to glass to read them—it says, 'Love, M.K.'

"Now then, that may not be a case—I'll admit there isn't enough yet. But it sure as hell is enough to warrant a further investigation. If you think it's too hot for you, I'm prepared to go to the attorney general and ask him to assume jurisdiction. He might, and he might not, but I think I've got enough to take a shot at it."

Gilardi lit a cigarette and inhaled deeply, hoping his bluff would fly. He personally had every reason to doubt that the attorney general would do any such thing, particularly with an election on the horizon.

Walter, smiling wanly at Gilardi, felt a mixture of frustration and defeat. "It occurs to me," he said slowly, "that intervention by the attorney general when I have been in office only three months would be a loud message to the public that I am incompetent to enforce the law in this county. I suspect that if that were to happen, Uncle Carl would make my life miserable for as long as he lives. What is your pleasure, Lieutenant?"

Gilardi sighed, and his features relaxed. "Look, Mr. Barrett," he said, trying to keep his tone respectful, "I think I know what I'm doing. I'll do a deal with you. You give me one week. Seven solid days. Let me exercise my sources. Very quietly, nobody but you and me and your uncle will know anything's up. I'll report back to you then. If you think the case is a bummer, I'll go with your judgment. No application to the attorney general. Fair enough?"

Walter was a little startled by the offer. Perhaps Gilardi did respect him somewhat after all. "That," he said, "I can buy. Today is June twenty-sixth. Seven days will put us at July third, right in the middle of the holiday weekend. Talk to me on July fourth, and we'll see where we are."

"Good," said Gilardi. "I think we can work together. If something breaks before the fourth, I'll call you. Otherwise, I'll meet you right here that evening. Same time, if it's all right with you?"

Walter nodded, shook hands, dropped a ten-dollar bill on the table, and left. Gilardi ordered another bourbon. A double.

As he drained the last of his second drink, Joseph Gilardi stared out the window of LeRoux' Cocktail Lounge at the fading light on the marshes of Ipswich.

Upon the stroke of midnight, he thought, it would be the second anniversary of the death of Gina Santoro, the sixteen-year-old daughter of his mistress, Felicia Santoro.

Gilardi had been married for nearly thirty years to

the former Christina Moretti, chosen for him in the old tradition more by his family than himself.

Together they had raised three very routine children, all of whom were married and living routine lives. Christina, following custom and a surfeit of pasta, had gotten fat, indolent, and gossipy. She saw very little of her husband except on Sundays and at family affairs. They had not slept together in ages. But Gilardi had been sleeping with Felicia Santoro for nearly twenty years.

They had met when he was a young officer, assigned to the vice squad on night duty. Felicia had been soliciting on Washington Street, and Gilardi had picked her up. Because she looked forlorn and broken, and because he was young, he had taken her to an all-night restaurant for a cup of coffee rather than to the station house. Three nights later he visited her at her tiny Back Bay apartment and made love to her. He had helped her find a job at City Hall through Boston's entrenched patronage channels and had gradually fallen in love with her.

Felicia thrived on the attention, filled out, learned to smile, and brought him joy every moment he was with her. They had been going together for two years when she announced apologetically that she had missed her period but would be willing to have an abortion. Even though such operations were still very much illegal in the Commonwealth of Massachusetts, Gilardi could easily have arranged one. He could not bear to do it, sensing correctly that Felicia desperately wanted the child. Gina was born eight months later, and although his identity as a father was kept from her, he managed to pick up enough street money on the job to help with her support. Gina had flowered into a beautiful, joyous child until she was fourteen. Then she came home from school one day in misery and informed Felicia that she had found that her father had not been killed in the service, that she had no father, and that she was not a "legitimate person." Felicia was too poor a liar to persuade her otherwise.

Gina, embittered, began to stay out at night. First, word reached Gilardi that she had become an easy piece. Then, that she was into drugs. A year later, after being missing for a month, she was found in an attic in East Boston, dead from an overdose of heroin.

Gilardi, in a cold rage, had pulled all the stops. Threatening, blackmailing, using the butt end of his .38 when necessary, he identified her pusher, a black man in his thirties. He persuaded the Suffolk County D.A. to get an indictment for murder and personally supervised the preparation of the case—from a suitable distance. Where the case was weak, he came up with witnesses who "remembered" that the black man had mentioned that Gina was a customer.

The verdict had come in at two-thirty in the morning after the jury had deliberated for nearly thirty hours. They had acquitted on the only charge before them: Felony-Murder. The Commonwealth's case had been chopped up handily by Michael Kilrayne, defending.

The news of the black man's acquittal had ignited Gilardi's temper. He slammed his hand so hard against the wall that the plaster had shattered. The hate that had filled him for the man who had destroyed his daughter surged, multiplied, and spread from defendant to defender. Had he had the opportunity at that moment, he would have killed Michael Kilrayne in one swift brutal rage.

Gilardi could not accept the result. A month after the verdict he had paid a call to an acquaintance in The Organization and cashed a heavy due bill. The following night the black man twisted the key in the ignition switch of his car on Blue Hill Avenue in Roxbury and a split second later met his maker as five sticks of dynamite splattered the car and its driver over half an acre. It was a pity, thought Gilardi, that Kilrayne wasn't in the car with him.

Whenever Gilardi felt a touch of regret at having taken a judgment so final into his own hands, he reminded himself that it would not have been necessary had it not been for the perverted talents of Michael Kilrayne, who was still alive. He would get back at Kilrayne one day, he vowed. However long it took, he would remember.

Walter Barrett forced himself to drive slowly toward his home in Beverly, feeling the glow of his three martinis. He was unenthusiastic about going home, mostly because he was not anxious to listen to his wife, Elizabeth. He had married her in his mid-twenties partly because she came from a good family, partly because Uncle Carl had judged her to be the "right" kind of girl, and partly because she was as pretty as a porcelain doll. He had learned to his dismay, as soon as the bloom had faded from their honeymoon, that her passion, warmth and tenderness were also consistent with a porcelain doll. She spent her time doting on their two daughters, socializing at the yacht and country clubs, and talking Walter's ear off whenever he came home from work. She enjoyed being the wife of the District Attorney and was not beyond giving Walter advice as to who should be indicted and who should not.

Walter put Elizabeth out of his mind. He tried to imagine himself greeting the press in his office, announcing the indictment of Michael Kilrayne for murder. His official statement would be sanctimoniously pure, of course—ethical constraints against trying the case in the newspapers, and all that nonsense. The details could be slipped "off the record" to those favored reporters who had written benignly of him when he was appointed. Walter's name would quickly become known throughout the county, the Commonwealth, and probably the national press as well. His colleagues at the bar would be stunned at his boldness in tackling a number one like Kilrayne. . . .

Suddenly Walter had a discomforting thought: his Uncle Carl's divorce! How long ago? Twenty years, a little more, maybe. Walter had been a teenager, and his mother had forbidden him to discuss the subject. Nonetheless, between what he had read and the gossip he had heard in law school, where Kilrayne was something of a folk hero, he remembered the goriest of the details.

His Aunt Edwina had had enough of her dour, sexless (she thought) husband, and had sought a divorce. She had soon discovered that Carl, although still a relatively young man, was a power at the bar; the big law firms made excuses. The fraternity was reluctant to attack one of its own.

Frustrated, she had sought the services of an even younger lawyer, a rangy, handsome, renegade Irishman named Kilrayne. He had quietly but thoroughly done his homework and in the end had turned up a mistress on Beacon Street who was salaried by Carl's firm as a "consultant," a large bank account in Nassau upon which taxes had likely not been paid, and a forty percent interest in a producing oil well of some substance in Oklahoma. In addition, he was prepared to show that Carl was the firm's "Bag Man," who handled the kickbacks to assorted state officials after the firm's clients were awarded juicy public contracts. He assured Edwina that if push came to shove, he was ready to carve Carl a new rectum on the witness stand.

He sent Carl a formal letter demanding a divorce and property settlement and requesting a conference. Barrett had responded with a cold, arrogant, and brief message on his heavily embossed letterhead, stating that Edwina had no grounds for divorce and that he had no desire to confer about a serious matter with a lawyer of such youth and inexperience. By acting as his own counsel, Carl Barrett had unwittingly lit the fuse of a stick of Irish dynamite.

With Edwina's blessing, Kilrayne had ignored the traditional grounds of cruelty and had filed suit in the Essex County Probate Court seeking divorce on the grounds of adultery. The shit had promptly hit the fan.

Barrett immediately made a formal complaint to the Bar Association of Boston, charging Kilrayne with malicious and unethical conduct. Simultaneously, he prepared a civil suit against his younger antagonist for abuse of process. He also—fortunately, as it turned out—retained the services of Monroe I. Spears, Esquire, the leading divorce lawyer in the legal community. Spears flattered Kilrayne by coming to *his* office for a preliminary conference.

After two intense hours, Spears had left. His youthful opponent had the evidence, and, thanks to Barrett's pompous-ass letter, the balls to wipe that evidence all over a public courtroom if there were to be a trial. Barrett had protested like a wounded piglet, but in the end had folded his hand at Spears's insistence. Edwina was granted an uncontested divorce, their lavish house with all the furniture, some valuable art, her Buick automobile, *and* the Bahamian bank account. The complaint against Kilrayne was withdrawn.

Was Uncle Carl capable of holding a personal grudge against another lawyer for more than twenty years? You bet your goddam ass, thought Walter. Would the press dredge up the incident and claim that Walter's pursuit of Kilrayne on a doubtful murder charge was really a vendetta to please his Uncle Carl? Perhaps. That goddam guinea Gilardi, Walter thought, had better come up with some goddam good solid evidence. . . .

3

NOSING AROUND
Monday, July 3

Detective Lieutenant Joseph Gilardi let himself into
Sarah Hansen's house on Marblehead with a pass key
from a cluster on a large ring—for the second time. On
this occasion, however, he had a duly authorized search
warrant from the Superior Court, which described the
search as "incidental to the investigation of a missing
person." For the next thirty minutes he went from room
to room observing every detail, making an occasional
note, but touching nothing.

When he had completed his initial tour, he started
back through, opening every drawer and chest, looking
behind the books in a large living room bookcase, examining every pot and pan in the kitchen, tapping the
walls in every room, being careful not to smudge any
latent fingerprints.

Sarah's house was not large by any standard: two
bedrooms, a bath and a half, a small dinette, and a living room overlooking Marblehead Harbor. Had it not
been situated on one of the most desirable pieces of real
estate in Massachusetts, Gilardi thought, it might be
worth sixty thousand or less. As it was, it would bring
over a hundred with one small ad in the local newspaper. It was decorated and furnished in simple but exquisite taste.

Gilardi was disappointed that he was unable to find

any mementos with the initials "M.K." other than the silver table lighter he had seen on his first visit.

After two hours of poking about, Gilardi returned to the bedroom. Kilrayne, he thought, must have enjoyed some hours of pleasant dalliance on the pastel king-size bed in the center of the room. Indeed, the large mirror over the low chest of drawers would have permitted a bit of voyeurism, had the parties been so inclined. Off to the side was a Sony television console with a Betamax recorder built in. Gilardi ran his hands over the walnut panels of the cabinet, pressing lightly, when suddenly a door on the lower left of the unit popped open. Inside were a half-dozen tape cartridges, neatly stacked.

Gilardi removed them and studied their titles. Two were marked "Sound of Music," Parts I and II. The next two were labeled "Gone With The Wind," also Parts I and II. The fifth and sixth cartridges were not titled, but one was marked "A" and the other "B." He pushed the power switch on the Betamax, turned on the television set, and inserted cartridge "A" into the machine. After a few moments of snow there appeared a typed title, "Sometime Sweet Susan."

Gilardi recognized it as a feature-length pornographic film he had seen two years before at one of the x-rated theaters permitted to operate in Boston's "Combat Zone" on Washington Street. He watched a few minutes of the tape and confirmed its identity. Then he rewound cartridge "A" and inserted "B." A continuation of the same adventure. Ms. Hansen, he thought, was a lady of pleasantly lustful inclinations. Suddenly he had an intriguing thought.

The manufacturers of videotape equipment were not above pointing out that their units were good for something more than viewing. Indeed, several had run startlingly forthright advertisements in men's magazines, suggesting that couples might perpetuate scenes of their lovemaking with the use of a compatible video camera, at modest extra cost. Gilardi examined the unit until he found the camera jack and discovered, to his delight, that it was sufficiently scratched around the holes of the cannon plug to indicate some use.

He retraced his steps throughout the house, examining once again every place large enough to store a video camera and tripod and possibly a set of floodlights. He searched each closet and went back through the basement but found nothing. Perhaps Ms. Hansen had borrowed the necessary equipment from time to time, he thought. Or perhaps her paramour would bring it with him. Or perhaps she had used the camera only for birdwatching. Or perhaps she had bought the unit used. A check of the local stores might be informative.

As a last resort, he went back to the large cedar-lined storage closet adjacent to the study. With a flashlight, he examined the wooden ceiling and noticed a hole just about large enough for a human finger. Somewhat apprehensively—perhaps the woman kept pet snakes, for all he knew—Gilardi hooked his index finger through the hole and gave a slight tug. A large panel in the ceiling dropped slightly. He pulled harder, and it swung down easily, with a creak of the counterbalancing springs. Nestled on top of the panel was a set of folding wooden stairs. As he swung them down, a bare bulb up in the hole illuminated, revealing a small storage attic.

Gilardi climbed two of the stairs until he could see over the rim of the hole and observed a number of stacks of old magazines. He examined several of them and found that they were back issues of *Better Homes and Gardens, House Beautiful*, and a series of trade catalogues for interior decorators.

He swung his flashlight around the attic and spotted a large object with a gray cloth draped over it. Crawling along the rafters, he reached the cloth and pulled it away, revealing a black steamer trunk secured with what appeared to be a rather new padlock.

He descended the stairway long enough to retrieve the cluster of pass keys from his briefcase and returned to the trunk. The padlock snapped open on the third try. He lifted the lid.

On the top of the trunk were some old blankets, which he pushed aside. Under the blankets were a video camera, a microphone with a long thin cord, a tripod, and three more cassettes. Each had a manufacturer's imprint indicating that they were of thirty minutes duration. There were no other markings.

He spread his handkerchief on the floor of the attic and gingerly lifted each cassette out of the trunk and onto the handkerchief, using his pocket pen to preserve any fingerprints. He then folded the four corners of the handkerchief to form a carrying sling and carried it down to the bedroom.

He selected one at random and slipped it into the receptacle in the Betamax. He pushed the "Play" button, but the spools did not turn. After a pause, he noticed that the takeup spool was full and rewound the cartridge. Then he hit the "Play" button once again. For a few seconds the screen was white—then a picture appeared. It showed the torso and legs of an adult male, lying on his back on the king-size bed. After several seconds, during which the picture moved slightly as though the camera were being adjusted, a blond woman came into view and sat on the bed. She had a pretty face and a startling body. Like the male, she was nude. The few pictures he had seen of Sarah Hansen around the house had not prepared Gilardi for what looked to be the figure of a woman in her late twenties.

The blond took a bottle of what appeared to be massage oil from somewhere off camera—the night table perhaps—and began to rub its contents on the stomach and thighs of her companion, smiling as she did so. In a very short while he had come erect—fiercely so—and she teasingly fondled his genitals. From there she indulged him, languorously, with every kind of lovemaking Gilardi had ever read about. At no time, how-

ever, did any part of his body above the middle of his
chest come into view.

Gilardi sat enraptured—and thoroughly aroused—
until the tape had played itself out. Without taking time
to rewind it, he played a second one. More of the same,
but a different male. The third cartridge held a similar
scenario, but with a third male companion. The first
and third had dark hair, the second was somewhat more
fair. The left buttock of the third male showed a curved
white scar, perhaps six inches long. Each of the male
partners seemed to be mature and lean, although the
fair subject showed a hint of a paunch in certain positions.

By the time Gilardi had sated himself with repeated
viewings of each tape, it was middle evening, and the
daylight was fading rapidly. Frustrated as he was at
being unable to see the faces of any of Sarah's lovers, he
nonetheless had some hope that perhaps Michael Kilrayne had a six-inch scar on his buttock. That might be
identification enough to tie him in.

Gilardi chuckled, in spite of himself. Helluva consti-
tutional question, he thought "Your Honor, as part of
the discovery to which it is entitled, the commonwealth
demands an inspection of the defendant's ass!" Kilrayne would probably start throwing things around the
courtroom.

He went once more to the attic and combed the trunk
carefully against the possibility that there might be more
tapes, but without success. He left the padlock open
since he intended to testify, if necessary, that he had
found it that way. No use getting mired down in techni-
calities. Then he closed up the attic, placed the cartridges in his briefcase, and secured the house.

As he turned his cruiser south toward the city, he
could not rid his mind of the images he had seen during
the last few hours. The agitation in his loins, he mused
to himself, would need relief this night. He would, he

resolved, cruise through Park Square and arrest a hooker, then let her bargain her way to freedom. Feeling mildly pleased with his day's work, he lit a fresh cigar and drove on.

4

THE PARADIGM
Tuesday, July 4

When Walter Barrett arrived at LeRoux' on the evening of July 4, Joe Gilardi was seated at a table by a window overlooking the Capstan Marina. He smiled pleasantly as Walter sat down.

"Have a nice Fourth?" he asked.

"No," said Walter wearily, "I did not. It was awful. Yourself?"

"One of the best ever," said Gilardi, smacking his lips after an incongruously delicate sip of bourbon. He had the look of a cat deliciously full of milk and mouse, with a dash of catnip thrown in.

"I trust," said Walter, "that in a mere eight days you have assembled evidence of premeditated murder so tight that Kilrayne's counsel will break down my office door importuning for a chance to plead to second degree?"

Gilardi ignored the sarcasm. "Not quite," he said easily, "the smart money says that at first they'll offer manslaughter."

"Who, pray tell, is the smart money?"

"I am, of course," smiled Gilardi. "Perhaps you never heard, but my mother, God rest her lovely soul, was once the smartest bookie in Revere. Now, would you like my report?"

"Why don't we do that," said Walter, trying to hold

his own against a jungle creature whose deftness and cunning, he scolded himself, he had better stop underestimating.

"Why don't we," said Gilardi, twisting the knife ever so slightly. "I have managed, by resort to a box or two of No-Doz tablets and many gallons of coffee in more conventional form, to put in close to twenty hours a day. I will give you a summary.

"First, pursuant to the search warrant you were kind enough to get from Judge Schwimmer, I scoured Ms. Hansen's home from top to bottom. Personally. I would like to tell you that I found a thick diary bound in the best leather, detailing in neon lights a love affair with Mike Kilrayne. I was not that lucky."

Gilardi paused to light a small, crooked stogie. He did not blow the smoke directly at Walter, but allowed it to float toward him without apparent concern.

"What I did find, however, after impounding our table lighter, with appropriate fingerprint protection, was the following:

"One, our victim used, according to her checkbook, only one travel agency—Bob Hallowell, in Swampscott. She has not booked any travel in the last three months.

"Two, Ms. Hansen had a device which enabled her to transfer calls to any number from her own phone. In other words, she could set the machine so that when her phone rang, and she wasn't home, it would automatically redial and transfer the call without the caller knowing. For instance, you might call her at home, and she would pick up an instrument at the end of Kilrayne's private line, and you wouldn't know the difference. Get it?"

Walter nodded. "Was this device specially built, or is it commercially available?"

"I could have bought you one ten years ago from the yellow pages," said Gilardi. "However, they never caught on. Their use is unusual, and therefore, probably for deceptive purposes. OK?"

"Go on," said Walter.

"Number three is," said Gilardi, warming to his task, "our Hansen woman was a sexual athlete of some considerable strength. To remind herself of this fact on rainy days, she used a J.V.C. video tape recorder to memorialize her better moments. I have, in the line of duty of course, viewed the more than one and a half hours of tape which I found in a trunk with an open lock in her attic. As a matter of fact, in the line of duty I have viewed them several times."

"The lock was what?"

"Open," said Gilardi in a low voice. "In any event, I viewed these tapes. Although Ms. Hansen can be recognized from time to time, her male friends' faces do not appear. She was a woman of at least *some* discretion, it seems. Nevertheless, the sex acts are most explicit and involve three different males, each appearing several times. One of these *could* be Kilrayne.

"Number five. I have all of Ms. Hansen's phone records for the past six months. She placed a call to Kilrayne's private number on an average of once every three weeks. The most recent was on June fifth, two days before she was last seen."

"Could you blow that smoke the other way?" asked Walter.

"Sure thing."

"Go on."

"Number six. Kilrayne was not in his office for four days commencing June eighth. He tried a murder case for ten days before that and got a verdict of manslaughter at 5:37 P.M. on June seventh. He had a number of Scotch whiskies at the La Strada Ristorante at seven to eight P.M., which the waitress remembers because several people congratulated him on the verdict—which they should have, by the way—the prosecutor blew an easy second degree case.

"Number seven—lucky seven—Kilrayne discussed a 'contract' to 'remove an annoying problem' two months ago with one Frankie LaPere, who is now in Walpole doing seven to ten for burglary. The proposed victim was a female, and she was to vanish without a trace. Frankie said that it wasn't his line, but he would try to find someone to recommend. He never did.

"Number eight—and this is secondhand and ought to stay that way for the moment—two other former clients have heard Kilrayne talking about having a woman killed. They are the brothers Tomasello, George and Eddie, who were in Kilrayne's waiting room in early May, in the evening, and heard him shouting what he wanted done to someone on the phone. Both brothers have records. George is awaiting trial on pornography charges, and Eddie is on appeal bond from an interstate hijacking conviction in federal court. He's due to be sentenced in two weeks."

Barrett stared at Gilardi, trying hard to believe that one man could uncover so much evidence in eight days' time.

"Why do you want to keep the Tomasellos on 'secondhand' status?"

"Because," said Gilardi, "if you should decide to indict, the first thing you have to do is, you have to give a list of your witnesses to the defense. *If* you know they're going to be witnesses. That would not include people I haven't talked to and who didn't appear before the grand jury. The Tomasello boys are on the street. Kilrayne would know how to remove them from the street. Permanently."

"What about LaPere?"

"Aah," said Gilardi with obvious satisfaction. "LaPere is no problem. LaPere is in custody and will be happy to accept strong custodial protection. A good friend in the justice department, who owes me a favor or two, has arranged for LaPere to be kept at the Coast Guard station on Thatcher's Island off Loblolly Cove in Rockport. You may remember that Joe Barboza—the hit man who testified so very well against all and sundry in the sixties—was kept there quite successfully when the price on his head exceeded the national debt."

" '*Has*' arranged, you said? Apparently the case is to go forward, is that it?" Walter suddenly realized, quite clearly, that the tail was about to wag the dog.

Gilardi looked at him evenly, but did not flinch.

"No," he said, "that will be your decision. My job is to be ready for anything and everything. That's all."

Walter gulped the remainder of his martini. "Okay," he said. "There's one problem. We, as the lonely often lament, we ain't got no body. Death, as I understand the law of this Commonwealth, is still an element of the crime of murder. Show me a death, will you?"

Gilardi smiled thinly through the cloud of smoke from the stogie, and then pounced.

"Walter," he said harshly, "I have been very truthful with you. I'm entitled to the same treatment. You know very well how death can be proved in this case."

"I beg your pardon?" Walter did not sound suitably indignant.

"Fact is," said Gilardi, "one of my cronies who hobbies in the law tipped me to a California case almost twenty years old. *People* v. *L. Ewing Scott*, was the name. I went to the Social Law Library to get a handle on the kind of evidence that nailed old Scott for killing his wife, without a trace of a corpse. Couldn't get that particular volume of the California reports, however, because it was checked out to a Walter Barrett. Had to finagle my way into the Harvard Law Library to read the Scott case. Read every word, along with the Australian and English cases it mentioned. Thing is, you prove that the defendant *acted* like the victim was dead, you kill two birds with one swipe. The jury can find circumstantial proof of death, and since only the defendant—in this case one Kilrayne, by name—*knew* it, he must be the one."

"I read the Scott case, Lieutenant Gilardi, and some others like it. Sure, you can prove death by circumstantial evidence. But it seems to me that it's a chancy way to go. In any event, let's just say we've got a problem. Like maybe one morning during the trial the judge gavels the court to order, and there's Ms. Hansen sitting in row number one. That would not help our case a great deal, you must admit."

Gilardi sighed elaborately, as if he was tired of stroking a spoiled child. "No," he said, "it really wouldn't help at all. I guess you could say that it might blow the case out of the water. Leave some egg on our faces, trying to prove that a stacked and fascinated courtroom spectator sitting in the front row was a dead broad, when even the judge might be anxious to demonstrate the contrary. We'd look pretty silly, wouldn't we."

"That's right," said Walter. "That's my point."

Gilardi drew heavily on his stogie, drained his glass, and glared at Walter. "Now you listen to me for just a whole minute, you flabby little piece of shit, because when I'm through I'm going to walk out of here in disgust. I've got better places to bend my elbow than with a guy who's got the balls of a stud field mouse, especially after I spent eight days breakin' *my* balls on this case while you had to prove one more time that you can't get along with your own family.

"Number one, I'm going to keep my word to you, mostly because the way I was brought up, breaking your word was a capital offense. Number two, you know and I know damned well that that woman isn't walking into any courtroom, 'cause Kilrayne referred to her as 'was,' whether we can use the statement or not—at least *we* know he said it. Number three, you worry too much about your own ass. If you look foolish in this case, you might not get elected, so you gotta go back to the practice and rake in nothing but money. Me, I've gotta look look forward to being a lieutenant until I retire, when there are four slots above me that are crying for a good man—and I'm the best they got. What you want is for me to bring you fingerprints, half a dozen priests as eyewitnesses, *and* a signed confession taken in the presence of the whole Supreme Judicial Court. Then you might have enough guts to get an indictment. You want an open and shut guaranteed conviction, that's all. Well sonny, that just ain't the way the cards shake out in this business. You got this much evidence against a bum like Kilrayne, you take a shot and put his feet to the fire. Maybe he does walk out. If he does, he's a couple of inches shorter than he was, and he doesn't walk so good anymore. That's the realities, Walter, that's the way this game goes down. Your uncle wants a boy to do a man's job. I am going to tell him tomorrow morning that he can take this case and you with it and shove them both up his fat ass."

Gilardi stormed out, leaving Walter furious, crimson, and speechless.

The phone next to Gilardi's bed snapped him out of his sleep at six-thirty the following morning.

"Yuh. What is it."

"This is Walter Barrett, Lieutenant. I'd like to see you in my office this morning at about nine. I'm going to submit the Hansen murder to the grand jury."

There was silence for a long five seconds. "Okay," said Gilardi. "At nine."

5

A JURY OH SO GRAND
Friday, July 7

The old Salem courthouse, successor to an earlier court where women were once condemned to death as witches, seemed to have drawn its architecture from that era. A two-story brick structure, halfheartedly maintained with an occasional dash of new paint around its windows, it contained a few offices and one large, dark courtroom in which Cotton Mather would have felt quite comfortable. The County Commissioners of Essex had turned down so many requests for air conditioning that no one bothered to apply anymore. Walter Barrett stepped from the grand jury room looking as though he had been in a sauna. He mopped his brow with a sopping handkerchief, then stuffed it into the back pocket of his trousers.

"They're jocking me around," he said to Detective Lieutenant Gilardi. "Hung up just where I thought they'd be. Is she dead? They just aren't sure. And this heat doesn't help. They want to get the hell out of here and go to the beach."

"Jesus Christ," said Gilardi, "who ever heard of a grand jury that didn't indict when they were told to. Who's the troublemaker?"

"No one juror," said Barrett, "although there's an accountant that thinks he's some kind of Perry Mason. They're not *refusing* to vote a true bill. They *are* suggesting that maybe another thirty days and our girl doesn't show up, it would be a stronger case."

Gilardi shook his head. "No good," he said. "Witnesses like LaPere and the Tomasellos get nervous when things don't happen on schedule."

"What do you suggest?" asked Walter.

Gilardi tugged his jaw. "That Supreme Court case a while ago," he murmured. "Where you can use stuff you find in an illegal search before a grand jury, even though it can't come in at trial. Wouldn't that apply to wiretaps as well?"

Walter thought for a moment, then nodded. "You know, it just might."

"We could find out," grinned Gilardi. "Sarah *was* a nice woman."

"Lieutenant," said Barrett, "you are the Commonwealth's next witness. Come with me."

Thirty minutes later Walter emerged from the grand jury room with a sweaty smile to see Gilardi standing there.

"We got it," he said.

6

THE DIGNITY OF DUE PROCESS
Friday, July 7

The large and reasonably modern auditorium was abuzz
with the excitement of more than seven hundred students and professors eagerly anticipating some profound
intellectual entertainment. Northeastern University, the
college of the Boston working class, could seldom command so distinguished a group of panelists for a single
event. The issue was a hot one: Is the Supreme Court of
the United States, as presently constituted, a threat to
individual liberty?

For the prosecution, supporting the Supreme Court,
there was Campbell Burns, District Attorney of Hamp-
den County, and an indefatigable spokesman for law
and order at any price. And for the defense, one of the
chief critics of the Supreme Court, Michael Kilrayne,
Baron of the Boston criminal defense bar.

Kilrayne, in his early fifties, made a formidable appearance because his six feet of height was matched by
the build of a linebacker who kept in trim by mountain-
climbing, playing only singles, and swimming vigorously
outdoors in summer, indoors in winter. The calmest exercise he took was gesticulating in the courtroom, for
which he was famous; when Michael Kilrayne raised
both hands toward the jury box, as a preacher might,

the jurors felt that they were the objects of instruction they had better accept.

The moderator for the evening was Frederick Lowell Osborne, a man just sixty, graying, distinguished in his carriage as well as his speech. His suits were invariably gray, the jacket buttoned except for those moments when he thought a flash of his Phi Beta Kappa key might be useful. Osborne was the senior trial partner for Boston's largest law firm—Benson, Howe & Proctor— and Chairman of the American Bar Association's Litigation Council. Most Boston lawyers thought he should have been appointed to the Supreme Court years earlier.

Just as Osborne began the introdutcion of the issue and its advocates, two huge state troopers, dressed in two-tone blue with scout hats, breeches, and highly polished puttees, stepped forward into the floodlights and positioned themselves on either side of Michael Kilrayne.

"Mr. Kilrayne," said the smaller of the two, his right hand resting on the butt of the pistol he wore on his hip, "pursuant to an indictment returned this date by the grand jury of the county of Essex, I arrest you for the murder of Sarah Hansen."

Kilrayne gasped, then began to grow livid. "You what?" he roared.

The trooper answered by slapping a handcuff hard against Kilrayne's right wrist. Its inner section swung a quick circle, and ratcheted tight. Before he could react, the trooper had cuffed his left wrist and with his colleague hustled him from the stage.

Osborne, at first aghast, recovered quickly. "Ladies and gentlemen," he said into the microphone, "assuming that this little scene was not staged by Mr. Kilrayne—and I am satisfied that it was not—I should say that he has scored a point for his side of our proposed debate. I regret that, under the circumstances, the debate must be discontinued. I shall look forward to a further opportunity to be with you some other afternoon."

Osborne hurried from the stage and located a phone in an adjacent dressing room. He dialed his private office number.

"Martha," he said when his secretary answered, "check the Superior Court schedule, and tell me who is sitting in Essex."

There was a pause of a few seconds. "Judge Kevin Sullivan is in the First Criminal Session—he's the only one in Essex for July. His number in chambers is 856-4392."

"Excellent. Now please call our good client Dean Simmons at Digitronics. Ask him as a special favor to have one of his Jet Rangers at the Nashua Street Heliport just as fast as he can. I'll be there in ten minutes."

Osborne hung up the receiver briefly, then dialed Judge Sullivan's chambers. The judge's secretary caught him in the parking lot, just about to drive home for the weekend.

"Yes, Fred," he said, "what can I do for you?"

"Judge, did the grand jury hand up a murder indictment against Mike Kilrayne in your court this afternoon?"

"Yes, about two hours ago. It was sealed, as a matter of fact. I was flabbergasted, to say the least. I was told the D.A. expected to sit on it 'til Monday."

"Judge, they arrested Mike ten minutes ago in front of a thousand students here at Northeastern. I presume he's on the way to Salem to be booked. I suspect that perhaps Mr. Barrett would like to keep him in jail over the weekend. I would like to impose on you to address the question of bail this evening, if possible—and I'm sorry for the imposition."

"I'll be happy to wait," said the Judge, frowning. "I assume it's going to take you some little time to get up here in the weekend traffic."

"With luck," replied Osborne, "I will be landing on the end of Nilsson's wharf in about twenty minutes. Per-

haps Your Honor would be kind enough to ask your secretary to order me a cab?"

"Certainly," said Sullivan. "I shall look forward to
seeing you again."

"Many thanks," said Osborne, and hung up.

Kevin Sullivan shook his head. "We'll be working a
little late this evening," he said to Edna, his secretary.
"Please notify the bailiffs and the reporter. Let Mrs.
Sullivan know that our trip to Maine will be delayed.
And send a cab to Nilsson's Wharf to pick up Mr. Os-
borne, please."

Sullivan had been on the bench for fifteen years. He
was tall, nearly bald, and powerfully built. He was re-
garded as a fair man, but the trial bar avoided provok-
ing his occasionally quick temper. He was a master at
reducing offending lawyers to jelly right from the bench.
"I wonder," he thought to himself, "what this horse's
ass Barrett is up to now." He was deeply irritated by the
misinformation he had been given about the proposed
time of arrest.

Osborne had locked his car and was waiting at the
gate when the yellow and brown helicopter fluttered
over the Charles River and touched down at the painted
triangle on the helipad. Ten seconds later the pilot lifted
off and cleared through Logan's control zone to the
waterfront at Salem. Osborne sat in the left seat, next to
the pilot, and studied the weekend traffic crawling
along toward the North Shore.

In just eight minutes, the Jet Ranger was touching
down on a clear spot near the end of the wharf. The
pilot handed a card with a telephone number scrawled
on it to Osborne. "I'll be at the Beverly Airport at this
number," he said. "The boss said to stay with you until
you're ready to quit for the day." Osborne thanked him
and slid into the back of the waiting cab.

Judge Kevin Sullivan's chambers consisted of a government-green room, trimmed in dark wood, with an ancient desk and a highbacked chair upholstered in brown leather that had cracked with age. One wall was lined with faded brown volumes of the *Massachusetts Report,* some of which were so burdened with dust as to suggest that they were not often consulted. The window behind the desk looked out on the courthouse parking lot and beyond to Salem Harbor. Judge Sullivan sometimes found himself standing in front of that window, looking out but unseeing, when wrestling with one of the hairline decisions that experienced trial judges universally dreaded.

When Osborne walked into the room, the judge was on the phone with Walter Barrett. His heavy brows were knitted into a scowl. He was obviously not buying whatever he was being told.

"Your claim that the decision to arrest Mr. Kilrayne this afternoon was made *after* you spoke to this court strains your creditability rather severely, I'm afraid. In any event, I expect to entertain an application for bail immediately upon his arrival. You will be present with any evidence you may wish to submit. Meanwhile, you are directed to make no statements to the press of any kind."

Osborne could hear a vigorous protest in response but could not make out the words. Judge Sullivan cut it short.

"Mr. District Attorney, you have heard my order. I will tolerate no deviation from it in any form. I will commit to jail without hesitation any transgressors. Instruct your staff accordingly." He hung up.

Sullivan stood up to shake Osborne's hand. "Edna," he called, "please get me the Commissioner of Public Safety at once. If he's not in, I will speak with his deputy."

"I appreciate the court's accommodation," said Osborne. "I hope Your Honor's weekend plans have not been seriously inconvenienced."

"Nothing that can't wait," said Sullivan. "Now, Fred, what the hell is this case all about?"

Osborne turned his palms outward. "I have no idea at all," he said. "I was about to moderate a panel discussion for a student group when a couple of state troopers snatched my star off the stage. Familiar as I am with the penchant of some of our prosecutors for Friday afternoon arrests in highly publicized cases, I thought it best to act first and consult with my client—if he wishes to retain me—second."

Sullivan grunted. "Deputy Commissioner Borelli is on the line," said Edna.

The judge settled back into his chair and picked up the phone. "Mr. Borelli," he said in a formal tone, "somewhere between Boston and Salem one of your cruisers is carrying Mr. Michael Kilrayne, presumably to this court. Please inform the driver by radio that I am waiting to set bail and that I will expect the trooper in charge to report to me that he used all deliberate speed, including siren and flashing lights, to expedite his arrival. Will that be done, then?"

There was a pause, as the judge listened without expression. "Thank you, Mr. Borelli. There is one other thing—could you please check and tell me when this assignment was given to the arresting officers, and by whom? No, that's all right—I'll hold."

Sullivan swiveled in his chair and looked out the window behind his desk. After several minutes of silence he said softly, "Thank you, Mr. Borelli. Your cooperation with the court is appreciated." He placed the phone in its cradle.

Edna entered the chambers with two mugs of coffee and set one before the judge. The other she handed to Osborne. "Cream, no sugar, I believe?" Osborne nodded his thanks. Practically every judge's secretary in Massachusetts had served him coffee in chambers, and

Edna was no exception. Osborne was treated with considerable deference by the bench, for good reason: when the Massachusetts Supreme Judicial Court decided to discipline one of the Commonwealth's judges for some misdeed, it usually appointed Osborne to prosecute.

Most judges were of the hope that, should such calamitous circumstances arise as to them, Osborne would be willing to defend, thereby leaving the second best to prosecute.

"Perhaps," said Osborne softly, "Your Honor would prefer that I take my coffee in your lobby. Mr. Barrett might not be above criticizing the Court for *ex parte*. . . ."

"Bullshit," said Sullivan. "Mr. Barrett is going to be much too busy explaining himself to worry about criticizing the bench. Relax. Tell me, except for this unforeseen legal matter, where might you have been off to for the weekend?"

Osborne sighed, and smiled. "I had in mind going up to Franconia Notch in the White Mountains, Judge. To stare at the Old Man of the Mountains and perhaps improve my wisdom."

Sullivan grinned broadly, his gray-blue eyes twinkling. "Perhaps," he said, "with all deference to the competence of our colleagues, we should hold our bar conventions there. We could all stand to improve our wisdom."

Ten minutes later, the noise level in the courtroom outside Sullivan's chambers began to climb, signaling the arrival of the press and Kilrayne. Osborne drained the last of his coffee from the mug and left the judge as Sullivan was slipping into his robe. As he entered the courtroom, he saw Kilrayne at the rear entrance, flanked by the troopers and harried by a gaggle of reporters. ". . . a goddam lousy frame," he was saying in harsh tones. "If you people will but find the room where this plot was hatched, I'll bet a case of twenty-year-old Scotch that you'll find one of Carl Barrett's offensive cigars in the trash can. I waxed him pretty good many years ago, and he is a man to whom vengeance is everything."

Osborne pushed through the crowd quickly, and whispered to his client, "Michael! Make no further comment please. Judge Sullivan has imposed a rather firm gag order on Barrett, and I'm sure he means to include the defense and its representatives."

"Okay," said Kilrayne, "but with these birds the best defense is a good offense. No point in letting them convict me before the trial. Say, how the hell did you get here so fast? These distinguished officers had the siren running for the last half of the trip."

Osborne winked. "A grateful client and the wonders of vertical flight," he answered. "I assumed without asking that you might want me to try to arrange bail?"

"Hell yes," said Kilrayne, in a hoarse whisper. The troopers had moved the press back a bit. "Matter of fact, I had intended to use my one phone call—when Captain Midnight and his sidekick here got around to letting me have it—to try to persuade you to take on the whole case."

"My firm will scream in their best Brahmin anguish," Osborne said, "but I think we can work it out."

There was a stir as Walter Barrett, two of his assistants and Lieutenant Gilardi entered the room. Barrett was looking sour. Before the press could descend on him, the bailiff gaveled the court to order, and Judge Sullivan mounted the bench.

"Counsel will state their appearances," he said briskly.

"Uh, Walter Barrett, District Attorney, for the Commonwealth," said Barrett.

"Frederic Osborne for the defendant," said Osborne.

"Arraign the defendant," said Sullivan.

"Michael Kilrayne," intoned the clerk, reading the

archaic phraseology of a Massachusetts indictment, "This indictment charges that on or about June fifth, in the year of Our Lord Nineteen Hundred and Seventy-Eight, within the County of Essex, that you did assault and beat one Sarah Hansen, and did thereby kill and murder the same Sarah Hansen, with premeditation and malice aforethought, against the peace and dignity of the Commonwealth of Massachusetts and contrary to the statute in such case made and provided. How say you to this charge? Are you guilty or not guilty?"

"Not guilty," said Kilrayne, loudly.

"If it please the court," said Osborne, "the defense moves the setting of bail."

"What says the Commonwealth?" Sullivan asked, looking at Barrett.

Barrett was whispering to Gilardi. "May I have a moment, Your Honor?"

"You may," said Sullivan. There was a buzz of whispered exchange from the press section. "Ladies and gentlemen," said Sullivan, "the court respects your right, indeed your duty, to observe and report the news. You, in turn, will respect the dignity of these proceedings and maintain silence until they are concluded." The buzz vanished abruptly.

"Your Honor," said Barrett, "the Commonwealth will not oppose bail in this case."

"In that event," said Sullivan, "there will be no need for a hearing. Does the Commonwealth have a recommendation?"

"We do, Your Honor," said Barrett. "The Commonwealth feels that bail in the amount of two hundred fifty thousand dollars, with double surety, would be appropriate."

"Bastard!" muttered Kilrayne under his breath.

Sullivan did not react to Barrett's recommendation. "What says the defendant, Mr. Osborne?" Kilrayne, who had used the word "defendant" for all of his professional life, winced at hearing it applied to him.

"I should think, Your Honor, inasmuch as Mr. Kilrayne has well-known roots in the community and no prior criminal record, that release in his own recognizance might be warranted." Because the public invariably infers something of the degree of guilt from the amount of bail set in a criminal case, Osborne was anxious to keep it as low as possible.

"Were the charge other than murder in the first degree, I would agree, Mr. Osborne. However, since as there is no absolute entitlement to any bail in such cases, I think that I will require Mr. Kilrayne to recognize in the amount of twenty-five thousand dollars, without surety."

Score one, thought Osborne to himself. He did not have to search his memory to know that nowhere in the history of the Superior Court had bail for murder one been set in such liberal terms. Perhaps the public would get the message. "Very well, Your Honor," he said. Barrett and Gilardi looked glum.

"I am assuming," said Sullivan, "that due to his peculiar circumstances Mr. Kilrayne may wish to exercise his right under federal and state constitutions to have a speedy trial . . ."

Kilrayne nodded his head vigorously.

". . . in which event a date should be calendared at the first possible moment so that pretrial matters may be scheduled with dispatch. I will therefore see counsel in this court at two o'clock on Monday next."

Barrett started to close his briefcase.

"Before this court is adjourned, however," Sullivan went on, "there is a matter which needs to be placed on the record. This very afternoon, when this indictment was handed up to me, I was told by the District Attorney that it was to be held as secret until Monday. In reliance on that representation, I was about to depart for the weekend when I received notice that the arrest warrant had been executed and that Mr. Kilrayne was in custody. Mr. Barrett has assured me, less than an hour ago, that his change in plans was made *after* his representation to the court. I find, however, that at ten o'clock this morning arrangements were made for this arrest with State Police Headquarters by Detective Lieutenant Joseph Gilardi, who now appears at the prosecution's table. I anticipate that this seeming anomaly will be fully explained by Mr. Barrett on Monday.

"Meanwhile, inasmuch as there may well be a speedy trial in this case, prospective jurors in this county will need to be protected from irresponsible speculation by those professing inside knowledge of the case. It would be most unseemly if counsel for either side, or their associates, were to make public and truculent announcement of their trial plans and ammunition. I therefore direct that all parties refrain from any discussion of this matter with the news media. And although I might ordinarily be troubled by First Amendment considerations in ordering a citizen not to publicly declare his innocence, in this case Mr. Kilrayne is a member of the bar. As such, I include him in this order. This court will be adjourned."

Sullivan rose and left the bench.

The press buzz rose in a crescendo, as newsmen tried to assimilate what had happened.

Osborne nudged Kilrayne. "I suggest we meet in my office in the morning at ten o'clock. Meanwhile, I can give you a lift—quite literally—back to Boston, if you would care to join me."

When Kilrayne and Osborne reached the heliport on the Charles, Kilrayne's Oldsmobile was waiting for him in the parking lot where Olivia, his receptionist, had left it for him. He dropped Osborne at his office. On his way to his home in South Boston, he stopped at the market in Boston's North End and bought a small basket of cut flowers.

At his home, an old two-story, wood frame house, Kilrayne found his wife, Lucy, sitting in the living room

having tea with her neighbor, Kathryn Mullaney. Lucy
Kilrayne was a pale, slight woman in her late forties,
showing still visible traces of the pretty, vivacious,
raven-haired woman she once had been. A sudden
stroke seven years earlier had changed all that. Partially
paralyzed, Lucy Kilrayne slipped in and out of the real
world around her in an unpredictable pattern.

Kilrayne cocked a questioning eyebrow at Mrs. Mullaney as he removed his suit jacket. She responded with
a barely perceptible shake of her head. Lucy was drifting again.

Kilrayne kissed Lucy on the cheek and set the basket
of flowers gently in her lap. She recognized him and
managed an oddly distorted smile.

The words halting and full of effort, she said slowly,
"You were in court today?"

He nodded.

"Did you win again, Michael?"

Kilrayne glanced sideways at Mrs. Mullaney, who
had heard the news reported on the radio and had
quickly turned it off. Again she shook her head.

"The case isn't over, sweetheart," he said, taking
Lucy's hand lightly in his own.

"You'll win, Michael," she said, staring at the setting
sun.

Mrs. Mullaney turned away. She was embarrassed to
see tears in a grown man's eyes.

7

A MATTER OF ETHICS
Saturday, July 8

Frederick Osborne's office was distinguished from that of most other senior partners in his law firm in that no paper was visible on his desk or anywhere else. Usually, only one accordion envelope could be seen on the cocktail table between the leather couch and two armchairs where he preferred to have his conferences. That envelope contained the papers relating to the case of the client he was expecting. The effect was one of concentrating on one person or case at a time and was always valued by the client, as much as Osborne valued the services of Miss Martha Brookstone who had been his loyal secretary and organizer for nearly thirty years.

Miss Brookstone knew that Mr. Osborne was expecting a visitor on Saturday morning and despite her previous plans to go shopping, she was at her station when Kilrayne arrived. She recognized him, of course, and stepping twice on the floor buzzer—her signal to Osborne that the visitor had arrived—she ushered him into the inner office.

Osborne, a glum expression on his face, put the newspaper aside and rose. "Ah, Michael," he said, holding out his hand. Miss Brookstone reached for the folded newspaper to withdraw it from the room when Osborne put up a cautioning hand. "Thank you," he said to her, "I may need to refer to it."

Miss Brookstone nodded her small head and disappeared.

"Cheer up, Fred," Kilrayne said, "I'm the one they're trying to burn."

"I'm afraid there are some people doing a burn right now," said Osborne, "and none too slowly at that. Have you read the coverage this morning?"

"Yes, and I caught the late news last night. I'd say we got the best end of it. Johnny Wembley on Channel Seven reported that Judge Sullivan practically called Barrett a liar and suggested that his indictment might not be much more sound than his word. Can't do much better than that. The defense usually gets killed in the first wave of publicity."

"I didn't mean that," said Osborne slowly. "What I do mean is that we may have to get you other counsel."

Kilrayne blanched. "You're kidding!" he exploded. "I thought you said you could tell your stuffed shirt partners to shove it?"

Osborne shook his head. "I could have, Mike. That isn't the problem. The problem is, I find that our firm represents the Multiwell Oil Company of Oklahoma and that Carl Barrett owns a controlling interest in that company. To make matters worse, we are representing Carl in a claim against the IRS for the recovery of some taxes he paid two years ago. That's the trouble with being a cog in a big firm—I have no idea who our clients are until I run a check on our computer. This time I didn't have to. My phone was ringing off the hook last night."

"What the hell has representing Carl got to do with this? His spaghetti-boned nephew is the D.A., not Carl."

"Quite true. But I think you're forgetting your statement to the press, the one you made just before I got to you. About Carl being the mastermind behind your indictment. Remember?"

Kilrayne slumped into a chair in front of Osborne's

desk. "Yeah. And I haven't the slightest doubt it's true. But that's not a defense likely to come out at trial."

"No, it isn't likely," agreed Osborne. "But you've handled enough homicide cases to know as well as I do that what may come out at trial is anyone's guess this early in the game. Let me ask you this: if you should come by some hard evidence that Carl *was* the architect of this whole mess, would you waive it, or would you try to get it before the jury?"

"I'd use it, of course," said Kilrayne. "With great pleasure."

"You wouldn't want counsel to withdraw at that point because of a conflict, would you? Or to ignore the evidence of a frame in final argument?"

"No."

"Well, trivial as it may seem, this firm can't very well vouch for Carl in a federal proceeding while calling him a liar in the Massachusetts Superior Court, can it?"

Kilrayne shook his head. "No, I suppose you can't."

"Which brings us," said Osborne soberly, "to a very sticky question. Flattered as I am that you would entrust your future to my talents, that seems out of the question now. You obviously can't defend yourself. That leaves pretty slim pickin's on the local scene, wouldn't you agree?"

Kilrayne nodded grimly. "We've got some fair talent in this city," he said, "but nothing really polished. I can't name a one of our colleagues with whom I would feel comfortable."

"Have you anyone in mind?"

"I'd feel pretty good about Paul Wilson in Washington," he said slowly. "He's as good as I am, to put it bluntly—maybe better. But I'm not sure I can afford him. I charge pretty good when I can, but Paul's out of sight."

Osborne shook his head. "When I knew I'd have to get out after those phone calls last night, I did my best to put myself in your shoes. I must admit it's a grisly experience. The ranks look pretty thin when your own ass is on the line. In any event, I thought of Paul and tracked him down at his summer place. He'll take your case and, as a professional courtesy, do so at a modest fee."

Kilrayne brightened. "No shit! That's great!"

"Not so fast," cautioned Osborne, holding up his hand. "There's a hitch. Paul cannot under any circumstances try this case before next spring. Are you willing to wait that long?"

Kilrayne's smile deflated like a punctured circus balloon. "Christ, Fred, you know I can't let this thing fester for nine months. I'd have no practice left. Besides, Barrett's going to push for a quick trial. He needs to get that wimpy face in the newspapers if he wants to get elected this fall. I don't think we could stall it that long if we wanted to."

"I agree," said Osborne. "Now, I have an idea. A wild one, admittedly. Tell me, what do you think the Commonwealth's case consists of?"

Kilrayne lit a cigarette. "I tapped a few sources last night," he said. "I couldn't find out a helluva lot, but I think they're pretty thin. The woman is missing, without question. There's no hard evidence that she's dead. I represented her for a traffic offense many years ago. I have seen her as a friend on infrequent occasions since, usually in public places. The word is, though, that a former client has testified that I tried to get him to take a contract. Don't ask me which client—I don't know. That's about it."

"Do you know why she disappeared, Mike?"

"No, I have no idea," replied Kilrayne evenly, looking straight at Osborne.

"You would agree, though, that if she doesn't turn up after all this publicity, the notion that she's dead is going to be increasingly easy to sell?"

Kilrayne nodded. "I suppose so."

"And if the prosecution intends to produce some perjured testimony, excellence in cross-examination and summing up are likely to be your best weapons?"

"Without question."

"What you and I know about those two intricate and difficult talents, we probably learned at the expense of our first clients since we have no formal schooling in either, wouldn't you say."

"Sure. That's true of every half-decent trial lawyer in America."

"Indeed. But there is a place where men are trained in such skills and trained very well indeed. At the Inns of Court in London."

"You mean the barristers?" Kilrayne was puzzled. "Sure. They're good. Damned good, from what little I've seen. But how the hell would I get a barrister admitted in Massachusetts?"

"Aha," said Osborne. "That's my wild idea. Five years ago I would have discarded it as impossible. But times change. Have you kept up with the speeches of our distinguished United States Supreme Court Chief Justice?"

"You mean about the incompetence of our trial lawyers compared to the barristers? Sure. That's about the only thing the old right-winged rascal and I have ever agreed upon."

Osborne's eyes twinkled. "It goes a bit further than that. The chief has made it pretty plain that he would like to see a few barristers appear in our courts so that our law schools might get a look at *real* professionalism and do a little meaningful training of their own. I feel fairly confident that if I were to sponsor one of our British friends, I would get some pretty heavy backing from on high. It's well worth a try."

"Mmmm. Sounds interesting. Anyone specific in mind?"

"I can think of several who are superb by our standards," said Osborne, leaning across his desk. "But one I've watched during numerous visits to London in the past ten years is an absolute master. He's now thirty-nine, and has been appointed Queen's Counsel."

"Your judgment is good enough for me, Fred. Do you think he would come?"

Osborne nodded, grinning broadly. "I contacted him just half an hour before you arrived. He'd like to come over and discuss the situation. I think he's quite interested, providing you don't insist on discussing Irish politics."

"I'm impressed with your efforts. You sure move quickly for a stuffy Bostonian."

"There's one more hitch. Barristers try cases; they do none of the preparation. Sort of like a batter who doesn't run. If my friend Anthony Everard decides to defend you, and if I can get permission of the court for him to do so, we are going to need a runner."

Kilrayne nodded. "And a damned good one. Melvin Belli once said 'If your investigator is good enough, most any lawyer will do.' That's a bit of an overstatement, but I've had a lot of cases on ice before the trial ever started. I can get Andy Kerrigan, I guess. Sonofabitch is good when he's off the bottle."

Osborne shook his head. "Not for this one, Mike. Andy's good when he's sober—I agree—but barristers need something more than a good investigator. Their cases are prepared by solicitors, who are members of the bar. That's what they're used to. I have a fellow in mind, if you're interested."

Kilrayne leaned forward. "Fred, I was interested in having you defend me. If I can't have that, then I'm interested in every single piece of advice you may have to give."

"Very well," said Osborne. "This is a chap named Daniel Shaw. He's thirty-six, former Navy flier, served a couple of years with intelligence. Works out of San Francisco, specializes in aviation law. Bright, resourceful, never misses a trick. He's good in the courtroom—damned good, as a matter of fact. I gave some thought to suggesting that he try the case. But civil trials don't equip a man for the jungle of the criminal courts. I'm afraid Dan might have to get bitten on the backside a couple of times before he decided to take the gloves off. And two times can be two too many in a case like this one is shaping up to be. For investigation, though, he's a tiger. Some of my colleagues on the ABA Litigation Council admit they hate to see him coming."

"I don't suppose," said Kilrayne, "that you've tracked Mr. Shaw down too."

Osborne smiled a sigh. "No. I tried, but Dan is off gallivanting for the weekend, it seems. He's a bachelor and flies around in his own Lear Jet. I've got a matter on in federal court Monday morning, and I'll be with you Monday afternoon up in Essex—my last formal appearance, I'm afraid—but I'll get hold of him sometime Monday. I think you should talk to him at least."

"Sure," said Kilrayne, lighting another cigarette. He held the smoke for a moment, then exhaled slowly, his expression distant and serious. "I appreciate all you've done, Fred, really. I know going to bat for me hasn't made you any new friends in the firm. I'll tell you, after knocking around the criminal courts for the better part of my fifty-two years, the prospect of being defended by a couple of youngsters is a little frightening. As a matter of fact, being defended by *anyone*, including you, is frightening. Juries are just so much roulette."

"My last thought before I went to sleep at about three o'clock this morning," said Osborne slowly, "was almost exactly that. Being defended for a criminal charge is frightening, no matter who you have. I don't envy you, Mike. Whatever I can do, without violating the canons of ethics, just call. I look at you, and remember that I came close to practicing criminal law exclusively on my own once, and I say to myself, 'There but for the grace of God go I'."

8

WHAT I MEANT WAS
Monday, July 10

Daniel Shaw leaned against the rail of the empty jury box in the United States District Court for the Northern District of California, stalking his quarry in the witness box with painstaking care. A shade less than six feet in height, Shaw was a handsome man with sandy brown hair and eyes of a clear, brilliant blue that many a reluctant witness had discovered were capable of unblinking penetration.

His client, the pilot of a small twin-engine plane that had collided with a Hughes Air West DC-9 at a runway intersection at San Francisco's International Airport, was sitting at the plaintiff's table, swiveling his head from lawyer to witness with each question and answer.

Judge Penfield Hewitt gazed intently at the obviously uncomfortable DC-9 copilot, observing his demeanor.

"You have told us," said Shaw slowly, "that you did not find the taxi clearance issued by ground control to be ambiguous or confusing. Is that correct?"

First Officer John Ortiz nodded. "That's right," he said.

"And you agree that as your captain added power to taxi through the intersection, the cockpit voice recorder of your aircraft discloses your own voice saying 'Sir, there may be some mistake, I think . . . ,' and then there is the sound of the collision, correct?"

"I didn't mean . . . ," Ortiz began.

"No no," said Shaw, cutting him off. "My question was, did you *say* those words at that time?"

Ortiz shrugged wanly. "If it's there, I guess I said it."

"Mr. Ortiz," said Shaw pressing, "this court has heard the tape. I am asking whether you, who have also listened to that same tape on numerous occasions, agree that the voice speaking those words is yours?"

Ortiz nodded.

"Mr. Ortiz," said Judge Hewitt, "you must articulate your answer for the record. The court stenographer must hear what you say in order to make an appropriate record of these proceedings."

"Yes, that was me," said Ortiz lamely.

"Very well," said Shaw. "And is it not a fact that you uttered those words because you thought that ground control had cleared another aircraft through the intersection at the same time as your own?"

Ortiz shook his head. "No, I don't think so."

"Then what did you mean by 'some mistake' when you spoke to the captain?"

"I think I was referring to our flight plan," said Ortiz.

"Really," said Shaw. "Tell me, Mr. Ortiz, do you know a former Air West mechanic named Rafael Sanchez?"

Ortiz looked puzzled. "I used to. I haven't seen him for some time."

"Did you," continued Shaw, "have some cocktails at the Sanchez home the night after this accident?"

"I don't know," said Ortiz. "I may have."

"And on that occasion," asked Shaw, reaching for a notepad on counsel table and pretending to read from it, "Did you say to Rafael Sanchez, in the presence of his wife Liz, and I quote, '. . . some asshole controller in the tower cleared us right into a Piper Aztec, nearly killed the poor bastard. . . .' Did you make that remark?"

Ortiz looked pale. He did not respond.

Judge Hewitt leaned toward the witness stand. "Mr. Ortiz," he said gently, "because this is a case against the Federal Aviation Administration of the United States Government, under the law I must be the jury as well as the judge. I must find the facts. Therefore, it is important that you answer questions properly put to you. Did you understand the question?"

Ortiz looked unhappily at the judge. "Yes, Your Honor."

"Are you able to make answer to the question?" asked Hewitt. "On your oath, of course."

Ortiz was suddenly frightened. He had tried to protect the controller as best he could, but there was a limit. The important thing, he realized, was to look out for himself at this point. Rafael Sanchez had a big mouth, but that was history.

"Yes, Your Honor," he said. "I remember making a remark to that effect."

Shaw pounced. "And was that because," he boomed, "you as a pilot with seventeen years' experience found the clearance to be dangerous and incorrect?"

"I guess so," said Ortiz unhappily.

"If this would be a convenient time, Mr. Shaw," said Judge Hewitt, "the court will take a ten minute recess."

"Certainly, Your Honor," said Shaw smartly. The bailiff said, "All rise, the court will be in recess."

When Hewitt returned to the bench, Shaw stood before him holding a note. "Your Honor," he said, "during the recess period I received a note from my office, as a result of which I have placed a telephone call to the east coast. Based on that conversation, I have an extraordinary request to make of the Court, and I apologize for doing so. I should like, at the conclusion of today's session, to adjourn this matter for the balance of the week. I would not make such a request except for the unusual and pressing circumstances which have just developed."

"Mr. Shaw," said Hewitt impatiently, "I had expected to conclude these proceedings tomorrow. Are you through with this witness?"

"I am," said Shaw.

"Do you have any rebuttal witnesses?"

"Just one," said Shaw, "and he will be brief. I would expect that we will finish in one more trial day."

"What is the position of the United States," asked Hewitt of the government lawyers.

Charles DeMatteo, Assistant United States Attorney, shrugged. "We have no more evidence, Your Honor. We would like to finish tomorrow too, but if Mr. Shaw has a life or death situation. . . ."

"In a sense," said Shaw, "my able colleague has put his finger almost precisely on the mark. If Your Honor would indulge me, I would be most appreciative."

Hewitt sighed. "I'm not sure that good practice would commend concessions of this sort, even to counsel who tend to roam in other jurisdictions as a matter of habit. However, in reliance on your representation that the matter is urgent, Mr. Shaw, I will allow you seventy-two hours. You will be here ready to wind this case up at nine-thirty on Friday morning. Understood?"

"I do, Your Honor," said Shaw, "and I tender my thanks to the court."

9

THE MANEUVERING
Monday, July 10

Walter Barrett and Detective Lieutenant Joseph Gilardi were in a cheerful mood as they walked together from Barrett's office to the First Criminal Session of the Superior Court.

"That gag order," said Gilardi, "is a blessing in disguise, Walter. Reporters can't ask why you brought the indictment."

"They can ask," said Barrett, smiling. "I just don't have to answer. And nobody's going to be able to dig around and find out about your testimony on that wiretap."

"You must be relieved not to have to face Osborne."

"Oh, I don't know."

Gilardi glanced at Barrett. The coward was damn glad to hear from his uncle that Osborne would be disqualified from participating in the trial.

"The best news," said Barrett just as they reached the courthouse steps, "is Boling's appointing Webster Lodge to preside."

"Yep," said Gilardi. Everything was going their way.

Webster Lodge, sixty-nine, and on the verge of mandatory retirement, was an old curmudgeon who could spread homilies about individual liberty across the record in elaborate rhetoric, while subtly knifing the defendant at every opportunity. Everyone knew Lodge had two natural enemies in life: alcoholic beverages and citizens of Irish descent. He had wailed profusely at the gradual takeover of Massachusetts politics by the "Irish Crude," as he liked to call them, and prided himself at having given a goodly number of their ilk staggering jail sentences. He had once confided to Carl Barrett—whom he liked, for reasons of his own—that all defendants in his court were entitled to the presumption of innocence, except for the Italians, who were allowed to start even, and the Irish, whom he invariably presumed to be guilty.

From the prosecution's point of view, if Lodge rode roughshod over the defense, who could do anything about it? Oh, the Supreme Judicial Court could reverse, but who cared? The public took jury verdicts to be the sweet blood of victory and appellate afterthoughts to be mere technical gibberish. If a jury said you were guilty, then by god you were guilty, no matter what tricks the shysters might pull on appeal.

"This could be Webster Lodge's last big trial," said Barrett.

"Right," said Gilardi, "and I bet he'd love to give Kilrayne a reaming that'd ignite the rebellion in Belfast all over again."

When Judge Sullivan mounted the bench, Gilardi and Barrett were seated at the prosecutor's table directly before it, joined by a young Assistant District Attorney named Samuel Wills.

With Osborne and Kilrayne at the defense table, was Stacy Barton, Kilrayne's understudy. Stacy, thirty-three and divorced, was a late bloomer in the world of law. She had put herself through law school at night without anyone's help, while working as an official stenographer of the Superior Court during the day.

She had been practicing for only three years but had sat through more trials than most lawyers see in a lifetime. She was a handsome woman, slender but well-proportioned, with light brown hair, a wide, expressive mouth, and brown eyes. She adored Kilrayne but had pretty well kept her distance from him, believing that an emotional entanglement would fly right in the face of her most cherished objective: to be the first woman trial lawyer in the history of American law who was really good in the courtroom and recognized as such.

"Good afternoon, counsel," boomed the judge. "We will next take up the matter of *Commonwealth* versus *Kilrayne*. Are both parties appropriately represented?"

"Walter Barrett, District Attorney, for the Commonwealth."

"Frederic Osborne for the defense."

"Very well," said Sullivan. "I have before me, among other papers, a motion for a speedy trial submitted by the defense. Perhaps that should be our first order of business."

Barrett was on his feet. "If it please the court," he said, "during our last session Your Honor directed that I report upon the seeming conflict between representations made to Your Honor that same day and certain arrangements made earlier for the arrest of the defendant Kilrayne." He paused for a moment, letting the words "defendant Kilrayne" grate on Mike's senses.

"When it appeared that an indictment was imminent," Barrett continued, "I asked Lieutenant Gilardi to have troopers available to execute the arrest warrant. Deputy Commissioner Borelli had troopers standing by. When the indictment was handed up to Your Honor, it was my intent to serve the warrant today, allowing ample time for a bail hearing without inconveniencing the court on a weekend. But after my appearance before you, my office had a call from a newspaper reporter who said that she wished to confirm a report that a prominent criminal lawyer had been indicted. I assumed that perhaps one of our grand jurors, or perhaps a court attaché, had been careless in mentioning the indictment. Rather than have such a story break in the press, casting suspicion on any number of lawyers, I thought it best to move swiftly."

"Thank you, Mr. Barrett," said Sullivan coldly. "We could have saved ourselves some trouble if you had told me all of this on Friday afternoon, couldn't we." Before Barrett could retort, Sullivan turned to Osborne.

"Has the defense a suggestion for a trial date?"

"I do, Your Honor," said Osborne. "I wish to disclose, however, that circumstances unrelated to this case may necessitate my withdrawal as counsel prior to trial. Therefore, I should like to record my request without prejudice to my successor, should there be one, to make application for an adjournment."

Sullivan frowned. "Your withdrawal will be the court's loss," he said. "But your position is of course acceptable. What date have you in mind?"

"I had thought that perhaps September seventh would be appropriate," said Osborne, "barring unforeseen developments. It is in the interests of both the defense and the Commonwealth to dispose of this case at the first reasonable moment. As Your Honor may imagine, Mr. Kilrayne has any number of cases docketed for the fall which will suffer while this one is pending."

"Thank you, Mr. Osborne. Mr. Barrett?"

"I would ask for mid-October, Judge," replied Walter. As his Uncle Carl had pointed out, each day between indictment and trial that Sarah did *not* show up would cement the notion more firmly in the public mind that she was a *permanently* missing person.

"Do you have any specific objection to the date requested by the defense?" asked Sullivan.

"No, Your Honor," said Barrett. "My office will be prepared to go forward whenever this court orders us to do so."

"All right," said Sullivan. "We will set the matter down specially for September seventh. Mr. Clerk, you will arrange for a special venire of jurors to be summoned during early August so that adequate notice is given them. Now, in view of the short time available for preparation, perhaps we can expedite discovery somewhat. Before I take up the motions before me, Mr. Barrett, would you indicate what evidence you are willing to turn over to the defense without orders from the court?"

"We have a list of the witnesses we now expect to call," said Barrett, walking back toward the defense table. "May the record show that I am now delivering a copy of that list to the defense." He dropped a sheet of bond paper with several dozen names in front of Osborne. "Beyond that, there is very little for the defense to discover."

Kilrayne scanned the list quickly and drew a circle around the name "LaPere."

"There's the former client," he said. "That bastard had his sister call me three days before the indictment and strongly suggest that I ought to try to get him out, on the cuff. Now I know why."

"Your Honor," said Osborne, rising, "in view of all the circumstances in this case, I should think that the prosecutor ought to deliver the minutes of the grand jury proceedings to the defense. It would save considerable time."

"What about that, Mr. Barrett?" asked Sullivan.

Barrett rose with a feigned apology. "I'm sorry, Your Honor, but our regular reporter was on vacation last week, and our efforts to find a replacement were unsuccessful. Inasmuch as there is no requirement that grand jury proceedings be recorded, we were forced to go forward without a stenographer. Therefore, there are no minutes to turn over."

"Bastard," muttered Kilrayne to Osborne.

"They've got all stops out," whispered Osborne. "What else do you want me to ask for?"

"Any evidence of death," said Kilrayne, "including the manner of death and the time of death."

Osborne made the request. Without waiting for the judge to speak, Barrett said, "The Commonwealth professes no knowledge beyond that set forth in the indictment."

"I take it," said Sullivan, "that you have no autopsy report?"

"We have none," said Barrett, as if an autopsy were a matter of small consequence.

"Anything further, Mr. Osborne?" said Sullivan.

"We would like copies of any witness statements."

"We have none," said Barrett.

"Nothing further at this time," said Osborne.

"If I may, Your Honor," said Barrett, "the Commonwealth would request the following from the defendant: a lock of hair from his head, a blood sample, a fingernail cutting, and an examination by a physician to be appointed by the court."

"Mr. Osborne?"

Osborne turned to Kilrayne. "What do we say, Mike?"

Kilrayne thought for a minute. "Let them have it all," he said.

"Agreed, Your Honor," said Osborne.

"Very well. You gentlemen work out arrangements among yourselves and bring to my attention those that cannot be resolved by conference. This session will be adjourned, but I will remain available to assist counsel throughout the balance of the month."

As Kilrayne left the courtroom with Osborne, shrugging the press aside, he wondered what in the world Gilardi had—or worse, what he was prepared to manufacture, beyond the testimony of LaPere.

10

THE PRESS
Tuesday, July 11

Editor Martin Hanlon sat behind a scarred oak desk in his office at the *Boston Chronicle*, his lively hazel eyes peering over the rims of his Ben Franklin glasses at the paper's two top criminal court reporters, Bill Guidetti and Charley O'Shea.

"To quote from the Ohio Supreme Court in *State* versus *Sheppard*," he said, "this case has it all: 'Murder, mystery, society, sex, and suspense.' Plus the likelihood, from what we hear, of a British barrister to defend. You both are assigned to the Kilrayne case, and nothing else 'til further notice. By any count, it will be a smasher. The public is going to want to know every angle, every nuance, every sidelight. Spare no efforts. Indeed, although I shudder to say it, spare no expense."

Guidetti patted the balding spot at the back of his skull. "My sources say this one smells like a compost," he said. "Joe Gilardi, god bless our Sicilian heritage, is masterminding this case and leading that wimp Barrett around by the nose. I wouldn't put it past Kilrayne to walk the bitch in right in the middle of the trial and thumb his nose at the lot of them." O'Shea nodded in agreement.

"Maybe so," conceded Hanlon with apparent displeasure. "I know you guys are both buddies with Mike over the years. If you feel that your objectivity has been impaired, I can import some pros from our sister paper in Detroit. I have a feeling—only a feeling at this point—that our friend Kilrayne has a serious problem, which is not to say that Gilardi hasn't massaged the evidence pretty good."

O'Shea glared at him. He had been the lead criminal reporter for longer than Hanlon had been on board. "Don't you worry about us," he growled. "We've been around long enough to sort things out as they come along."

"Okay, Charley, okay," said Hanlon. "No offense. Have at it, both of you. But Charley, one thing. . . ."

"What's that?" asked O'Shea.

"Last time I gave you an unlimited expense account, you managed to exceed it in four days. Easy this time, huh?"

O'Shea slammed his battered felt hat over his gray hair, smiled, and followed a chuckling Guidetti out of the room.

Hanlon waited for Tom Severenson to come on the line. For five years Tom had been his prodigy and disciple on the *Chronicle*, a sure bet for city editor when Hanlon retired. But Tom had been impatient for a top post, and Hanlon had helped him land the editor's position at *Far West* magazine, a monthly slick based in Los Angeles. Under his guidance, it had done well.

"Marty, you old bastard," said a familiar voice, "how's the corruption in Bean City?"

" 'Bout the same as you left it," retorted Hanlon, "despite our vigorous editorial exposés. Listen, Tom, are you people going to cover this Kilrayne thing out here?"

"What's that?"

"Word is that Daniel Shaw of San Francisco is going to be a key guy for the defense."

"Oh, that case! Hell yes! Shaw's becoming the biggest box office draw in courtrooms out here."

"I'm not sure we've heard of him east of the Rockies," said Hanlon. "What's his background?"

"Basically, he started out as a specialist in aviation cases. Very little criminal experience, from what I understand, except when he was in the Navy doing courtsmartial, but a zinger on every other count. Sharp as a Wilkinson Sword Blade. Made more money than anyone out here except perhaps Belli, and I wouldn't bet on that. Thirty-six, a bachelor, attractive, bit of a jetsetter—matter of fact he flies his own—good in the courtroom, crackerjack investigator, good copy all the way. You bet your bippy we'll be covering."

"I don't get it," said Hanlon. "The story is they're bringing in a barrister from England, too. What's up? They supposed to split the work?"

"I doubt it," replied Severenson. "You're behind on the culture in the mother country, ignorant colonist. Barristers try cases in the courtroom, they don't prepare them. Solicitors do. And our bet out here is that Shaw will be Kilrayne's lead solicitor."

"Hmm. Look, Tom, I need a favor. I've got Bill and Charley on this thing, and you know what they can do when they're right. But they're both drinking buddies of Mike's. Might cause them to miss a few things, especially Charley. I wouldn't trust an Irishman, including myself, twenty feet when one of his kin has his ass on the line. I wonder if you could have your man give me a call when he hits town. I'd like to have an independent source just to check on things, if you know what I mean."

Severenson laughed softly. "Sure, Marty. I owe you my life. Except that 'my man' on this case is a twentyeight-year-old, sexy, stacked, red-headed wizard named Patricia Perrin who'll blow your socks off and make you wish that old zipper of yours hadn't gotten rusty. I'll have her get in touch."

"Thanks, Tom. I'll try to stay cool. And have her

keep a tight lip, if you will. Charley and Bill would grind my ass if they knew. . . ."

" 'Nuff said, my friend. You taught me the business, remember?"

"Thanks, Tom. Be in touch."

Hanlon hung up. He underlined the name Patricia Perrin several times with his pencil, then thought better of it and tore the top half-dozen sheets off his scratch pad, crumpled them, and threw them in the waste basket. He reflected upon Severenson's description of his reporter and subconsciously glanced down to see if his belt could be hitched in one more notch. It could not.

11

OUTRUN THE SUN
Tuesday, July 11

Anthony Everard sat next to the left window of British Airways Flight 3, in a row number twelve, looking as always as if he were being photographed for an ad for an expensive product only gentlemen of considerable means could afford. In actual fact, the dark blue suit he was wearing was one of two that he had had made on Savile Row nearly ten years earlier, and which he habitually alternated on business days so that he would not have to concern himself with something so trivial as what to wear that day. His shirt was white as always, his tie was Harrow, his gold cuff links a present from the one client he had ever allowed to present him with a gift: Penelope Odgers, daughter of the late Sir Frederick and Lady Odgers, who had been the victim of a scheme to deprive her of her inheritance. The solicitor she consulted chose Everard as his barrister. Everard succeeded in court and in courtship, and Penelope had become his wife three weeks after he had declined the cuff links. He accepted them to wear at the wedding and had worn them ever since whenever he embarked on a new venture.

The aisle seat next to him on his right was vacant, for which he was grateful. The Concorde was without question a splendid machine—indeed, he wondered how many of the tax pounds he and Penelope paid each year were tucked into the anything but commodious seat in which he was sitting. Still, he had never flown before in any aircraft that could overtake the sun.

The captain was speaking in courteous but terribly British clipped phrases. "Following our takeoff," came the voice over the speakers, "we shall accelerate to point nine five Mach, or ninety-five percent the speed of sound. In consideration of our Irish neighbors, we will climb at that speed until we have passed over the Atlantic Ocean."

Irish neighbors. A fitting thought. Everard wondered what his Irish client might hold in store—certainly the practice of law, even in murder cases, was a quite different affair in the courts of the States. Would Everard give a good account of the British bar or get caught in some sort of rough trap and play the fool? It was a chance he had agreed to take. If Osborne, whom he knew and understood, were typical of the breed, he felt on safe ground. If not, then he might find his comeuppance.

"Once we are over the ocean, and still climbing," the captain went on, "we will ignite the afterburners again and accelerate through the speed of sound to one point seven Mach. You may expect a slight increase in the sound level when the afterburners come on but very little sensation other than that. When we have reached that speed, we will shut off the afterburners and gain further speed rather slowly until we are cruising at Mach two, or two times the speed of sound. Our average altitude will be about fifty-seven thousand feet, depending upon our air temperature. The normally strong winds encountered by westbound jets will not trouble us as there is little or no wind at our cruise altitude. Assuming that we lift off at eleven-fifteen, on schedule, we should be at our gate at Kennedy Airport at ten o'clock, eastern daylight time, after three hours and thirty-one minutes in the air. We hope that you will enjoy our flight."

Everard looked out of the four by six inch window to his left, but could see very little. The thick glass, designed to hold very heavy pressure from inside the fuselage, distorted the grass beside the taxi way. A steward in his middle fifties was demonstrating the use of the life vest and oxygen mask. He maneuvered within the confines of the narrow center aisle with practiced agility.

As the captain announced that they were taking the runway, Everard glanced about the cabin.

Behind him by one row, and to his right on the opposite aisle seat, was a middle-aged man whose black eyes seemed to dart about with a look somewhere between apprehension and alarm. Everard laughed to himself. The poor bugger was probably nervous about flying. Everard gazed out his tiny window once again. The sound of the engines rose sharply, and the Concorde began to move forward, its nose pointing high even before it had begun to gain speed. As the ground roll continued, Everard thought about how he might report the sensation to his wife and son when he returned. Nothing out of the ordinary, really. Just a routine jet takeoff.

The Concorde lifted off and seemed to wallow. Everard watched the Mach meter at the front of the cabin begin to climb, slowly, from Mach point three seven. In a few minutes it steadied at point nine five. The deck angle of the aircraft continued to be steep. After about fifteen minutes, the captain declared that the afterburners were about to ignite, and the noise level increased slightly. As the Mach meter passed through one point zero, Everard felt a slight buzz—then it receded. As promised, the increase in speed to one point seven was a matter of a few minutes only; then the sound level dropped, and the changing numbers on the Mach meter became sluggish. Oh well, thought Everard, so much for supersonic flight.

The front cabin stewardess—a trim brunette in her mid-forties had been quietly moving down the aisle taking dinner orders and offering an invitation for a brief visit to the cockpit. Many of the passengers accepted eagerly. Everard did not. If ever it became his lot to try a lawsuit involving the Concorde, he would need many more hours in the captain's seat than this short flight would allow, even if he were the only passenger. Until that time, he had no wish to clutter his mind.

He noted, however, that the frightened gentleman to his right accepted very quickly the invitation to go forward—accepted, and yet looked terribly uncomfortable about the whole idea. As the stewardess passed on down the aisle, Everard thought he glimpsed a dark object with the initials G-U inside the man's coat, near his right armpit. He could not be sure. And yet it struck him as odd.

The cocktails and hors d'oeuvre were quite splendid, despite the cramped cabin, and Everard was beginning to enjoy himself. The Mach meter showed one point eight two, climbing slowly, and the first meals were being served to the front rows. The passenger in row thirteen, the aisle seat, had gone forward, either to use the toilet or to make his cockpit visit. Everard was prepared to savor the Quiche Lorraine he had ordered, when suddenly the chief steward came marching slowly down the aisle, his eyes glazed, looking at no one. Everard felt a sudden discomfort in his system.

"I say," he said as the chief was about to pass by him, "might I have a word with you, sir?"

The chief snapped to attention momentarily, put his fingers to his lips, and shook his head.

"I insist," said Everard firmly.

The chief glanced back over his right shoulder and leaned over the empty aisle seat toward Everard.

"Is there some trouble?"

"Oh no, sir," said the chief.

Everard had had too much experience in examining lying witnesses to accept the answer. He motioned the chief to bend down so that they would not be over-heard.

The chief really didn't want to get into a conversation with the gentleman, but his years of service had accustomed him to recognizing authority in a man's voice and manner, and this passenger seemed to have both. He could be someone truly important.

"I happen," said Everard, "to be a friend of the Chairman of British Airways, and I would not like to report to him that you told me a falsehood unless it was in the interest of the safety of the aircraft. Is there a problem with this plane?"

The chief's eyes darted left, then right. No one was paying attention to their whisperings.

"Oh no, sir," he said. "Not the plane."

"Then you are having trouble with a passenger, I presume," said Everard.

"I wouldn't exactly say that, sir."

"Would you say that there was some interference with the captain's plans?"

"His flight plans?" asked the chief, looking a bit flustered.

"Exactly."

"I really have to go now, sir," said the chief.

"Where are we headed?" Everard thought of the lawyers awaiting him in Boston.

The chief whispered in his ear. "Not to be alarmed, sir."

"I'm not. You seem to be." Everard pointed at his ear.

The chief's mouth was an inch from Everard's head, when he whispered, "Dakar," then straightened up.

"Very well then," said Everard, seeming entirely composed, and motioning the chief down again. "Is he armed?"

"I'm afraid so, sir. Yes. May I go?"

"One moment, chief. Is *it*"—he emphasized the word—"dark black in color?"

"It is, sir," said the chief. "Flat sides and a wide handle. That's all I noticed. I really couldn't say more."

"Very well then, chief. Would you fetch me a torch? A heavy one, preferably."

"A bit later, sir."

"Now," said Everard, with all the skill he could muster to make the one word a command that could not be denied.

"I'm sure we have one amidships."

"Then be quick about it." Everard smiled. "Perhaps I can be of help."

"Right away, sir," said the chief, hustling toward the rear of the aircraft. In a few seconds he was back, holding a long, silver, three-cell flashlight. "Will this do, sir?"

"Nicely, I should think," replied Everard. "Now would you please do what you have to do, but take your time about it."

"Very good, sir," said the chief.

Everard stood up in the aisle, tucked the flashlight butt first on the right side of his waistband under his jacket, and strode casually toward the cockpit. When he was fifteen feet from the entry door, the nervous passenger turned toward him, spinning the hapless stewardess in front of him as a shield.

"Do not come any farther," he said.

"Nonsense," said Everard, "I'm on your side. I had some part in arranging for you to come aboard. Do not interfere with my orders, or I will have you executed as soon as we land in Dakar."

The man was obviously jolted. His psyche had suddenly been cast from the boat into waters that might be infested with sharks. If there were no sanctuary for him in Dakar, he was undone. He could not understand why this Englishman claimed to be a confederate, but in his fuzz-gray world one ignored nothing, listened carefully to everything.

"I do not understand," he said, faltering.

"You are not using your wits," said Everard coldly. "Unless our friend the captain turns south at once, we will not have enough fuel to get to Senegal. Why have you allowed him to ignore your orders?"

"He has told me he takes a few minutes to reset his route, then he turns."

"He lies," said Everard. "He should have turned south at once, then calculated his exact course. You are letting him fool you."

The captain, twisted in his seat about six feet forward of the Arab, stared at Everard with wide-eyed puzzlement. He nodded at the first officer, who twisted the heading control of the autopilot to one hundred eighty degrees. The Concorde began a gentle turn to the left.

"I do not know you," said the Arab. "Return to your seat at once or I will kill this woman." Miss Langford, already pale, began to look a bit green.

"My friend," said Everard with mock exasperation, "without my assistance you would never have gotten that pistol by the metal detector." The Arab began to protest, but Everard cut him off. "Further, you idiot," he went on, harshly, "you will shoot no one unless the hammer is cocked and the safety off, both of which you have forgotten."

The Arab cast his glance down at the weapon for a fraction of a second. It was enough. With one sudden motion, Everard snatched the flashlight from under his suit jacket and brought it down hard on the Arab's right wrist with a sharp crack. The pistol clattered to the deck, as the Arab, howling with pain, stooped to get it. Everard swung the flashlight again, hitting the Arab hard at the base of the skull. He slumped with a groan, and lay still.

"What the bloody hell, . . ." blurted the captain, starting to rise from his seat.

Everard scooped the pistol from the floor and handed it to the bewildered captain, butt first.

"You need not worry about this weapon," he said

quietly; "it is really quite harmless. If you examine it with care, you will observe that it is a detailed plastic replica, not a firearm."

The captain confirmed what he had been told, and looked quite relieved, then somewhat irritated. "How could you have known? That was a bloody awful chance to take with Miss Langford's life, I should say."

Everard smiled. "No chance at all. This gentleman was seated across from me, and I noticed an object inside his coat which *looked* like it might be the handle of an automatic pistol. There was a stamped imprint on the butt of the handgrip with the letters "G-U," which I recognized to mean the Guntsler-Uphoff Company in Stuttgart, which specializes in making replicas of popular firearms. When our friend balked at my suggestion that I had helped him fool the metal detector, it was because *he* knew that he had smuggled no metal aboard. When he failed to cock the hammer or release the safety catch, there was no question left. Miss Langford was never in actual danger although all of you were supposed to believe that she was."

The captain shook his head, fingering the letters "G-U" on the bottom of the weapon. "Extraordinary. Are you a firearms specialist, sir?"

"No, I'm afraid not," replied Everard, chuckling. "I'm a barrister. Unfortunately for our skyjacker here, I defended an accused for armed robbery several months ago. The so-called 'weapon' used was an exact duplicate of the one you are holding. I tried to persuade His Lordship that since it was not a true firearm, the charge should be reduced to unarmed robbery. I was not successful, but my memory of the plastic replica is quite keen. Perhaps if I had been a better loser, I would have forgotten those letters and we should all be on our way to Senegal for a bit of West African cuisine."

The first officer turned the autopilot back to the west and removed his belt to bind the hands of the still unconscious Arab. "I wonder," said the captain, "whether this chap has any actual confederates aboard?"

Everard shook his head. "I doubt it," he said. "No organized terrorist would make an attempt of this nature without a real weapon. I think the authorities will discover that this gentleman is of marginal sanity, with a real or imagined grudge against England, British Airways, or some passenger back in the cabin. However, if you have any morphine aboard, I would give him a healthy injection. The mentally ill become quite violent when frustrated, and there is precious little room up here for jousting about, wouldn't you say?"

The captain agreed, and reached for the first aid box.

12

A BRACE OF COUNSEL
Tuesday, July 11

Stacy Barton had been looking forward with great anticipation to greeting, on the same day, two of the finest
trial lawyers her generation could proffer. By the time
she had picked up Anthony Everard and Daniel Shaw
in successive trips to Boston's Logan Airport and delivered them to Kilrayne's office she was exhausted.

She had expected the pressure from the press but
had, of course, not anticipated that Everard would be
greeted as a national hero. On landing in New York,
the British Airways captain had, for an Englishman,
been lavish in his praise of Everard's cool and wit in
aborting the first attempted hijacking of an SST, and
the American press gobbled it up. The wire services had
already fashioned a bloody cockpit battle as part of the
saga.

Mobbed by the Boston press when he got off the
plane from Kennedy, Everard, accustomed by his discipline to keeping a tight lip except when in the courtroom, referred all questions to British Airways.

The men were seated with Stacy and Kilrayne in his
conference room when Osborne arrived. He greeted
both friends warmly and sat down.

"Everard," said Osborne, "I guess you're a transat-
lantic hero now. I'm going to Beirut on business next
month. Will you fly with me?"

Everard laughed, and Osborne got down to business.

"Gentlemen," he began, "as I have said to both of you by telephone, it is with great personal sadness that I learned that due to a technical conflict typical of a large law firm, I am unable to defend Mike, who is my friend. When confronting that situation, I asked myself what my first choice would be were I accused of a serious offense and faced with the unnerving prospect of trial by jury. This meeting is the result of that reflection." Osborne paused, and glanced from one to the other soberly.

"As to procedural matters, I see no problem. In your case Dan, your admission *pro hac vice* will be permitted as a matter of course. As to Tony, if he decides to join us, the Chief Justice of our Superior Court, the Honorable Patrick Boling, will personally preside tomorrow morning in Salem at his admission to defend this case, technically as associate counsel.

"Indeed, I am pleased to say that he has been authorized to extend a warm welcome from the Chief Justice of our Supreme Judicial Court, as well as the Chief Justice of the United States."

"What about Barrett?" asked Kilrayne. "He'll scream like a castrated bull. I can't imagine a bush leaguer agreeing that Ted Williams can be a designated hitter for the other team."

"That, ah, problem has been confronted and solved," said Osborne. "A mutual friend has advised Walter that a number of Essex County's most influential citizens trace, or at least claim, a long British heritage, and might be deeply affronted by opposition on his part. As an aspiring candidate, Walter has reportedly seen the wisdom of assent."

Everard clasped his hands behind his head and smiled. "Life," he said, "apparently hasn't changed here in the Colonies."

"I'm told," said Shaw with a wink at Kilrayne, "that the only living cannibals in America are quartered here in the witch-hanging country. Some of them, I suspect from recent experience, are reporters. Meanwhile, brother Everard, it seems that our friend Fred Osborne has tucked us into a trial date less than sixty days down the road. At some point I need to know what this case is all about, how long the trial will go, and what Mike expects of us."

"Of course," said Osborne softly. "I think it inappropriate that I participate further except to move the admission of counsel. I shall leave you to your own business and wish you well. Mike, I bow out with deep regret, but I leave you in the best hands I've run across in sixty years. Godspeed."

Osborne shook hands with all three men, and with Stacy, and left the conference room. For a few moments, no one spoke.

Kilrayne stared at the tablet of foolscap before him. "I guess," he said, "Mr. Shaw's questions deserve answers. The short facts are these, as best I can put them together.

"I had a client some years ago named Sarah Hansen. I defended her for driving under. She was acquitted, largely because she is—or was, as things may turn out—a stunning woman. I was lucky enough to put an all male jury in the box for that trial.

"Sarah is an interior decorator of substantial talent. She had more independence than John Hancock. She earns a good income with no help from anyone. She is very private, very vivacious, and much sought after. I suspect she has a number of close male friends.

"I have had a drink or two with Sarah from time to time, over the years," Kilrayne went on. "The prosecution will try to prove more than that, I'm sure. They will also prove that Sarah hasn't been seen since last June seventh. They have no positive evidence of death."

"Pardon me," interjected Everard. "Do I understand that actually there is no corpse?"

"There's a strong inference that they have none,"

said Kilrayne wryly, "since there is no autopsy report."

"Extraordinary," said Everard.

"It is extraordinary," agreed Kilrayne, "indeed I would have thought it impossible. But there is one California case in this country, one Australian case, and," he added, "unhappily one case from the mother country, my esteemed colleague, where convictions for murder have been upheld with no direct evidence of death. I don't want to become fourth on that list."

"May I ask," said Everard, "whether your relationship with Ms. Hansen has been such that she would in some secret spot observe that you were going to be tried for her murder and yet not come forward to disclaim her own death to save you the inconvenience?"

Kilrayne looked at him, then at Shaw. "No," he said, "I have no reason to believe that could happen. Sarah is, from all that I could tell, very stable, and we have never uttered a disagreeable word between us. I think we should assume that she is either dead or in captivity where she knows nothing of the indictment or cannot come forward if she knows."

Everard glanced at Shaw. "Very well. Please go on."

Kilrayne nodded. "I will. Your next question, or one of them, will ask why I was indicted. If you ask me questions of fact, I'll answer as directly as I can. But a 'why' question is going to be muddied by my own legal analysis. I don't want to do that. I've defended a few lawyers and found the experience to be a pain in the ass. Defending me may well be a pain in the ass. I apologize for that and assure you that being defended is just as big a pain in the ass."

Shaw grinned. "I have had both experiences, Mike, although when I was the client it was a gripe before the bar association and not an indictment, and I agree."

"I am the neophyte in this business," said Everard. "I defended a solicitor once, and he was a lamb. He was also a blithering fool. Had he been a worthy advocate, I'm quite sure he would have been a nuisance and also a much more defensible client. But do tell us about the reason for your being accused. I'm afraid you Americans have a good bit more politics mixed in your system than we are used to."

"I'll put it as simply as I know how," said Kilrayne, "and it's as thin as I hope their indictment is. The District Attorney of Essex County is a weakfish in his mid-thirties named Walter Barrett. He was put in the job by his uncle, Carl Barrett, who despite the fact that he is a total discredit to our profession, is a big man in local political circles. Many years ago, when I was mostly comprised of piss and vinegar, I represented his wife in a divorce case that the establishment didn't want. Carl wrote me a particularly insulting letter—sort of master to serf—which riled my Irish corpuscles. I took him to the cleaners. I am sure he remembers the whole incident bitterly. I think he is somehow behind this indictment. That's really all I've got."

"How would this Barrett know the woman was missing?" asked Everard. "More particularly, how would he be so sure that she wouldn't turn up that he would risk a murder indictment?"

"I don't know," said Kilrayne, shaking his head. "For the life of me, I have no idea."

"If Walter Barrett is a silly, as you say," asked Shaw, "who's the heavy in it with him? There's got to be somebody on the scene to control the case—his uncle can't very well do that on a moment-to-moment basis?"

Again Kilrayne shook his head. "I don't know. There is a Lieutenant from the State Police Detective Division named Gilardi assigned to the case. He's headquarters, not Essex County Staff, although there is a regular from that division assigned as there is at every D.A.'s office. Gilardi's a heavy. Bright, streetwise, and knows how to knuckle a witness. He's been in court at Walter's elbow. He could be the mastermind. But Gilardi and I have no score to settle—at least none that I'm aware of. With a cop, you're never sure. I might have embarrassed one of his buddies one time, for god's sake, and he could have it in for me. But I don't think so. I always figured that if Gilardi got jammed up, he'd come right here quick looking for a defense at a discount. I could be wrong."

Everard caught a small reaction from Stacy Barton out of the corner of his eye. He could not let it pass. "Pardon me," he interjected, "but if we're going to make progress in this difficult matter, I think we need every small bit of information. Mrs. Barton, do you have something about this Leftenant Gilardi?"

Stacy hesitated, then looked at Mike. He nodded with the slightest movement of his eyes. She replied. "I hadn't mentioned this to Mr. Kilrayne yet, but when I was at the airport today, waiting for Mr. Shaw, a friend came to talk with me. He's a corporal in the state police, on airport detail. We were talking about the case. He said that Lieutenant Gilardi had told a sergeant he knows that Mike Kilrayne was going to get taken down pretty good. The sergeant said he was kind of gloating about it. I'm not so sure he hasn't got a grudge."

Kilrayne frowned. "Did the corporal elaborate at all?"

"No," said Stacy. "That's all he could tell me."

"Okay," said Shaw. "All that you've told us wouldn't make out a case against anyone for homicide even if she *is* dead. Where's the zinger?"

"I have only one clue as to that," replied Kilrayne. "One of the listed witnesses is a two-bit hood named Frank LaPere. Frank is in his late thirties. Unfortunately, he looks more like a bank vice president than a criminal and can handle himself pretty well when he puts his mind to it.

"Six years ago I defended Frankie for an armored truck heist. He was acquitted but never paid the balance of his bill. Late last April he made an appointment to see me, to ask that I represent him in a burglary case, with payment to be made immediately after the acquittal. I refused. His case was plenty triable. In fact, despite the fact that he went to bat with a comparatively inexperienced public defender, the jury just barely hooked him. He drew seven to ten in Walpole. A few days ago I got a call from his sister, who said Frank felt that if I had tried his case, he would have gotten off. If I would take his appeal 'on the come,' she said, he would feel much better about the whole thing. I refused again. Next thing I know he's a witness.

"My friends at Walpole say that Frankie was hustled out of there last week late at night, and not even the guards know where he is. He's squirreled away somewhere for 'protection,' meaning that if he is pressed on cross-examination about his special treatment, he will claim that I am a killer and that he is in great fear.

"What will he say? Christ knows. My experience tells me that he will claim I asked him to kill Sarah Hansen or to arrange for her to be killed. Nothing less would explain why Barrett's going forward."

"Would there have been anyone present during your last talk with this LaPere chap?" asked Everard.

Kilrayne shook his head. "The receptionist brought him in to my office," he said, "but we were alone together for a good thirty minutes. That's one of the risks, I suppose, of being in this business. Client conferences are usually head to head because *they* want them that way—and then there are no witnesses."

"You people play rough," said Shaw. "How do you suppose they got to this LaPere?"

"The same way they would have gotten to him in San Francisco, Dan'l," said Kilrayne with a tolerant smile. "Slip the word out through the prison network that evidence was needed against Michael Kilrayne and see who would come forward and what he had to trade. LaPere, like most of Walpole's finest, would like to get out. An off-the-record assurance of help in getting early work-release would be enough. Gilardi is an expert at fashioning such deals."

"But what about the prosecutor?" asked Everard. "Would he be a party to such an agreement?"

"Some would," said Kilrayne. "Some would arrange not to know about it and be grateful for the evidence without much caring whether it was the strict truth or not. Our criminal justice system seems to be driven by the philosophy of Vince Lombardi, who was a famous football coach in this country. He coined the phrase 'Winning isn't the important thing, it's the *only* thing.' A lot of our lawyers regard that attitude as gospel."

"Is LaPere the only such creature in this case?" asked Everard.

"So far as I know, at the moment," said Kilrayne grimly. "Gilardi's probably still sniffing around, looking for reinforcements. All he needs is a list of my dissatisfied clients, which means every psychopath who won less than he expected to."

Shaw looked at his watch. "Perhaps," he said, "Tony and I could adjourn to the hotel and discuss things for awhile. We could meet for breakfast and work out any details before the court proceeding in Salem. Would that be agreeable?"

"Whatever you like," smiled Kilrayne, wanly. "I'm just a client looking for counsel—the very best I can get."

"I wonder," said Everard, "if your Mrs. Barton would like to join us. I assume she would be working with us?"

"You could say that," said Kilrayne, his eyes twinkling slightly. "In fact, technically speaking, the reverse would be true. As the only lawyer with a Massachusetts license, she will be listed as lead counsel, I'm afraid. But Stacy's pretty reasonable. I don't think she'll try to hog the show."

Stacy smiled. The men gathered up their notes and departed with her for the Ritz-Carlton Hotel.

13

THE CONTRACT
Wednesday, July 12

"Good morning," said Kilrayne as he slipped into a booth in the hotel dining room next to Shaw and across from Everard, who was sipping at a cup of tea.

The waitress and a breathless Stacy Barton arrived at the table at the same time. "Sorry," said Stacy to Everard as she slipped in beside him, "traffic in this city is pretty impossible."

"I'm afraid the tea is equally impossible," said Everard.

After everyone was settled and breakfast orders had been taken, Shaw began. "I take it that you would prefer to go forward at the first possible moment?"

"As a general rule," said Kilrayne, "phony cases are best tried quickly. As long as this thing is hanging, I might as well lock my office doors. I'd rather get it over with."

"Okay," said Shaw. "Tony and I have kicked things around, and we'll be glad to work together with Stacy in defending you. I'll do the preparation, Tony will handle the trial. He's tied up 'til late August, but we've arranged to meet in London around the middle of next month. We'll have to rely on Stacy to handle any motions that have to be filed and argued as we go along."

Kilrayne nodded. "Sounds good. Indeed I'm very

grateful. Let's get to a necessary evil, if we may. What will the fee arrangements be?"

"Neither of us, I'm afraid, knows very much about fees in American criminal cases," replied Shaw. "I can't very well charge you a third of an acquittal. Tony's usual fee is four hundred pounds a day for trial. I can live with a per diem of five hundred dollars. In view of the heavy travel expense you're going to be stuck with, we thought that these figures might be fair."

"That's very fair indeed," Kilrayne said. "I hope I never have to return the favor."

Everard raised his teacup in mock toast. "Amen," he said.

There were few empty seats in the First Criminal Session in the Essex County Superior Court when Osborne ushered Everard, Shaw, Kilrayne, and Stacy Barton to the defense table at ten-thirty that morning. All three networks found the idea of a lawyer charged with murder worth covering. The *Daily News* had sent Theo Wilson; the *Post*, Helen Dudar; and *The New York Times*, Wallace Turner. *Time, Newsweek,* and *People* had their Boston correspondents on hand, and every local paper had reporters jostling for seats.

Walter Barrett, who was already at the prosecution table with his staff, walked over with a warm smile and greeted Shaw and Everard. "Welcome to our humble surround," he said grandly, just loud enough for the press in the front row to hear.

Shaw and Everard nodded pleasantly.

"Well, Dan," said Barrett, "I guess I ought to have your name for this one. 'Daniel in the lion's Den.' "

Shaw winked. "Naw," he said, affecting a country twang. "We're just a couple of good ol' boys here to learn about criminal law in the east. 'Walter in the chicken yard' might be more like it."

If Walter caught the point, he didn't let on. Being a subject of national news coverage had him beaming to the point that the status of his opponents was of second-ary moment. Gilardi nodded politely to the newcomers but did not come over.

By his very appearance and demeanor, Supreme Court Chief Justice Patrick Boling was a credit to the Commonwealth of Massachusetts and the judiciary gen-erally.

A large, handsome man, with thick gray hair and chiseled features, his blue eyes sparkled youthfully from under bushy eyebrows. He moved gracefully and spoke articulately in a mellow, resonant voice.

When the bailiff had called the proceedings to order, the judge gaveled once lightly and beamed out at the crowd. "The court apologizes for our limited facilities," he began. "Our courtroom here is small, but venerable, dating back several centuries. I hope our representatives from the media will be able to enjoy adequate comfort during this short session."

"It's venerable, all right," muttered Theo Wilson to Helen Dudar. "This is where they used to sentence women to be hanged for being witches. God help Gloria Steinem if she'd been around then."

"There are before the court," the judge went on, "three motions: two for the admission of counsel, and one for the withdrawal of appearance by Mr. Osborne. We shall proceed in that order."

"Your Honor," said Osborne, "I am pleased to pre-sent to the court Daniel E. Shaw, Esquire. Mr. Shaw is a member of the Bar of the State of California and has been for about ten years. He is admitted to the United States District Court for the Northern District of Cali-fornia, many of the United States Circuit Courts of Ap-peal, and the United States Supreme Court. He is a trial lawyer of wide-ranging experience and has practiced in a dozen or more jurisdictions other than California. I am pleased to vouch for his qualifications and to move his admission, *pro hac vice*, as associate counsel for the defense in this case."

"Mr. Shaw," said Boling warmly, "I am pleased to welcome you to this court, even as the judges of your great state have graciously extended similar privileges to members of the Bar of the Commonwealth. That motion will be granted."

"Thank you, Your Honor. Next, in a somewhat unprecedented step, I should like to move to admit, also as an associate defense counsel, a gentleman who although not a practitioner in this country is a most distinguished barrister from a nation to whom we owe much of our legal heritage. Anthony S. Everard, Esquire, Your Honor, Queen's Counsel, has a most exemplary trial record in the courts of England. I have had the pleasure of watching him work as an advocate on more than one occasion and can personally say that he deservedly has a reputation in the English courts that is superb in every respect. I believe that Mr. Everard would bring honor to this distinguished court."

"The court accepts and endorses your view," beamed Boling. "I am privileged to have among my judicial colleagues several of the Justices of the Queen's Bench, and Mr. Everard's accomplishments have been mentioned to me.

"You are right, of course, that the admission of counsel from beyond our national borders is extraordinary. But not entirely without precedent, perhaps. In discussing this matter with my disinguished colleague Roger Goodrich of the Supreme Court of Erie County, New York, I find that on one occasion a barrister from Toronto was permitted to appear on a civil case there.

"Even without that incident, however, the court is of the opinion that it can and should grant this motion for a variety of reasons. First, it is generally recognized that the barristers of England are probably, as a group, the best trained of all the advocates found in the Anglo-American systems of jurisprudence. It is a highly desirable training, which concerned members of the bar and bench have recently begun to study much more closely.

Certainly, this court could not help but benefit from the experience of having Mr. Everard before it.

"I am most pleased to say," said Boling, winding up with a flourish, "that the chief justices of both our state and federal courts share these views. Mr. Everard, the court welcomes you. The motion is granted."

Everard nodded his thanks. "The final motion," said Osborne, "is much less pleasant. After filing my appearance in this case, with a purpose to defend my friend and colleague, Mr. Kilrayne, throughout the trial, I have discovered circumstances unrelated to either the charge or the accused that suggest the possibility of some conflict of interests down the line. To guard against that possibility, however remote, I must reluctantly seek Your Honor's permission to withdraw."

The judge studied Osborne for a slow moment, then sighed.

"With equal reluctance, Mr. Osborne, your motion is granted. The court would have profited, I'm sure, from the benefit of your wisdom and judgment in assisting the guidance of these proceedings. This court will stand adjourned, pending the further orders of Judge Sullivan."

Wrote Ezra Reed in his column in the evening edition of the Boston *Chronicle* that same day:

The big question is how the public will react. It is unlikely that any court anywhere in the Commonwealth could have assembled a jury that would not have viewed Frederic Osborne with confidence and respect. Instead, this jury will be confronted with a silken-voiced superstar barrister, aided by the legal whiz of the west, backed by the cunning and experience of the formidable Michael Kilrayne, who has something more than his reputation at stake, and can be expected to fight with more of everything than he has ever done before.

On the other side is Walter Barrett, newly appointed to a vacancy normally filled by popular vote. His trial credentials are slender at best. His evidence, a closely guarded secret thanks to a suffocating gag order issued by Judge Kevin Sullivan, is rumored to be skimpy. And although no one underestimated the dogged brilliance of Detective Lieutenant Joseph Gilardi in putting together a case from loose ends, in this case he is in the position of a good, steady pitcher, facing the Yankees' old murderers' row.

The public, however, is notoriously for the underdog. The lopsidedness of this contest might just suggest overkill to the sports fans who find their way to our jury boxes. In going so conspicuously first class, Mr. Kilrayne may have risked outsmarting himself.

On the other hand, it is difficult to criticize one who *thinks* he may have a heart problem for consulting a Dr. Michael DeBakey, if he can. And any murder charge is at least as dangerous as a heart problem.

Whatever the shakeout of this case, which is shaping up as a humdinger by any account, any smart businessman would give his right arm for the popcorn concession at the courthouse.

Walter Barrett and Gilardi read the column in Barrett's office with some satisfaction. "Not too shabby," said an elated Barrett. Gilardi grunted in reserved agreement.

Michael Kilrayne stared out the window of his office, while Stacy read the column to him. "That's the bullshit," he said. "No jury is going to hook me for murder because they're feeling sorry for poor little Walter."

"I hope not," said Stacy. "You have to admit, though," she said, "that Walter was born to be an underdog."

Carl Barrett read the column as he sipped his after-dinner coffee in his home on the Manchester waterfront. "I think," he told himself, "that we may have to get Walter some professional help."

14

JUDGE ME NOT
Friday, July 14

Michael Kilrayne was standing just outside the Third
Criminal Session on the ninth floor of the Suffolk Superior Court in Pemberton Square, smoking a cigarette
and waiting to be called to begin a hearing on a motion
to suppress evidence illegally seized in a cocaine case.
He pondered the manner in which his colleagues and
the court personnel handled the awkward matter of his
indictment. Most pretended to ignore it—business as
usual—while others took a whispered aside to express
their condolences and support.

"Anything I can do, Mike, just call, . . ." some
said. Others assured him that the legal community
viewed the whole affair as a cruel joke, and Walter Barrett as a publicity hungry fool. Kilrayne wondered
whether these same people were as supportive when
they were gossiping together, as they obviously were.
Lawyers, he reflected, seem to experience envy on a
more regular basis than those in other professions.

He stepped on the cigarette, and was about to push
open the courtroom door when Erma Coolidge, a vet-
eran of thirty-two years in the Court Clerk's Office,
touched his elbow. Erma had liked Mike since she had
first met him when the ink was hardly dry on his license
and had done him small favors over the years.

"Could I buzz in your ear for a moment, Mike?" she asked softly.

"Anytime, sweetheart," smiled Mike warmly, walking with her toward the elevators. "What's up?"

"Two bad breaks, I'm afraid," said Erma, frowning. "A little bird told me that your case was going to be specially assigned to Judge Brogan," she began.

"Bad break! Christ, that's anything but. Brogan's just about the best on the bench, with enough balls to throw this thing out."

"No, no, Mike," she protested. "That's just it. Judge Brogan disqualified himself because he feels that he would be leaning toward you subconsciously in his rulings. He said the whole thing was a fraud in his opinion, and therefore he couldn't sit."

Kilrayne lit another cigarette, unnerved by the news. Very suddenly, it dawned on him that *most* of the judges he considered to be competent were his contemporaries and friends, and might step aside for similar reasons. *That* was going to become a real problem, because drawing a decent judge was critical. A bummer could bury him, step by step, either through incompetence, malice, or both.

"What else does the bird say?" he asked, unhappily.

"The word is," said Erma slowly, "that the case will be assigned to Webster Lodge."

"Oh my Jesus!" groaned Kilrayne. "Webster Lodge? Christ, he's on record as doubting my integrity. How in hell did the chief ever pick him?"

"No one's really sure," said Erma. "There is some talk that Webster requested the assignment. He turns seventy in December and has to retire. His last big case, that sort of thing."

Kilrayne thought for a moment. "Erma," he said slowly. "Something very, very important. Is there *any* talk that Carl Barrett put him up to this? Any hint at all?"

"I don't think so," replied Erma. "Unless Carl suggested it to Webster and Webster went to the chief. He is pretty close with Carl, if anyone is."

"You're a doll," said Mike, patting her cheek affectionately. "You hear anything from that bird, let me know." He headed for the courtroom.

That afternoon Stacy Barton returned from the Industrial Accident Board with a client. As she entered the office Olivia, the receptionist, gave her the high sign. "Excuse me a moment," Stacy said to the young man who was with her. "I'll be with you in just a minute or two." She walked back to Kilrayne's office and found him pacing the floor, fuming.

"Close the door, Stacy," he said. "We have been screwed to the wall. Destroyed!"

"What happened?"

"Boling is assigning Webster Lodge, the Brahmin hangman, to sit at the trial!"

Stacy blanched, "Lodge! Oh my god. Why him? Is Boling trying to bury you?"

"No, I don't think so," said Kilrayne. "Pat and I have always gotten along, even before he was appointed. They say Lodge came to him and requested the assignment, on some notion that his days are numbered and by seniority he ought to have it. I'll swear his good buddy Barrett put him up to it, but that's something we'll never know. I've gotta come up with some way to get rid of the sonofabitch."

"Let me get rid of this client," said Stacy, "and then we can put our heads together."

Thirty minutes later Kilrayne's intercom buzzed. "Mike," said Stacy, "would you mind if I had dinner and a few cocktails with Charley O'Shea this evening?"

"No, I suppose not," said Kilrayne, "so long as you go to some foreign country and get Charley's word that he'll never mention it. I don't want him being seen with you and then printing something that's going to irritate

Sullivan. He's our man for the next two weeks at least."

"Two weeks only," said Stacy. "He's assigned to Barnstable next month—must have plenty of clout with the chief to get Cape Cod duty in August. Anyway, Charley will be okay. And I don't think anyone will see us. I'm having him up to my apartment."

"Okay. But watch out. Charley's an old smoothie, and you're just a kid."

"I'll be good."

"Have a good weekend. And tell Charley for me he's got good taste."

Patrick Boling was reviewing his fall Superior Court schedules on the following Monday morning when his secretary informed him that a Mr. O'Shea of the Boston *Chronicle* would like to see him on a matter of some urgency. Boling normally had little direct contact with reporters but decided that perhaps he ought to speak with O'Shea. Probably something to do with his admitting the barrister, Everard, to defend the Kilrayne case. Boling had gotten rather good marks from the press for his handling of the ceremony. With O'Shea, there might be more of the same.

"Good morning, Your Honor," said Charley heartily as he entered. "I trust you had a pleasant weekend." O'Shea's affability was in direct proportion to his desire to please Stacy, which was very great.

"Oh, very nice indeed," said the Chief Justice cordially. "Mary and I had the grandchildren down to the place on Nantucket. Wonderful wealther. What can I do for you this fine Monday morning?"

Charley, as innocent as a lamb, said, "I'm trying to follow up on some information that came in over the weekend. I don't like to bother Your Honor, but this information is somewhat troublesome, and I thought it might be better to bring it to you directly."

Boling frowned. It had been a mistake, he told himself, to allow the interview. O'Shea had not come to spread more accolades. He was deadly serious about something, probably something unpleasant. Now there was no convenient way to terminate the interview, duck the problem, or issue a stiff "no comment."

"Yes, what is it, Mr. O'Shea?" Boling affected a somewhat more formal tone of voice.

"Our information is," said O'Shea almost apologetically, "that Justice Webster Lodge is going to be handling the trial of the Kilrayne case."

Boling frowned. "Justice Lodge is among those under consideration," he replied. "No definite assignment has been made yet. The clerk will be publishing the schedule when an affirmative selection has been made."

"Oh. Our informant thought the matter was final. Well, Bill Guidetti—that's my partner—has been going through some of the clips looking for background, and came across a couple of public statements, in open court, I think, where the Justice was pretty critical of Mr. Kilrayne." As Boling started to flush, O'Shea hurriedly continued. "But that's not the reason I'm here. The information was that the prosecutor's uncle was somehow involved in suggesting Judge Lodge. That's what I was told to follow up on."

Boling leaned across the desk, his eyes blazing. "Mr. O'Shea, I assure you that I have had no conversation whatsoever with Carl Barrett, assuming that's who you mean, since this indictment was returned ten days ago. None at all."

"Oh no, Your Honor," said O'Shea hastily. "There is no suggestion of *your* involvement. Our editors know Your Honor's reputation far too well to think that there might be any collusion involving *this* office. I can't reveal my source without getting fired, but I can call Your Honor's attention to an ironic twist that might be helpful."

"What's that?"

"One of the editorial writers pulled the Sacco-Vanzetti file, the whole thing, on Saturday. There are some parallels involving the judge in that case which were thought to be provocative." O'Shea was beginning to perspire, despite the air conditioning.

"I see. And what do you intend to publish at this point?"

"Nothing, immediately," said Charley. "When the assignment is made firm, there may be something depending on how this source checks out."

"I'm glad to hear that," said Boling, relaxing a little. "You have my assurance that I will personally look into the matter. It looks like this trial will be carefully watched across the nation, and I am determined that the Superior Court will show its excellence in full measure. Not even the hint of a taint will be permitted. I appreciate your calling this matter to my attention, even though it may well be groundless."

"Very well, Your Honor. I thank you for seeing me and apologize for bringing unpleasant news. I'd hate to see any cloud cast on the judiciary after what everyone—including myself—thought was a splendid proceeding before you last Wednesday up in Salem."

Boling was smiling, a little stiffly, as Charley O'Shea made his way out the door. Charley was shuddering a little. If his editors could see him now, he would soon be at the bottom of Boston Harbor tied to a twenty-foot steel I-beam. He prayed that Boling would not contact one of them personally.

Charley's heart would have stopped had he remained as a fly on the wall. From the moment he had mentioned Sacco and Vanzetti, Patrick Boling's mind had begun to race. With the possible exception of the execution of women in Salem as "witches," Massachusetts had no blight on its entire judicial history that could hold a candle to Sacco and Vanzetti. So shabby had been the trial which led to the two men being electrocuted in Charlestown's old state prison that Governor Michael Dukakis had issued a decree pardoning both of them, albeit forty years after neither could have cared.

And the judge who had presided—*Webster* Thayer—had been generally vilified by historians writing about the case, many of them. His unjudicial conduct—speaking out at his country club against the defendants to whom he had owed a fair trial—had damned near caused the governor then in office to order a new trial. What had O'Shea been trying to tell him? Was Webster Lodge shooting his mouth off at some social gathering about how he had been chosen to preside at the mighty Kilrayne trial? It was an ugly thought.

I wonder, thought Boling as O'Shea was departing, if I'm going to read about an exclusive interview by the Boston *Chronicle* with the Chief Justice. Could O'Shea be trusted to stick by his word?

"Mrs. Johnson," he said as soon as the door had closed, "get me Martin Hanlon at the *Chronicle*."

She was punching the last number of the seven digits when Boling changed his mind. "Forget that for now. Get me Vincent Loring. I think he's sitting in Worcester."

Moments later Mrs. Johnson stepped into his office. "Line two," she said. "He was on the bench. They're getting him now."

Boling punched the second button and picked up his phone. "Vince? Look, I'm sorry to interrupt, but I've just had a most disquieting visit with a reporter. I want to ask you something off the record. Have you heard anything about Webster Lodge saying he was going to be on the Kilrayne case?"

"Not directly," said Judge Loring. "One of my bailiffs said this morning that there was a rumor to that effect."

"Hmm. Listen. Do you by chance know if he belongs to any country clubs?"

"I think so. One out in Dover, or near there. Has he been talking out of school?"

"I don't know. Perhaps. It's a risk I'm beginning to

worry about. Webster doesn't drink, but he'd getting on. Likes to ramble a bit. I *was* going to appoint him—the old rascal even requested the job—but we can't afford even the slightest degree of indiscretion in this one. The press is going to take even the littlest incident and put it on both wires." Boling paused for a moment.

"Look, Vince, you may be next in line. Any problem with sitting on the case?"

"I'm afraid so," said Loring. "Mike represented a young girl who put my wife's nephew in Walpole for statutory rape about ten years ago. Little bastard deserved it too. But if he should get convicted—Mike that is—someone would surely take a look at every one of my rulings and say I was trying to get even."

"I see. No, that wouldn't be good. Any suggestions?"

There was a moment of silence. "I think," said Loring, "that it's a tough one. Most of us know Mike, and most will have some feelings about him, pro or con. I think the best bet is one of the newer judges—someone who's had little or no contact with him."

"Well, that's right," said Boling, "except I hate to throw someone without much experience that deep into the pit. These two chaps I admitted last week are both extraordinary lawyers. They could macerate a neophyte. Hell, I don't even use a new man with Kilrayne himself when he's defending."

"It's a Hobson's choice, Pat," said Loring. "But I don't think either of these counsel is the type that would deliberately sandbag a judge to make him look bad. If you get someone with decent judgment, they'll probably help him along. If he gets reversed on appeal, what the hell. The Supreme Judicial Court isn't going to ream him unless he goes absolutely haywire somewhere along the way. On the other hand, if you assign one of the old guard, either a judge that's looked cross-eyed at Kilrayne, or shaken his hand more than three times, *someone* is going to scream that the bag is in. I don't envy you."

"Hmm. I think you may be right, Vincent. The lesser of two evils. Let me think. What do you think of Gary Somerville? He's on the short side of fifty and only a year on the bench, but fairly steady. Had one homicide, I think, a small one. Tried a fair number of cases defending insurance companies. I don't think Kilrayne's ever been in his court, except on very minor matters. Nothing I've ever heard of."

"You could do worse. I don't think he'd embarrass anyone, certainly."

"Good. I'll give him a little thought. Thanks very much, Vince, I'll let you get back to work."

"Sure thing. Good-bye."

Boling hung up the phone and pulled open the large file drawer on the left side of his desk. He kept track of his judges rather thoroughly, a fact of which he was quite proud. The public had little idea just how sensitive his responsibilities were or how conscientiously Patrick Boling attempted to discharge them. Secretly, he wished that he could personally preside at the trial. But he would be criticized for grandstanding and frowned on by the judges in the two-tiered appellate courts above him. He was supposed to be an administrator, which allowed no time for lengthy trials keeping him from his office.

He perused Somerville's file for a few minutes. There was very little in it. His original résumé, some commendatory letters from judges and lawyers supporting his appointment, and a few notes in Boling's own hand. Nothing terribly significant. Some tendency to get in deep water, but at least he knew how to swim. No way to tell how well he could swim with sharks and barracudas.

Boling filled his pipe, lit it, and mustered up in his mind all the reasons he could think of for rejecting Judge Somerville for the Kilrayne case. None, he found, were of sufficient countervailing importance to obscure

Somerville's main attraction: no material prior connection with Michael Kilrayne. Lawyers who defend insurance companies and lawyers who defend people seldom even meet each other. He finished his pipe, called Somerville in Nova Scotia, where he was vacationing, and closed off the last possible avenue of disqualification.

"Gary," he said, "I'm sorry to bother you during a well-deserved rest. I have one question for you, one of great consequence. I am considering assigning you to the Second Criminal Session in Essex in September."

Somerville gasped very slightly. "Would that be the Kilrayne case, Chief?"

"It would. I'm confident you can handle it to the obvious credit of the Superior Court. My question is, have you ever had any significant contact, one way or the other, with Michael Kilrayne? Anything the press might be able to play with?"

"No, Chief," replied Somerville, "I hardly know the man."

"Thank you, Gary. I'm going to announce the assignment this afternoon. You're in Middlesex next month, but I'm going to direct that all pretrial matters come before you, rather than Judge Carlson up in Essex, to give you a good grip on things. Go back to your rest. You may need it."

"Thank you, Chief. I'll do my best."

"I'm sure," said Boling benevolently; "from what I've heard that will be more than adquate. Good-bye."

Boling rose and stepped to his office door. "Mrs. Johnson," he said, "please prepare a memorandum for the press room and have it posted at four o'clock this afternoon, announcing that Mr. Justice Gary Somerville has been appointed to preside at the trial of *Commonwealth* v. *Kilrayne*. Should there be inquiries as to why he was selected, you may say that I am unavailable and that the appointment was routine."

At 4:15 that afternoon Stacy Barton burst into Kilrayne's office. He was pouring himself a Scotch at a small service bar built into his credenza.

"Make that a double, Mike," she said happily. "Justice Gary Somerville has been appointed to sit in September. Who is he, by the way?"

Kilrayne, grinning from ear to ear, filled the tumbler. "I barely know him," he replied jubilantly, "but Lucifer himself would be better than Lodge. Who told you?"

"Charley O'Shea, two minutes ago."

"A monumental accomplishment," said Kilrayne pontifically. "And I assume a benign coincidence. You didn't let old Charley push you into the sack, did you? Sounds like he outdid himself."

"That, Michael Kilrayne, is none of your business."

"Charley, I suspect, has been instrumental in rendering a great service to mankind—this mankind in particular."

Webster Lodge was in the study of his home, waiting for the early news at five o'clock to come on the television. His wife told him that Carl Barrett was calling.

He listened with sagging jowls as Carl told him the news. "I assure you, Carl," he said, "I have breathed no word of my assignment to anyone but you. I can't imagine what prompted Boling to change his mind."

"It is a grave disappointment to learn that a judge of your distinguished experience will not preside and of your replacement by a comparative newcomer to the bench. I wonder who is behind the switch."

"I've no idea, really," said Lodge. "Actually, I shouldn't say that. I have strong suspicion that Kilrayne himself may have had something to do with this. As I have told you in the past, he is a man who is not to be trusted. A shanty Irish for all of his days, I'm afraid."

15

DIGGING IN
Tuesday, July 18

There was a light ran falling as Sam Watkins, sitting in the left seat of Daniel Shaw's Lear Jet, flared for touchdown at Boston's Logan Airport. Delicately, he feathered the wheels to the runway so smoothly that a casual passenger in the rear would have been hard put to say just when ground contact was made. Watkins, Shaw's copilot and sometime investigator, grinned slightly but said nothing.

"Stop looking so pleased with yourself, Sam," said Shaw who was sitting next to him. "Any numbnuts can grease one on with a wet runway. Try that in Albuquerque sometime when the temperature is ninety-five."

"An accident on my part," retorted Watkins. "Actually, I was trying to slam it on, like you taught me. Kinda hoped I'd drive the landing gear struts up through the wings, so you'd be proud."

"Attaboy," said Shaw. "You've got the right attitude. Never outshine the boss." As Watkins cleared runway four left, Shaw keyed the microphone.

"Boston ground, Lear one thousand alpha, taxi to general aviation please."

"Roger, one thousand alpha, taxi via the inner, watch for an Eastern DC-9 outbound."

Thirty minutes later Shaw and Watkins entered Kilrayne's office. It was just after six o'clock in the evening. Kilrayne and Stacy Barton were sitting in Mike's office when the receptionist brought them through.

"Brother Kilrayne," said Shaw, "your Boston weather here is unacceptable. Just stopped by to tell you we're going home. Sam Watkins, here, who was going to help us with this case, just gets all confused flying through these clouds and all."

"Bullshit," replied Kilrayne, "anyone who lives in San Francisco has nothing to yell about when it comes to fog, rain, and other inconveniences. Someday we're going to send you folks a little snow and destroy thirty thousand automobiles the first day. How are you, Sam. Thanks for coming. Scotch?"

"Thank you," said Watkins, shaking hands. "Fact is, the FAA won't let him fly without me."

Stacy Barton handed both men Scotch over rocks, with a splash, and winked at Shaw. "He's right, you know," she said to Kilrayne. "But only because Lear Jets require two pilots. I had a date with a Lear Jet pilot, once. He talked about airplanes until I had a headache. When I have a headache, I say goodnight."

"You'll find some Alka-Seltzer in my briefcase," said Shaw, returning the wink. "What's happening?"

"Well," said Kilrayne, "we played a little game of musical judges for a bit over the weekend but wound up okay. At least I think we did. They've assigned a fellow named Gary Somerville to preside. Just over a year on the bench, insurance defense type before that."

Shaw wrinkled his nose.

"Despite that poor background," Kilrayne went on, "he checks out as a decent guy. Forty-nine, stable marriage, two kids, a little shaky on the rules of evidence in criminal cases, but runs his own court. Has a pretty good idea of what lawyer's ethics ought to be and gets tense when he spots a breach. I figure that's a plus for us. A friend who used to work with him says that Judge Somerville thinks British barristers are the cat's meow."

Kilrayne passed his glass to Stacy for a refill.

"Anyway, he's a far cry better than the old slug they tried to set us up with. Guy named Lodge who keeps a toy guillotine in his night table and thinks that Irishmen and Mephistopheles deserve one another."

"Sounds good," said Shaw. "Would you join me in the reckless undertaking of leaving Sam here with Ms. Barton for a minute?" He stepped just outside the office with Kilrayne.

"I've been working a few of my sources from the old days in intelligence," he said. "Funny how the camaraderie of the illicit seems to hang on through the years. In any event, I learned two things through a disenchanted FBI agent, who knows my guy. First, your boy LaPere is being kept at some Coast Guard Station near Cape Ann—an island, I think."

"Sure. Thatcher's Island," Kilrayne said. "It's a forlorn chunk of rock off Loblolly Cove in Rockport, about a mile. Nothing there but two old stone lighthouses, a few Coast Guard people, and Frankie. That's bad. The feds kept Joe Barboza there when he was doing in some of my Italian friends some years ago. That sonofabitch killed at least twenty-six people personally, then lied through three trials and sucked in every judge and jury he talked to. Putting Frankie there, that's bad news. Means Walter Barrett's got some help."

"Not Walter," corrected Shaw. "The Bureau wouldn't give Walter the steam off you know what. It was arranged by Joe Gilardi.

"The other thing is, we ought to expect some trouble from a party named Tomasello. That name mean anything to you?"

Kilrayne scowled. "The name does. Twice, as a matter of fact. Two brothers I've represented off and on. They're both in trouble at the moment, but I couldn't help them." He looked at Shaw. "Shit," he said, "the formula again. Clients with their ass in a crack. What the hell are *they* supposed to say?"

"No info," said Shaw, "only that they won't be helpful."

Kilrayne thought for a moment. "Okay," he said. "I think I know where to go. Have Stacy take you and Sam over to the hotel, and I'll meet you back here in the morning at nine-thirty. I have to meet with some people."

"Good enough," replied Shaw. "By the way, before I get *my* ass in a crack, what are the rules as to Stacy. I came here to help, not to be in the way."

Kilrayne grinned. "Stacy is free as a bird," he said. "She's a big girl, and a person of quality. Just don't screw up my defense, if you know what I mean."

When the three had been seated in the elegant dining room of the Ritz-Carlton Hotel, Shaw, without consulting the others, ordered a round of caviar and a magnum of champagne. Stacy raised an eyebrow. "The boss," she smiled, "is going to gag a bit when he gets the bill for this one."

"He won't," chuckled Shaw. "Dinner tonight is courtesy of Hughes Air West Airlines. The Federal Judge in San Francisco who was kind enough to interrupt a trial to let me come here initially was also kind enough to return a substantial damage award for my client. We won't hit Michael with this one."

When dinner was over, Sam Watkins went to his room. Shaw and Stacy Barton said good night to him, and walked down the hall to Shaw's suite for a nightcap. Shaw produced a bottle of Cutty Sark from his luggage and fixed them both a Scotch and water over ice. Stacy noticed that the bucket of ice was fresh and wondered for a moment how it had gotten there. Then she remembered that during their after dinner coffee, Shaw had stepped to the house phone momentarily. Pilots are trained, she reminded herself, to think ahead.

"Tell me," said Shaw, "what's Mike's relationship to

the local organized group, the boys whose names end in vowels?"

Stacy lit a cigarette and inhaled deeply. "Distant, but quite amicable, I would say. Mike doesn't represent them on anything like a regular basis and tends to keep his hands high when dealing with them. Doesn't want to get mixed up in any attempt to reach a juror or a prosecutor, which happens occasionally. But once in a while when one of the important ones—like Angelo Giordano himself—gets bound up, and there is no alternative but to go to trial on the merits, they'll call for Mike. His record has been good, and they respect him. I'm sure that they want him to stay available, which means they don't want him convicted."

Shaw sipped his drink thoughtfully. "Reason I ask is, some of the information we'll be looking for might be hard to come by. Sometimes a little help from the boys in the rackets can be worth a lot. Would they do that for Mike?"

"I'm sure they would, within reason," replied Stacy. "There's one risk though—Mike's contact is all with the upper echelon. As far as the boys on the street go, I would have to say that Joe Gilardi fits pretty well. He was brought up right in the middle of that society and keeps his contacts working. Does them favors from time to time. Any information we got might well end up in Gilardi's hands pretty quickly."

"Mmm-hmm. That's not good. I wonder if that would work in reverse," said Shaw. "I've got an idea."

"I'll try anything," said Stacy.

"Including some of Mike's contacts?" asked Shaw.

"Why not?"

"Is that a role for a lady?" asked Shaw.

"I stopped being a lady when I became a lawyer," said Stacy.

At a little after ten o'clock, Stacy drained her second Scotch and announced that it was time to go.

"I wonder," said Shaw evilly, "just what your blood-alcohol count is right about now?"

"What?" said Stacy, startled by the remark.

"Blood-alcohol," said Shaw. "You've had about four Scotches now this evening and a brandy with your coffee. You know that new California case, the one that says where the host feeds liquor to the guest, and the guest drives into someone, the host can be made to pay the damages? Now if you hit someone with that little Volkswagen of yours, they could come to California and sue me. Perhaps I have a duty to offer to put you up for the night—purely for legal protection of course. . . . "

Stacy smiled. "I did read about that case," she said, "and from what I remember, you could solve the problem just as easily by sending me home in a cab."

Shaw sighed reproachfully. "As easily, perhaps, but not as pleasantly. After all, I have plenty of room here, just going to waste."

Stacy leaned forward in her chair, exposing a hint of breast through the vee of her blouse. "Daniel," she said, "you're very sweet and I'm flattered. But I'm afraid you underestimate the Boston press corps. I'd bet my nickel that there are reporters down in the bar right now, watching my car. If it doesn't leave at a reasonable hour, the public will be told that you and I are working up this case in the bedroom. If I leave in a cab, it will be reported that I was intoxicated beyond the point where I could drive. Neither story would help our client very much. Besides, I'm quite sober. I could stay here and drink you under the table, but tonight's not the night."

Shaw grinned. "You win. A rain check, perhaps?"

"Perhaps," said Stacy, picking up her purse. As he walked her to the door, she kissed him lightly on the cheek. "Just to show you that I'm not all bad," she said.

16

UNWRITTEN RULES
Wednesday, July 19

George Tomasello, pornographer and liar-for-hire, was terribly nervous as he waited outside Danny Giordano's little office on Richmond Street in Boston's North End. A message that Danny wanted to see you was generally considered to be bad news. Worse, George was rather sure he knew the nature of the request for a discussion. He was going to have to do some fast talking.

Danny was in his late forties, the youngest of the three Giordano brothers, and the one who policed things around town. Though Angelo, the eldest, made most of the decisions, Danny usually carried them out. Danny, a tall, wiry fellow, wore conservative suits. His dark eyes peered through glasses that seemed to get thicker each year. The word was that his sight was failing rapidly, a notion that made any number of people silently wish that the process could be accelerated. Perhaps then Danny would be forced into a more peaceable line of work.

When George was called in, he sat in a straight wooden chair in front of the little table that Danny used for a desk. George smiled unctuously as he shook hands and started to inquire about Danny's family, hoping to ease the situation with a little small talk. Danny cut him off abruptly.

"George," he said, "I believe you know our very

good friend, Mr. Kilrayne, the lawyer?" The emphasis on the word "very" told George that the next few minutes would not be pleasant. "We feel," Danny went on, "that Mr. Kilrayne is the victim of a frame. If Mr. Kilrayne lands in the can and we need a good lawyer, a very good lawyer, we can't use one that's in the can, understand? Now, that brings me to my point. I want to know whether you or Eddie have spoken to Joe Gilardi in the past few weeks."

"I haven't," said George, "and I don't think Eddie has."

"Then why would I be getting information that you and Eddie might be witnesses for the state—good information, George, not just small talk."

"What happened is," said George looking at his hands, "this guy what's a friend of the lieutenant, he talked to both of us. Said he thought we might know something about Mr. Kilrayne having some girlfriend hit, and if we did it could be good for us, y'know."

"How could it be good for you, George?"

"Well, Eddie gets sentenced this Friday on that case he got hooked on in federal court, and the feebies say that he's gonna get buried. Then I got this little crummy beef for sellin' a few fuck films, don't amount to a pound of shit, but this guy, name's LaCarva, he's tellin' us he can make things go pretty good for us if we have anythin' what helps Gilardi, you see the play there?"

"What play, George?" Danny looked positively fierce.

"Well, what we said was, we was standin' just outside Mr. Kilrayne's private office with the door open just a crack, y'know, and we hear him tellin' some guy 'I don't want her killed.' "

"So how does that help Gilardi?"

"It don't. So this LaCarva says, he tells us, 'You know, that ain't too bad, I think the lieutenant will like that. I'm going to give him my report about what you guys heard, but I'm leavin' out the word 'don't,' and that way you guys might be pretty valuable.' So Eddie says to me, 'Christ, maybe we play these bulls along a little, I could hit the street insteada Lewisburg,' which Eddie likes because some guys up in Lewisburg he jammed with a couple times, he ain't lookin' forward to goin' there."

"You must have heard more than just one sentence when you two were listening in on your lawyer," said Danny coldly. "What was Mr. Kilrayne talking about?"

"Oh, some niece of his got some dough, she went and bought herself some kinda speedboat with two hot rod engines, he was talkin' like it would be too dangerous for her, that's all."

"So this LaCarva wants you to tesify that you two birds heard Mr. Kilrayne say 'I want her killed,' and leave it at that, am I right?"

"That was his play, Danny. Now of course I don't do any shit deals like that for nobody, especially against a guy who helped us sometimes in the past. I mean this Mr. Kilrayne is an all right guy, and me, Christ, if I pull some house of correction for the dirty movies, why, I can do that time standing on my head, y'know?"

"Sure you can, George. But Eddie doesn't want to go to Lewisburg, you said. What's Eddie's plan?"

"Well, Eddie told me maybe he can con this Gilardi, get the street from the feds, then sort of lose his memory before Mr. Kilrayne's trial, that's what he told me. I told him, I said 'Eddie, you're playin' with some people, the kind of people they are they'll ream you pretty good if you pull a switch on them,' but Eddie, he kind of thinks he knows everything, like law and all that, he tells me once he gets probation they can't come back and make it worse, he's goin' to suck them in all the way."

"This LaCarva," said Danny. "Who is he?"

"He's a feebie," said George, "some buddy of Gilardi's, is what he said. That's why Eddie, he got turned on to this guy, because LaCarva says he's got some clout with the U.S. Attorney, which he probably has."

Danny Giordano leaned across his table and stared hard at George Tomasello. His voice grated when he spoke. "George," he said, "your brother Eddie is a stupid little shit. He's always been stupid. That's why he's in a jam to begin with. Rippin' off liquor trucks went out forty years ago, but Eddie, he's slow to catch on. Now you go find Eddie, tonight—tonight, not tomorrow night or some other time. You tell that little asshole that Gilardi ain't stupid like he is. He plays a game with the fuzzy people, they win every time. He ain't going to get no sentence at all, he makes a deal with those people. They're going to postpone the sentence until after he's done his little act. The act turns bad, Eddie goes to Lewisburg for twice the time he woulda got to begin with. You understand what I'm sayin'?"

"Sure Danny," said George hastily. "I see the play there. What they do is, they keep Eddie on the string until *after* he's a witness, then if he's no good, they croak him. Those guys ain't dumb. I told him, I said 'Eddie, you screw around with this guy Gilardi, you're crazy, that's all I can say,' I says. Eddie don't listen to me very good anymore."

"He better listen to you tonight, George, he better listen good. You tell him I don't want to read in the paper that he got probation, and I don't want to read that his sentence got postponed. You get me? I don't want to read either of those things. You know what the penalty is for lyin' in a murder case?"

"I know, I know," said George, the perspiration beaded on his forehead and on either side of his nose. "I told Eddie, I said, 'You can get life for that,' is what I told him."

"You're close, George. If Eddie lies in Mr. Kilrayne's case, he could get a little worse than that. You understand what I'm telling you?"

"Sure, Danny, sure. Look, I'll get Eddie tonight, like

you said, and I'll tell him." George fingered his hat for a moment, searching for the right words. "There's just one thing, Danny. . . ."

"What one thing?"

"Eddie, like I told you, he knows it all. He could just say, he could tell me, 'George, you go shit in your hat, I know what I'm doin', I'll handle this situation with these dumb people,' that's the way Eddie is with me sometimes."

"You give him strong advice, George," said Danny. "The strongest you know how. You understand? You tell Eddie I'll be reading the newspaper."

"I'll tell him, Danny. I'll tell him good, like you said." George Tomasello was very happy to leave.

17

A LITTLE BOATING
Saturday, July 22

Eddie Tomasello was sitting in a booth at the Friar's Tavern on Summer Street. He had one hand on Angela Corso's thigh and the other hand on a mug of beer. He had just finished explaining to Angela how stupid his brother George had been. Eddie told Angela how he decided to ignore George and put one over on the Federal Bureau of Investigation by getting his sentence postponed until October.

Angela, a voluptuous dark-haired girl in her middle twenties who worked for the Post Office, was troubled. "But what happens when they call you as a witness? What're you going to do then?"

"What'll happen is," said Eddie, "I'll do pretty good when the prosecutor calls me, then when that English guy gets me on cross-examination, he'll make mincemeat out of me. You know, I'll be all confused, and like that."

"But that's what I don't understand," said Angela. "When you do all that and hurt their case, how come they won't zap you after that?"

"Because I got my head on straight, that's why," said Eddie. "They come after me at that point, all I gotta do is complain they asked me to lie. They can't stand that. So they're screwed, and your Eddie is on the street, no

Lewisburg, no letters for them screws to read, I'm fat. Get what I mean?"

"I guess so," said Angela, doubtfully. "It just seems awful complicated, that's all."

Eddie was signaling the waitress for another mug of beer and trying to get his finger inside the crotch of Angela's panties, when two stocky men stopped next to his booth.

"Hi Eddie. I'm Nick, this here is Vito. We got a message for you from George. He needs to see you right away, like. He's outside."

"I don't think I know you guys," said Eddie, his voice quavering a bit. Both men wore navy blue trench coats, gray felt hats, and dark glasses. It was a uniform Eddie had heard about. "You from outta town or somethin'?"

"We're friends of George. He wants to see you now, and he ain't jerkin' around. Let's go." Nick let his coat open far enough for the butt of his .45 automatic to show in its shoulder holster. "George, he ain't got much time."

"What's wrong with George?" asked Eddie, now beginning to shake a bit.

"He's pretty sick," said Vito. "Come with us. You can bring the doll if you want to."

Eddie felt better. If these boys had some rough stuff for him, they wouldn't want Angela along. That wasn't the way the heavy guys operated. Eddie threw a ten dollar bill on the table, took Angela by the hand, and followed the pair out of the tavern.

As soon as they were on the sidewalk, Vito stepped behind Eddie and poked something hard into the right side of his back. "That car there," he said, indicating a dark blue Chevrolet sedan parked at the curb. "Get in."

Eddie got in the back seat with Angela. Nick climbed in behind the wheel, and Vito sat beside him.

"Where's George?" asked Eddie, barely able to control his larynx. "I thought George would be here," he whined.

"Don't worry about George, Eddie," said Vito. "He's going to be okay."

"Then where are you taking me and Angela?" asked Eddie. It was not a question. It was an attempt to plumb the depths of what was to come.

"Y'know," said Vito, "in order to help George, we're going to have to take this little boat ride. You like boats, don't you Eddie?"

"Oh, sure," said Eddie. "I grew up around boats, George shoulda told you that. It's Angela. She gets sorta seasick, you know what I mean. . . ."

Angela had not been close to the head of the line when the powers that be were handing out brains. "Oh, no," she said. "Eddie's wrong about that. I was brought up on boats too. My father was a lobster fisherman. I used to help him pull the traps." The words were no sooner out of her mouth than she regretted them, partly because Eddie was pinching her thigh as if his life were depending on the strength of his fingers. It was too late.

"That's what we like," said Nick, "a girl who knows what the ocean is all about. We're goin' to take an ocean trip, ain't that right, Vito?"

"Yeah."

Forty-five minutes later Nick pulled the car in between two large boats that were sitting in cradles at Colonial Marina in Plymouth Harbor. Vito got out first, and stuffed the pistol in his raincoat pocket. He herded Eddie and Angela down to the dock and onto a large sport fishing yacht. Nick started the engines and cast off the lines while Vito kept Eddie and Angela seated together in a bunk in the forward cabin. Nick moved the shift levers into forward gear and eased out of the harbor. Once past the breakwater, he opened the throttles, and the ship rose out of the water and began to plane at eighteen knots. Thirty minutes later, Nick cut the throttles to idle and turned the searchlight on and off three times. Within a few minutes a small outboard-powered runabout pulled alongside. Eddie felt the engines stop and could hear the outboard idling.

Several minutes went by, and then Nick poked his head through the companionway opening. "Let's go," he said to Vito.

Vito nodded. "What we're gonna do is, we're goin' to pick up George. Then we'll be back. George, he's kinda jammed up, you know what I mean. One thing, though. Don't get no smart ideas like you might like to take off. This here is a tough boat to handle, you and the girl could get in trouble. Am I right Nick?"

"Yeah, yeah, come on. We're runnin' late."

Vito grinned as he got up to leave the cabin. "You two wanna get it on while we're gone, you'll have to do a quickie. We're comin' back real soon."

Eddie watched through a porthole as the two men climbed into the outboard. The man at the wheel was wearing yellow oilskins with a large fisherman's hat. Eddie tried to see his face, but there was not enough light. The outboard sped away to the east, showing no running lights. When he could no longer hear the sound of its engine, Eddie began to breathe more easily.

"Come on," he said to Angela. "I know how to drive this tub. Let's get outa here."

"Supposing they come back and chase us?" said Angela. "Those men have guns. I saw one."

"That's right, baby. I don't know what game they're playin', but I'm thinkin' it's one I ain't gonna like. We're splittin'." Eddie climbed up to the cockpit, located the starter buttons, and fired up the starboard engine. When it was idling smoothly he pushed the port starter button.

He perceived only a blinding, searing flash as twelve sticks of dynamite, wired to the coil of the port engine, blew the boat to kindling wood. Eddie and Angela, hurled upward by the blast, were dead before they hit the water.

Less than two miles away, Nick and Vito watched from the outboard. "Like they said," said Nick, "that Eddie, he's the kinda guy won't listen to nobody. We tole him not to mess around, and look what he does."

"Yeah," said Vito. "Now lemme see, that's three big ones for the insurance job on the boat and another two for friend Eddie. Sorta like killin' two birds with one stone, like they say."

"Right," said Nick. "Let's get the hell back on shore. Me, I'm headin' in town, see if I can pick up a little ginch at one a the joints. That little broad, she kinda reminded me I ain't had a piece in a while, her and them big knockers and all."

"She was built all right," said Vito. "Too bad she hung around with a guy like Eddie. She was just like he was, I guess."

"Whaddaya mean," asked Nick, raising his voice to be heard above the scream of the outboard.

"Dumb," shouted Vito. "Very dumb."

Vito and Nick would have been a bit more concerned about their incidental murder of Angela Corso had they been local boys rather than imported hit men. They would have known they would at some point have to reckon with Angela's kid brother, "Big Sal" Corso.

Salvatore Corso, twenty-three, prided himself on being every inch a Sicilian. Nearly six feet tall, and 190 pounds of muscle, he had thick black hair, intense brown eyes, and an incendiary temper. His only desire in life was to be a model mobster. He dressed the way he thought a mobster ought to dress. His well-molded women looked their part, and he always had a fat roll of street cash in his pocket to flash when needed. Though it was unlikely that he would ever be much more than a soldier, Sal hoped for advancement. In the meantime, he would be the best soldier of all time—the toughest, the most dependable, and the most loyal.

Word was out that Danny Giordano was slowly going

blind. Big Sal's ambition was to one day fill at least part
of Danny's shoes, policing those who were getting out of
line. Unknown to Sal—it would have shattered his ego
had he been told—he had already been passed over for
any position of serious responsibility. His flashfire temper and his dull-witted judgment simply made him unacceptable. It was generally assumed in the upper eche-
lons that one day Sal's immature swaggering would
irritate the wrong party, and he would be blown away.

Unaware that he had been written off, Big Sal hung
around at what he considered to be the right joints and
practiced intensively with what he thought were appropriate weapons: brass knuckles, a shot-filled leather
sap, a .45 Colt automatic, and a Winchester double-
barrelled sawed-off shotgun, which he had cut down
himself. He liked to practice with the latter by drawing
it suddenly and firing both barrels with only his right
hand.

Moreover, the truth was that Sal and Angela had a
secret. Though guilt-stricken, Big Sal and Angela Corso
had continued having sexual intercourse on a regular
basis since they were teenagers. Every time they promised each other that this would have to be the last, and
every succeeding time their resolution turned to sand
before the onslaught of their mutual affection and passion for one another's bodies. Big Sal never worried
about his parents finding out. They were innocent old-
world peasants, glad to see brother and sister so fond of
each other. Big Sal had stopped worrying about what
God would think; he hadn't been struck dead by light-
ning, and he and Angela'd been at it for nearly ten
years. He was worried about what might happen if the
mob bosses found out. Their moral standards were in-
flexible.

Angela recognized her younger brother's intellectual
limitations and would assist him in making decisions
whenever his judgment seemed stymied—which was often. At the same time, she enjoyed the almost total pro-

tection her bull-strong younger sibling lavished on her. Ever since they had first been intimate, Sal had reacted fiercely to any affront, however slight, to Angela. His contemporaries swiftly—and sometimes painfully—learned that in Sal's world Angela was hallowed ground, period. Sal had once slowly and deliberately twisted a classmate's arm until the bone snapped for merely boasting that he had fondled Angela's bare breast—which he had. On another occasion Sal had beaten an older and larger friend so badly with his fists that the boy lost the hearing of his left ear permanently. His transgression amounted to a description in a bar of how Angela had gratified him orally one night on an almost empty Delta 727 to Fort Lauderdale—which was also true.

Nick and Vito were unaware that one of the sources of Big Sal's murderous temper was his difficulty in adjusting to the fact—even after all these years—that he enjoyed his private relations with his sister more than with any girl friend or prostitute he consorted with. He tried to diminish his unconscious guilt feelings by letting Angela go with others. But his hope was one day to have her—somewhere—for himself alone. Nick and Vito wouldn't have been the only ones concerned. Stacy Barton and Michael Kilrayne might have been troubled also. Once Big Sal learned that his sister had been blown away, he could be expected to erupt like an angry volcano.

18

THE EMBALMER
Sunday, July 23

Carl Barrett was seated on a small porch on the back side of his home, overlooking Manchester harbor, when Walter arrived to keep his appointment. With Carl was a short man in his late fifties with gray, thinning hair and gray eyes.

"Walter," said Carl, "I'd like you to meet an old friend of mine, Phil Durham. Phil was First Assistant out in Worcester County for better than twenty years. Just came by for a little visit."

Walter shook hands, and accepted a martini from his uncle. "Looks like you've got yourself tied into a helluva case," said Durham. "One *helluva* case."

Walter smiled proudly. "We're putting the pieces together rather nicely," he said. "Lieutenant Gilardi and I have been spending a great deal of time going over all of the details. Of course, the burden of proof is very heavy—but then, I guess you know all that better than I do, after twenty years in the business. Are you in private practice now?"

"Some," said Durham. "I bought a little real estate over the years, enough to keep the wolf from the door. I handle the odd case now and then and play a lot of golf."

"Walter," said his uncle, lighting a fresh cigar, "I've been doing a little checking on your two opponents.

Particularly this English chap. I'm told that he's very, very good."

Walter nodded. "That's what I hear. Very quiet and low keyed, they say, at least compared to our lawyers."

"The British," said Durham, "can take the legs out from under a case before you figure out what's going on. I've watched a few trials at the Old Bailey in London. Slick operators, they are."

"Your big problem, as I see it," said Carl, "is not necessarily going to be the lawyers themselves."

"How's that?" asked Walter.

"What Carl is saying," said Durham, "is that in a criminal case, once the defendant takes the stand, everything the lawyers have done up to that point tends to fade in the jury's mind. If they like the defendant, if they believe him, the ball game's over. If they think he's lying, though, they'll sometimes convict even though the case is very thin. You can almost bet that Kilrayne will testify. And while most lawyers make lousy witnesses, he won't. He did insurance adjusting when he was going to law school and learned to be a good witness before he ever passed the bar. His testimony will be your big problem, as I was telling Carl before you arrived."

Walter felt somewhat deflated. He was beginning to sense that his uncle had staged the meeting for something more than mere cocktails.

"The thing is," said Carl, "that you're going to have your hands full being the general in this case, keeping track of your evidence and all that. I thought perhaps you might like to talk to Phil a bit about the business of cross-examining Kilrayne. Phil's a master at that part of it. Matter of fact," Carl went on, smiling expansively, "about ten, fifteen years ago, Phil was trying a famous case out in Worcester—contractor named Cameratta, accused of killing his wife and burying her in a gravel pit. The prosecution didn't have too much to go on until Cameratta took the stand. Phil just cut him to ribbons, by all accounts. After the case was over I had lunch with old John Willis, who was presiding, and he said 'Carl, I've heard people say that Phil Durham is a killer when it comes to cross-examination. But they're wrong. Durham's an embalmer. When he kills them, they stay dead. Never saw anything like what he did to that contractor.' "

"Well, certainly," said Walter. "I'd be happy for any advice Phil could give me. There's no doubt, Kilrayne's going to take the stand and deny any knowledge of what happened to the woman. That will be a critical point, I agree."

"What you might want to consider," said Carl, "is exploring the possibility of signing Phil on as a special prosecutor for the trial. Nothing like an experienced hand to help out when the pace gets heavy." Carl looked at Walter with his half-lidded stare.

"Well, . . ." Walter hesitated. His uncle had put him in a very awkward position, and he was fuming. "An expert would be nice to have," he said, "if you don't think the voters would feel that I was hiding behind someone's skirts, so to speak."

"Nonsense," said Carl. "Not at all. Look at it this way, Walter. Everyone knows the defense is loaded for bear. If the jury lets Kilrayne go, the editorial writers are going to lionize the defense lawyers and point to your lack of trial experience. With someone like Phil here to share the load, nobody's going to put you down if you don't win a conviction. Just an exercise of good judgment, people will say."

"Maybe you're right," said Walter reluctantly. "Still, there's not a whole lot of room in the budget for extra expense. . . ."

Durham chuckled. "After the many years of service I have given the good people of the Commonwealth," he said, "I would expect to be quite reasonable. Say, three hundred dollars a day for trial, forty an hour for preparation."

"I guess we could handle that all right," said Walter.

"I suppose maybe I ought to mention the idea to Joe Gilardi, just as a courtesy."

"You'll have Gilardi's enthusiastic approval," said Carl. "I talked about Phil with him the other day on the phone. Joe has worked with Phil in the past once or twice, and considers him first-rate, he told me."

Walter had an impulse to suggest that Carl try the case himself, since he seemed to be running the show. Instead he smiled, and nodded agreeably.

When Stacy Barton brought the news that Philip Durham had been appointed a Special Prosecutor the following day, Kilrayne and Shaw were in the library studying the L. Ewing Scott case in the California reports.

"Doesn't surprise me a helluva lot," said Kilrayne. "I couldn't imagine old Carl letting a lightweight like Walter take on the likes of Tony Everard."

"What's the book on this Durham?" asked Shaw.

"Phil is a very skillful lawyer," replied Kilrayne. "His manner is gruff and heavy-handed, a very intimidating style, no mercy whatsoever. He takes every case very personally and would prosecute his grandmother if he caught her jaywalking. He's been single all his life, supports an invalid mother, and has icewater in his veins."

"Have you gone against him?"

"Several times. The last was about five years ago, before he retired from the office. Rape case, question of identification. Phil murdered my client on the stand, got him ten to fifteen in Walpole. The kid was innocent, so far as I know, but that wouldn't matter to Durham."

"You think he'd put the blocks to you just for the exercise, even if he thought you were getting shafted?" asked Shaw.

"Without batting an eye," said Kilrayne. "Phil thinks all defense lawyers should be in jail on general principles, and he's no fan of mine. He'll have to be watched like a hawk every minute, or he'll be slipping things into evidence that are prejudicial as hell, and have nothing to do with the case."

Shaw sighed. "Forewarned," he said, "is forearmed. I hope."

19

THE REPORTER
Thursday, July 27

When Daniel Shaw, dressed in his shirtsleeves, answered the door to the living room of his suite, he had expected the interviewer who had made an appointment to see him to be a reasonably attractive young lady. He had not expected the air to fairly crackle with her electricity.

"Thank you for seeing me," said Patricia Perrin, flashing a warm smile. "May I come in?"

"Indeed you may," said Shaw, unable to refrain from running his glance up and down once quickly as he stood aside. She was petite, with auburn hair and shining blue eyes. Her skin was fair, with the hint of a freckle or two here and there. She wore a pale blue blouse, open to the cleavage point, and a brown cotton skirt. Shaw estimated that she would go a hundred and five, soaking wet, distributed in a fashion that had helped to make Hugh Hefner a millionaire many times over.

"Won't you sit down," he said, indicating the sofa.

"Thank you," she replied, taking in the room as she sat. "This is very nice. I hope you will have a few minutes to spend. . . ."

"Sure," said Shaw easily in a low voice. "I have the time. What would you like to talk about, other than the case?"

"As I mentioned on the phone," she began, "the case

is secondary in a way. *Far West* is a monthly feature magazine, as you know, and I want a profile of you. Readers want to know what you're like behind the scenes, what your hobbies are, how the excitement of a case like this affects you, what foods you like, what your taste in women is, how you fly your airplane, what makes you tick. I understand the restrictions of the court order about not discussing the details of the trial, and I will respect them. Beyond that, I simply want to get to know you as well as I can as quickly as I can."

Shaw, slouched in his chair, gazed at her with an amused smile. "Sounds like a fascinating undertaking," he said, making no effort to conceal the leer in his voice.

She glanced at him sharply. "You are thinking, perhaps, that I mean that too literally—like maybe a short cut to familiarity might be accomplished in yonder boudoir?"

"Not exactly," said Shaw, "but I must admit the thought flashed by. I didn't mean to be rude. You are an extremely attractive woman, and I am appropriately impressed. Just that, nothing more. You won't need tin pants."

"Thank you," she said. "I think I've read most of what's been written about you so far, and the articles fall into two extreme categories: Each one is either a hatchet job or a butter job and ignores the likelihood that at the botom line you are probably just a smart, able, real person who gets frightened by things that go bump in the night and puts his trousers on one leg at a time. At least that's what I'm hoping and expecting to find."

"Fair enough," laughed Shaw. "I agree with your appraisal of what others have written. Ask me halfway reasonable questions, and I'll try to give honest answers. Just one rule, though."

"What's that?"

"At any time when we're talking, that phone may

ring. Just hearing my half of the conversation might make you privy to things the press should not hear. I'm a guest of the Massachusetts Court and don't need the judge on my back for leaking to a reporter, no matter how pretty she is, so I'll take my calls in the other room behind a closed door, understood?"

"Perfectly," said Patricia calmly. "In fact, you take your calls here. I'll go into the other room."

"Thank you," he said.

She waved it away as if it were nothing. But in her chest she felt a tightness.

"Now then," she said, taking a notepad and pencil from her purse, "perhaps we could begin. By the way, supposing from time to time I feel the need to ask a question that is more outrageous than reasonable. What would be my penalty if I did that?"

"Simple," said Shaw. "You'll get a matching answer."

20

OF A SUNNY AFTERNOON
Tuesday, August 1

Daniel Shaw gently eased his head and shoulders into the hell hole in the belly of his Lear Jet and checked the gauges and lines. Satisfied, he ducked back down and continued his walkaround preflight inspection. Patricia Perrin followed him, watching his every move with fascination. He peered into the right tip tank, secured the cap, and headed for the entry door on the left side. "Okay," he said, "I guess we're ready."

She climbed in ahead of him, and sat in the copilot's seat. Shaw closed the clamshell doors, locked them with the electric locking motor, and slid into the left seat next to her.

He had spent about five hours with her so far and had gained respect for her skill as an interviewer. She moved quickly from one topic to another, her pencil moving swiftly over the notepad scribbling in her own form of speedwriting. Shaw had challenged her one time after a particularly long and involved answer, and she had read his words back to him almost verbatim. He had kept his hands to himself and found that he was growing quite comfortable with her. Only when she had asked "What kind of women do you prefer?" had he bounced her a bit.

"Exquisite little redheads with sumptuous bodies who

penalize their interviewees by refusing to take off their clothes while asking questions," he had said airily.

"Touché," she had replied softly without looking up. "You warned me." On her pad she wrote, "Any healthy attractive female whose heels are suitably round."

She had prevailed on him to let her have a crack at finding out first-hand what it was like to ride in a Lear Jet. She had shown him her current private pilot's license and a third-class medical certificate and explained that she had flown just over a hundred hours. He had decided to take her for a short spin on a day when the weather was good, thus eliminating the need to carry Sam Watkins, his copilot and chief investigator, along with him. She would be a legal copilot under visual flight rules, as long as the purpose of the flight was for "training." At least that would be his excuse if anyone caught him at it.

Shaw moved the start switch for the right engine to the down position and watched the right tachometer as the turbine began to wind up. He brought the right thrust lever around the horn, saw the fuel flow meter begin to register, heard the snap-snap of the igniters, and watched the tail pipe temperature begin to climb, just as the deep "Vrroooom" of the lightoff reached his ears. "We have a light," he explained, pointing to the tail pipe temperature gauge. When the turbine had stabilized at idle, he flipped the starter switch to "generator" and began to taxi away from the general aviation ramp.

"Boston ground," he said into the microphone, "Lear Jet one thousand alpha taxi for takeoff. Request permission to shift to clearance delivery."

"Approved," boomed the speaker above his head. "Taxi to two-two right, call when you're back on this frequency."

"Roger," said Shaw, resetting his transceiver. "Boston clearance, Lear one thousand alpha here, requesting clearance northeast out of the TCA for a round robin to

Bangor, Maine, VFR. Ask center if we can cruise at two-five-oh, please."

"Roger, stand by." A minute passed. "One thousand alpha, you're cleared as requested, hold runway heading after takeoff for vectors out of the TCA, climb and maintain fifteen thousand, expect two-five-oh five miles after departure, squawk four-three-zero-one, departure control on one two four point two."

Shaw read back the clearance, returned to ground control, and continued toward the active runway. There were four commercial jets lined up ahead of him.

"This is a sweet old bird," he explained to his enraptured guest, who had never been at the controls of anything larger than a small Piper. "I say old only because it was built in 1965," he went on. "The original model twenty-three is still the lightest and fastest of all the Lears. This one has new engines, new paint and interior, all the current modifications, and avionics that are tuned to a hair's edge." He patted the glare-shield with undisguised affection. "She's demanding and thirsty," he said, "but treat her right and she's a beautiful lady." He glanced sideways at Patricia, who smiled and wrinkled her nose.

"Why are we only using one engine?" she asked. Shaw pointed to the fuel gauge. "We have less than three thousand pounds of fuel," he explained. "Less than half a load. Each engine uses about six hundred pounds of fuel an hour idling on the ground, so we taxi on one, and light the other a minute or two before we roll."

Patricia shook her head in wonder. "In what this burns in one hour taxiing I could fly a Cherokee for more than ten hours. Amazing."

Shaw chuckled. "That's true, sweetheart—but this old girl can do a few things that would be a hard act to follow in a Cherokee." As the American 727 ahead of them was cleared into position, Shaw fired the left engine, let it stabilize, then rechecked the freedom of the controls.

"Lear one thousand alpha," called the tower, "position and hold. Wind zero-six-zero at eight." Shaw acknowledged and aligned himself with the dotted line in the center of the runway.

"One thousand alpha, caution wake turbulence behind the departing American Boeing, cleared for takeoff."

"One thousand alpha rolling," replied Shaw, moving the thrust levers forward smoothly but crisply. The Lear leaped ahead as he released the brakes, the engines bellowing a deep tortured howl. Patricia Perrin was forced back in her seat by the acceleration. After rolling just a little over one thousand feet Shaw drew back on the yoke and snapped the landing gear switch to "up." As the airspeed indicator moved through one hundred fifty knots, he raised the flaps, and lifted the nose of the aircraft thirty degrees above the horizon. The rate of climb indicator pegged at six thousand feet per minute, and the altimeter began to unwind like a clock with its springs gone haywire. Sixty seconds after liftoff he was hurtling through fifteen thousand feet, cleared to cruise altitude. In one more minute he eased the nose over, leveled at two-five-oh, and punched the auto pilot engage button, then the heading mode, then the altitude hold. He reduced the power to ninety percent, then, with a perfectly straight face, unbuckled his seat belt and began to climb out.

"Be back in a little white," he said nonchalantly.

Patricia Perrin regained her mesmerized senses with a jolt.

"Daniel," she screamed, "where the hell are you going?"

Shaw feigned surprise and sighed elaborately. "You writers," he said wearily, "are all alike. No sense of humor. Fellow can't even take a brief snooze, you want to make a federal case out of it."

Patricia rolled her eyes upward and shook her head.

"You," she said with a half-smile, "are a proper bastard. First you scare the living shit out of me with your Cape Kennedy takeoff, then you leave me alone with this monstrous blowtorch." She wiped her eyes with the back of her hand and muttered softly, "My god, what a machine. . . ."

"There, there," soothed Shaw with mock paternal affection. "Not to worry. She won't bite." He leaned over and kissed her gently on the tip of the nose.

She stared at him without speaking, her eyes soft and moist, her lips slightly parted, her breathing a little labored. Shaw looked back at her, unable to unlock his gaze, all the joking gone. He leaned over and kissed her again, this time on the lips.

I am sliding, sliding fast, she thought as she moved ever so slightly to him. Because I want to, I guess. . . .

I am falling off the deep end, thought Shaw, a deep end five miles above the coast of Portland, Maine, like some kind of crazy man, and it's all so wrong, I should level with her, tell her there's no use, but I. . . .

What might have been a dramatic high altitude reverie was interrupted by the blare of the radio speaker above their heads.

"Attention all aircraft this frequency, this is Boston Center. A fog bank that has been hovering off the coast of New England is now moving onshore because of a wind shift. Flight Service advises that low ceilings and visibilities may move in swiftly to cover coastal airports. Planning for inland alternates is advised."

Daniel Shaw snapped to attention as if he were back in Navy uniform. He glanced at the fuel gauge. There were slightly over fourteen hundred pounds remaining. He switched the DME to Boston. One hundred sixty miles out. No sweat. He thumbed the red button on the left side of his control yoke, which disengaged the autopilot, and rolled into a forty-five degree bank to the left, pulling hard in the turn as if he were back in a Navy A-4.

"What's the matter?" asked Patricia.

"Nothing," said Shaw. "A little fog coming in unexpectedly. Boston's fickle that way, like San Francisco. Since you don't have an instrument rating, I'd prefer to get in before it hits the field. After all, if I set us down in some strange city, you'll think I planned the whole thing just to set the stage for a final move to the jugular."

She smiled and touched his shoulder but did not respond.

"Boston Center," said Shaw into the microphone, "this is Lear one thousand alpha at two five oh. Based on your advisory, we're aborting our round robin and turning back to Logan. Request descent in two zero miles."

"Roger, one thousand alpha," replied the controller, "two zero miles. Are you landing Boston?"

"We'd like to," said Shaw. "Request clearance to leave the frequency momentarily."

"Go ahead," said Boston Center. "Check in when you're back."

Shaw turned his primary transceiver to 120.6 megacycles.

"Boston Approach, one thousand alpha inbound your station. What are your local field conditions?"

"One thousand alpha, Boston Approach. The fog bank is moving across the field from the bay at about fifteen knots. Ground vehicle at the approach end of runway three-three estimates two hundred feet, one-half mile, occasionally sky obscured and one-sixteenth in patches."

Shaw frowned. "What about adjacent airports. Have you any info?"

"Roger. Hyannis is closed, runway visual range six hundred feet. Portland ditto. New Bedford one hundred and a quarter, Providence three hundred and one, and lowering. Navy Weymouth is two hundred and one-half, GCA is operating. That's pretty much the picture."

"What about Hanscom field?" asked Shaw. "The fog shouldn't get there for an hour."

"Hanscom is presently closed to traffic," said the approach controller. "Weather's okay, but there's an emergency in progress. Air Force T-39 Sabreliner with V.I.P. from Washington has an unsafe indication on the nose gear. Tower's trying to check it visually on low passes. Might open up soon, though."

"Thanks Approach. We're switching back to Center. See you in a few minutes."

"Boston Center, one thousand alpha back with you. How's the traffic into Logan?"

"Looks like you'll be about number eight," replied the controller. "Descend and maintain six thousand, Victor one thirty-nine to Tonni intersection, hold northeast, right hand turns."

Shaw read back the clearance, thumbed the autopilot pitch control gently forward, and drew the thrust levers back until the turbines stabilized at eighty percent. The fuel gauge showed eleven hundred fifty pounds.

Patricia Perrin watched Shaw's face with growing apprehension. In all the hours she had spent with him, he had always been totally relaxed, totally in control. Now the muscles at the hinge of his jaw bone were knotted, and the lines in his forehead were furrowed with concern.

"Daniel," she asked, "are we low on gas?"

His features eased, and he grinned at her. "We are indeed. In fact, we have none at all." Her jaw dropped.

"However," he went on, "we have enough *kerosene* to get us on the ground. Now, if you'll keep your ears open and your eyes peeled, you may learn something about instrument landings. We're going to do this one on the autopilot, almost to the ground. Once 'George' gets locked on to the glide slope, he can fly a better approach than any human pilot. I'll watch 'George' and the gauges. You watch the radar altimeter. Starting at five hundred feet call out every hundred. At two hundred feet, forget the cockpit and look for the high intensity approach lights. They're a series of flashing strobes running toward the threshold of the runway. You should see them through the fog. When you do, just say 'I have the rabbit running' and I'll set her on the runway. Okay?"

Patricia nodded. "Whatever you say, Captain." She did not sound thoroughly convinced.

"And stop worrying," said Daniel. "If the boys jock us around too much, we can shoot over to Hanscom field, about fifteen miles west. We might have to declare an emergency, but we can get in, no sweat.

"As a matter of fact, Patty-cake," he went on, "I staged this whole deal. By making you a little anxious, I am causing your system to demand increasing amounts of oxygen.

"This, in turn, causes your chest to heave. With luck, one or two of the buttons on your blouse will succumb to the strain, and pop off. Pretty neat, huh?"

Patricia slid her hand slowly and seductively to his right thigh and suddenly pinched him hard between her thumb and forefinger.

"Ouch," he yelled.

"Now," she said sweetly. "Please get your mind out of your pants and fly this goddam airplane!"

Shaw, subdued somewhat, turned his attention to the increasing level of chatter from Boston Center, which was issuing advisories as to the progress at Logan.

Delta's Flight 721 from Tampa had gotten in. Eastern's shuttle from LaGuardia had missed and gone back to New York. United's 94 from San Francisco had broken off the approach at the middle marker, and diverted to Hartford. An Air New England Twin Otter had spotted the runway a shade too late, and was going around for a second try.

Shaw frowned. Air New England had in effect pushed him back one slot. His fuel gauge was now reading less than one thousand pounds, and he was floating slowly down through eight thousand feet. He calculated that the Tonni intersection, an electronic pinpoint eighteen miles east of Logan, was less than twelve miles away. The prospects of diverting to Hanscom were beginning to become a bit more real.

Without saying anything to Patricia, he tuned the secondary transceiver to Hanscom Approach, hoping to learn that the Sabreliner had landed safely, and that the field was open.

He monitored Hanscom's frequency for thirty seconds and heard no traffic, which he took to be a good sign. He turned the speaker for the secondary transceiver off so that Patricia would not catch wind of what he was checking.

"Boston Approach," he said "Lear one thousand alpha is leveling at six thousand, entering the holding pattern at Tonni. What's our position in line please?"

"One thousand alpha," said the controller, "you are presently number five. Air Force Two is now leaving Whitman for the outer marker. He has exercised his priority. Air New England is outer marker inbound. American's Detroit flight has just landed, reporting that the field was two hundred and one quarter at breakout, but runway visual range three thousand feet at touchdown. The field is pretty much up and down in drifting fog patches."

"Roger," said Shaw. "We'll take a couple of swings around the pattern and see how things are."

"Sonofabitch," he muttered.

"What's wrong?" asked Patricia.

"Nothing serious," he sighed. "Air Force Two is the Vice President of the United States. Paper said this morning he was due in Boston for a speech tonight. He has the right to take landing priority from any aircraft but Air Force One, and he's using it. And I'll bet the best part of my ass that he's got at least two hours of spare fuel. Sonofabitch."

"What will we do?"

Shaw studied the fuel gauge. It was slipping below eight hundred pounds. His speed was one hundred sixty knots. He twisted the autopilot heading control, and turned to the inbound leg of the holding pattern. Air Force Two reported the outer marker, and Trans-World 17 was six miles behind. Eastern 93 was leaving Whitman, and Allegheny 41 was descending from four thousand to follow. Air New England had landed on the second pass.

Shaw tried to estimate his chances of being cleared in with only one more swing through the holding pattern. They did not look good.

"I guess," he said to Patricia, "we'll take a look at Hanscom."

"Boston Approach," he said to his microphone, "Lear one thousand alpha would like to divert to Hanscom. I believe the emergency has terminated?"

"Negative," said the controller, "Hanscom is closed. There's a Sabreliner with a folded nose wheel on the runway, disabled right at the intersections. They estimate thirty minutes to pull him out of there. By then they'll be down with fog."

"Roger," said Shaw. "I checked the frequency at Hanscom approach and heard no action. I thought that their problem was over."

"Negative," said Boston Approach, "they were working him on a military frequency, UHF. Expect approach clearance in seventeen minutes."

Shaw, for the first time, faced himself squarely in the mirror of his mind and admitted that he was in trouble. Bad trouble.

He had seven hundred pounds of fuel. By the time he hit the outer marker, he would probably be down to four hundred—about sixty gallons. That would allow one pass. If he missed the approach, he would flame out before he could shoot another. He might ditch in Boston Harbor and survive since a Lear with no fuel will float like a cork.

But sitting next to him was a writer. Way down where he kept his most private secrets, he knew that he had been trying to impress her. He could have carried more fuel but had wanted to climb like a rocket. He could have diverted inland but didn't want her thinking he had lost his cool. He *should* have realized that Hanscom's emergency would have been audible *only* on UHF but had forgotten.

He glanced sideways at Patricia, who was looking rather stonily at the instruments in front of her—particularly the fuel gauge. There was no use in trying to kid her any further. She knew that they would not be in the air much longer.

He quickly pondered his choices. In a moment he would have to turn outbound in the holding pattern and fly east, away from Logan Airport. He could declare an emergency for low fuel and start his approach immediately. If he got in, there would be forms to fill out and a lot of questions by the FAA. The news media would pick up the incident and draw attention to his declaration of panic. Patricia Perrin would report the incident in breathless prose in her article. One way or another, the bureaucrats would launch an in-depth probe. If they went deep enough, he might never fly again.

"Pat," he said, "switch Nav one to one-ten-three. We'll land in turn with no sweat. Let's just check the ILS to make sure it's working."

Patricia turned the primary navigation receiver as she was told. Shaw slid his left hand to the circuit breaker panel beside his seat and quietly pulled the breaker that controlled his gyro compass and horizontal situation indicator. A red flag popped out of the corner of the instrument.

"Oh-oh," said Shaw. "We've got a problem. Tune number two."

Patricia set one-ten point three megacycles in the secondary navigation receiver. The red flag didn't move.

"Boston Approach," said Shaw to the microphone.

"Lear one thousand alpha has the four right ILS inop, intermittent at best."

"What's the matter?" said Patricia, alarmed now.

"Part of our instrument landing system receiver's screwed."

"What are we going to do?"

Shaw silenced her with a wave of his hand. Into the mike he said, "Request an immediate vector to Navy Weymouth. Tell them to have the GCA unit standing by. Departing Tonni now on heading two-four-zero, six thousand feet."

If Patricia was nervous, the Boston Approach controller had the cool of a lizard.

"Roger, one thousand alpha. Take up heading two *five* zero for GCA approach to runway eight, Navy Weymouth. They are standing by. Descend at your discretion to two thousand. Do you have a fuel problem?"

"No," said Shaw evenly. "We don't. And we don't want one."

"Understood," said approach. "Navy Weymouth has granted permission for an unscheduled landing. You have agreed to hold them harmless for any mistakes which might be made. At least I told them you would. Are you familiar with GCA procedures?"

"Affirmative," growled Shaw. "Tell Navy Weymouth that Lieutenant Commander Daniel E. Shaw, U.S. Naval Reserve, Miramar, California, is commanding this aircraft and current in GCA. I do not expect to make a second pass. And tell them to forget the legal bullshit. I am also a Judge Advocate."

"Roger," the controller seemed gleeful. "They have the message. They are monitoring this frequency. They are ready to take you on one-two-six point two. And Commander—good luck. Kenneth Arnold, Bo'sun's Mate First Class, United States Naval Reserve."

"So long," said Shaw, shifting to the new frequency. He lowered the nose of the Lear without changing the power setting and watched his speed build to two hundred seventy knots as his vertical speed indicator showed a descent of one thousand feet per minute.

He estimated that he had twenty miles to go before the GCA controller turned him on final—about four and one-half minutes. He might have just over five hundred pounds when he started down the chute.

"Lear one thousand alpha, this is Navy Weymouth. Radar contact. We have you drifting slightly south. Make that heading two-five-five degrees, maintain two thousand."

"Roger, Weymouth," said Shaw, "two-five-five and two thousand."

"Daniel," said Patricia, "what is a GCA?"

"The Letters," he said, "stand for Ground Controlled Approach. That's military lingo for what civilian pilots call Precision Approach Radar. In other words, instead of flying down a radio beam like the Instrument Landing System, which we can see in the cockpit by the two crossed needles on our ILS indicator, we'll fly down a very similar groove in the sky which the controllers can see on two different radar screens. I won't be able to know that I'm high, low, left or right of the glide path, but they will. They just talk me down—all the way to the runway if necessary."

"Is that as safe as an ILS?" she asked.

"There's very little agreement about that," he replied. "Airline pilots would probably tell you they prefer the ILS—gives them control in the cockpit, instead of relying on some guy on the ground. Navy types like myself are comfortable with GCA, particularly after a lot of carrier flying. Actually both are very safe. For a totally blind landing, GCA has the edge, I think."

"Are we going to land blind?"

"I doubt it," said Shaw, "but we can if we have to."

"Navy Weymouth, one thousand alpha here. What have you got at the moment?"

"Stand by," said the controller. Then, a few seconds

later. "One thousand alpha, Weymouth now two hundred over, one-half mile, variable one hundred sky obscured with one-sixteenth. Are you equipped with radar altimeter?"

"Affirmative," said Shaw. "Turn the runway lights up full, please."

"Roger, one thousand alpha. We have you passing north of the field, five miles. Turn left to one-seven-zero degrees, descend to fifteen hundred feet. What will be your final approach speed?"

"One hundred and five knots," said Shaw.

Down in the GCA trailer parked on the north side of the touchdown point of runway eight, Radar Specialist First Class, Alan Poe, glanced up at his supervisor, Lieutenant Michael Klein.

"Jesus Christ," he said. "A hundred and five. Our friend the commander must be running on fumes!"

Lieutenant Klein scowled. "Perhaps. He said he didn't want to make a second pass. At one oh five, he has a thousand pounds of fuel or less. I think, Mr. Poe, you'd better milk him down in one shot, right on the money." Klein peered out of the window of the trailer. "And I mean *right* on the money. By the look of this stuff, he's going to feel that runway before he ever sees it."

"And supposing he don't make it," said Poe. "What then?"

Klein stroked his jaw, and shook his head slowly. "No options, I'm afraid. Normally he could pull up to a fast intercept of Logan's four right ILS and take one last shot. But his receiver's inop, he says. I suspect he'll pour on the coal and grab all the sky he can until flame-out, then dead stick it into the water. I'll get the Coast Guard on the land line and have them start a cutter out toward Roosevelt Roads just in case." Klein glanced at the radar scope. "You'd better turn your boy," he said, reaching for the telephone.

Poe nodded. "One thousand alpha, turn left to one-two-zero to intercept the final approach path. Start reducing to final approach speed. Now turn further left to one-zero-zero." Sweat began to speckle Poe's forehead.

"Further left now to zero-eight-two," he said. "You need not acknowledge any further transmissions. You are intercepting the centerline nicely, coming up on the glide path. Prepare to begin a descent at three hundred feet per minute. You are five miles from touchdown, intercepting glide path now. Begin your descent."

Inside the cockpit of the Lear, Shaw was a study in concentration. His left hand was on the control yoke, his right on the thrust levers. His eyes moved mechanically and quickly as he scanned his flight instruments in a set pattern. Gyro attitude good, wings level. Gyro compass, steady on zero-eight-two degrees. Air speed one-twelve. He put a slight rearward pressure on the thrust levers. Rate of descent, 350 feet per minute, barometric altimeter 1,400, radar altimeter twelve-forty. Check—Weymouth is one-hundred sixty-one feet above sea level. Shaw's mind became his instruments.

"Pat," he said, "keep your head up for the last three hundred feet. Call if you see a rabbit or the runway."

"All right," she said in a low, frightened voice. "I will."

"You are holding nicely on the centerline," said Poe's voice, "and slightly above the glide path, but drifting down to it . . . you are on the glide path now, on the centerline, three and one-half miles from touchdown. Check your gear down and locked, and complete your final landing check list."

Without taking his eyes from the primary instruments, Shaw reached out and flicked the landing gear switch to "down." As they were falling into place, he added a slight amount of power to compensate for the increased drag and hold his rate of descent. Momentarily three green lights glowed on the panel. "Gear down and locked, pressure up," he said to no one in particular, out of long habit.

"Pat," he said, "We are all set except for the rest of the flaps. We're using half now, and I don't want any more than that until landing is assured. If you see the runway, push the flap lever all the way down. If you don't see anything by the time the radar altimeter shows two hundred feet, push it down anyway. Okay?"

She tried to answer, but terror had clogged her larynx. Shaw heard only an unintelligible, coarse whisper. He glanced at her quickly, saw her head nod forward slightly, and saw her left hand reach out and rest on the flap lever.

"You are drifting to the right of centerline," said Poe, "turn left to zero-seven-niner degrees. Holding nicely on the glide path." He glanced at Klein, who was standing to his right and staring intently at the scopes.

"This guy is some kinda smooth," muttered Poe, "but he'll need luck."

"Lots of it," said Klein. "The visibility out there is absolutely nothing. I hope he did some blind landings in all-weather school. Tell him to stay with you 'til touchdown. It's the only chance he's got."

Poe nodded. "You are correcting nicely back to the centerline, rising slightly above the glide path. Turn right to zero-eight-zero degrees. I am going to talk you all the way to the touchdown point. Do not acknowledge. Should you make visual contact with the runway, take over visually and disregard my instructions. Once again, runway eight is six thousand three hundred feet long, and two hundred feet wide. The lights are max intensity. You are coming down onto the glide path . . . you are now on the glide path, on centerline, one and one half miles from touchdown. Field visibility conditions at the touchdown point are limited and variable."

Shaw nodded to himself grimly and glanced at the radar altimeter. It was falling slowly through 320 feet.

"Just slightly below the glide path now," said Poe, "on the centerline, one mile from touchdown."

Shaw looked at his airspeed, and saw that he was 5 knots fast. He touched the electric trim on the left horn of his control yoke and lifted the nose a hair.

"Drifting slightly to the right of centerline, turn left zero-seven-eight degrees. You are on the glide path, correcting back to centerline. Right on the money as you approach minimums, very nice and holding."

A yellow light next to the radar altimeter flashed on and glowed steadily, indicating that he had passed through two hundred feet. "Pat . . . ," he started to say, but before he could get to the second word she pushed the flap lever full down. Shaw did not touch the power but lifted the nose further and watched the airspeed bleed off to 100, then 95, then 90 knots. He wiggled the thrust levers forward a fraction to hold 90 knots.

"On centerline, on glide path, passing the threshold of the runway, one-quarter mile from touchdown, 90 feet over the centerline, and descending nicely. Begin your flare to a landing altitude, stay on your present heading, now forty feet above the runway, speed looking good, position good, runway braking should be fair to good, coming up on touchdown now, roll straight ahead."

The combination of a very slow approach speed and a wet runway surface eased what might have been a hard landing into a reasonable touchdown. As the main wheels hit, Shaw flipped the spoiler switch on the power quadrant, let the nose fall through rapidly until he felt the nose wheel slam onto the runway, riveted his attention to the gyro compass, and stood on the brakes. The Lear started to swerve alarmingly to the left, and out of the corner of his eye Shaw saw the dim orange glow of the lights on the edge of the runway flash past. Quickly he kicked the right rudder and eased the left brake slightly, then came down hard on it again. He could feel the anti-skid system cycling as the main wheels threatened to lock up from the brake pressure, then were automatically released as the sensing device cut in to prevent the skid. The Lear came shuddering to a stop, still on the macadam.

From force of habit Shaw closed the spoilers, lifted the flaps, and shut down the right engine. He taxied gingerly until he found the runway edge lights, then a blue one indicating a turnoff. As soon as he had cleared the runway he shut down the left engine and turned off all the switches except the battery and the number one transceiver. The fuel gauge read 180 pounds. Had he tried to taxi to the ramp through the dense fog his engine would have flamed out half way. Flaming out would require a detailed written explanation. Shutting the engine down, for a lack of familiarity with the field, would not.

"One thousand alpha is down and off the runway on a taxiway on the north side. Request ground vehicle with towbar to meet us here. I am not familiar."

"Will do, Commander," said Poe, the relief in his voice a subtle contrast to the terse, disciplined assurances and instructions he had been transmitting moments before. "And by the way, thanks for making me look good."

Shaw smiled. "Roger." He looked at Pat. Her normally robust face was pale, and she was taking great, deep gulps of air almost in spasms, as if her lungs were fighting for life. She had held her breath for a full minute before her senses told her that Shaw had the aircraft under control. She sensed a tingling feeling, as if a limb had gone to sleep from staying in one position for too long. She did not realize that she was hyperventilating.

Shaw turned in his seat, and put his arms around her, patting her gently on the shoulder. "You're okay, hon," he said softly. "Just slow down a bit. Try to breathe slowly."

Gradually her eyes filled with tears as her heaving

chest eased a bit, and she began to quiver. Then she leaned against his shoulder and fell into a series of great, silent shuddering sobs. He held her until they had gone.

It took more than an hour for their taxi to grope through the fog to the hotel. She had been almost totally silent enroute, cuddled against his side. When they got to his suite, he poured two tumblers of straight Scotch, and handed one to her. She shook her head.

"I don't think I could keep it down just yet," she said. She fumbled in her purse and withdrew a small, white cigarette. She lit it and inhaled deeply.

Shaw started to remind her that she was in Massachusetts, not California, and that the great state that had once hung women as witches was still treating marijuana as a serious crime; however, he said nothing, and drained his glass in one gulp. The liquor felt warm in his stomach.

There was silence for a few minutes as Pat took four consecutive hits from the cigarette, then snubbed it out. She closed her eyes for a while, letting the relaxing tingle slowly flood her senses. She turned on the couch on which they both were sitting, put her arms tightly around Shaw, and kissed him deeply and softly, her breasts pressed against his chest.

"Daniel," she murmured. "I feel all clammy. Either from the fog or from being scared half to death. How about you?"

Shaw grinned. "Damp is what I feel. From the fog, of course," he lied. "What do you suggest?"

Her eyes had softened to a dreamy glaze. "I was thinking a bath might be nice," she said, looking at him like an affectionate doe. "Just the two of us." Without waiting for his response, she began to unbutton her blouse.

"Yes," he said, feeling the first stirrings of arousal

beginning, "a bath would be just the thing." He reached for her hands, placed them on his shoulders, and smiled. "Here," he said, "you must be exhausted. Let me do that."

21

MEN IN A BOX
Friday, August 18

Walter Barrett's office was boiling. He was anxious to get home to a cool drink, but Philip Durham had insisted on a meeting to evaluate the posture of the prosecution's case against Michael Kilrayne. When Durham arrived with Gilardi in tow, he was obviously in a dark mood. He was in his shirtsleeves, perspiring heavily and complaining about the lack of air conditioning in the old courthouse.

"I have learned," he said coldly, "that brother Shaw left for London, yesterday. I assume that he is briefing our barrister friend on what he had learned in his investigation. If he knows everything we know, the two of them must be very puzzled at this point."

"How's that?" asked Walter. Gilardi stared uncomfortably out the window.

"Because," said Durham furiously, "this goddam case is a shambles. I've never seen anything like it. How the hell you ever got a grand jury to buy *this* mess is beyond me, and I've sold grand juries some awful crap myself—but nothing like this. You must have somehow disqualified every grand juror with an I.Q. in three figures."

"Well, we . . ." Walter was about to explain to Durham about the wiretap evidence when he caught a dark frown that said "No" from Gilardi. Gilardi was afraid that Durham might well feel compelled to disclose the illegal evidence to Judge Somerville, who might in turn dismiss the indictment and bar the evidence from further use. Were that to happen, Gilardi was convinced, it would be impossible to get a new indictment from another grand jury, and he and Walter Barrett would be a laughingstock, with Kilrayne doing most of the laughing.

"The grand jury was persuaded, and they voted to indict on the evidence we presented, which we've told you about," Walter lied. "We can convince a trial jury the same way."

"Bullshit," exploded Durham. "Indictments are based on a lopsided presentation where nothing is challenged, voted by the people who've usually become the buddies of the prosecutor. Proving something beyond a reasonable doubt to a bunch of strangers is a different ball game as you should have learned in law school!"

"Wait a minute," said Walter, his voice rising. "You seem to forget the reason that my uncle maneuvered you into this case. We agreed that once Kilrayne took the stand, everything would hinge on his testimony. *You* are here to rip him to shreds, remember? When he stumbles on the witness stand, together with what we've got, that will be enough. Am I right, Joe?"

"Jesus," said Durham, "forget this 'am I right, Joe' crap for a minute. Has it ever occurred to you, Walter, that this case is so thin that an old fox like Kilrayne might *not* testify? Then where are we, for god's sake?"

"If I may, Phil," interrupted Gilardi quietly, "I have a little information on that score. Martin Hanlon, the editor of the *Chronicle,* does a little elbow-bending with a friend of mine who's a private detective. We keep it quiet, but I work pretty closely with this guy, getting information for him that he can't get and so on. He's helped me break a few cases, so it works out pretty good. Anyway, he told me Kilrayne feels he has to testify come hell or high water. Thinks his practice would fold if he didn't—jurors in other cases for his clients might think he was covering up something, and his track record could turn sour in a hurry. No wins, no business. I think we can count on him taking the stand."

Durham looked somewhat assuaged, but far from happy. "In that case," he said, "and bearing in mind that I am relying one hundred percent on what you are telling me, I'm going to have to save something as a hold-back to hit him with in the middle of cross. I think the table lighter with the initials might fill the bill."

"I thought we were going to have to turn that over for inspection by the defense," said Walter, plainly puzzled. "How are you going to surprise Kilrayne if he's already seen it?"

"We will *not* turn it over," said Durham firmly. "If we classify it as rebuttal evidence, we probably don't have to. It's a risk I'll have to take, and if Somerville blows his stack so be it. By the time I flash it in front of the jury, there'll be damned little he can do about it without letting the press think he's favoring Kilrayne, which is a problem he's going to have throughout the trial. If you birds hadn't presented it to the grand jury, we could have Joe march in with it in the middle of cross as if he had just found it on a return trip to her house. But that's out now—one of those grand jurors is likely to come forward, even though there is no record of what they saw and heard. I'll just have to play it as I outlined."

Walter did not look convinced. Gilardi tugged his ear, fearful that Durham was perilously close to pulling out of the case. That would be a disaster.

"I think Phil's right," Gilardi said. "It's worth the risk. If Kilrayne falters even one little bit when that lighter is shoved under his nose, his credibility is going to take a hard tumble. He will never be able to explain why he didn't candidly mention that little gift in his direct testimony. And since he probably won't tell his lawyers about it, that may come through to the jury as well. A man who doesn't tell his lawyers the truth certainly wouldn't hesitate to lie to a jury to get himself off the pin."

Walter nodded unhappily. "See you Monday," said Durham wearily, as he walked out of the office.

That evening Carl Barrett, at Gilardi's suggestion, called Durham at his home.

"Evening, Phil," he said when Durham answered, "just thought I might check with you on the progress of things. Trial starts in something less than three weeks, I guess."

"It does," replied Durham gloomily, "and our case-in-chief stinks something awful. I'll tell you, Carl, I've been giving some serious thought to resigning. I'm afraid the profession is going to think that I'm some kind of horse's ass for going to bat with a toothpick. Christ, Carl, we can still get kicked out of court for lack of proof of death!"

"I'm sure you'll prevail on that score, Phil. Somerville is new to the bench and fairly inexperienced. He'll let the case go to the jury, rather than let the public think that he was protecting a fellow trial lawyer."

"I'm not so sure," said Durham. "I've been doing a lot of checking on him, and I'm getting two differing opinions. One says that he's a mild guy sort of feeling his way along, especially in criminal cases: The other says that underneath he's all balls, and if you put his feet to the fire, you're going to find asbestos skin and a backbone of stainless steel."

"You'll handle it, Phil," Carl soothed.

"I'm not convinced," said Durham coldly, "and I *am* considering pulling out."

"I wouldn't," said Carl.

"What's that?"

"I don't think you should. The press would surely say that you were overwhelmed by the barrister and afraid

to oppose him, or Kilrayne himself, or all of them together. It wouldn't look good for you, Phil."

"Perhaps," said Durham, wishing at that moment
that he had never answered Carl's call back in July. "I
came into this case to put Kilrayne in a box. You're
telling me that in a way I'm in a box myself. I'll remember that. Good evening, Carl." He hung up.

22

GROUND RULES
Wednesday, September 6

The day before jury selection was to begin, Judge Gary Somerville called a meeting of counsel at two o'clock in the afternoon. In order to avoid continual interruptions, he invited Kilrayne to be present so that Everard would not need to leave chambers to consult with him.

When all were in attendance, with a stenographer, he bade them good afternoon and said, filling his pipe, "Let's get to the problems which we can expect to confront tomorrow. First I should like to address the matter of press seating." He indicated several volumes of the United States Supreme Court Reports which were lying open on the credenza behind his desk. "I have been studying my authority to give preferential press seating. In the *Sheppard* case, with which I'm sure you are all familiar, it has been widely assumed that Sheppard won a new trial because of press misconduct. My reading of the case suggests that while the conduct of the press was abysmal, and perhaps the worst example of yellow journalism in our history, the reversal turned in fact on the point that the trial judge let the press take over his courtroom and that the fault was laid at his feet. Do you gentlemen share that view? By the way, for purposes of this afternoon's discussion, I invite any comments Mr. Kilrayne might like to make, provided Mr. Everard does not object."

"Not a smidgeon," said Everard with a wry smile. "I must confess that since we are considerably less tolerant of any press interference in legal cases in England than America seems to be, I should think Mr. Kilrayne's expertise in this area to be more helpful than my own."

"Thank you, Mr. Everard. Gentlemen?"

"I think Your Honor is correct," said Durham.

"I think Your Honor is *precisely* correct," said Kilrayne with a smile.

Somerville colored slightly. "Very well, gentlemen," he said, "I will assume the responsibility of assuring total decorum from the press section. In fact, looking at the roster of those who have asked for reserved seats, I would estimate that we will have one of the most highly professional groups of criminal trial reporters ever assembled in attendance at our proceeding. If the youngsters from the local media will follow their example, I would expect no difficulties. Which brings me to my second point.

"Some recent rulings of the Burger Court, if I may call it that, seem to hold that although the press has the unfettered right to print anything it can get its hands on, newsmen and women have no special right of access. The ruling had to do with a desire of some reporters to visit a jail, but carried to its logical extreme it could mean that newspeople ought not to be given assigned seats at trials of great public interest but should wait in line with general spectators and take their chances.

"This disturbs me, because like every other trial judge in the past fifty years or more I have granted specific seats to named reporters. Perhaps I no longer have the power to do that. What says the Commonwealth?"

"We think," said Durham, "that Your Honor is well within his rights. Surely the press is entitled to a seat without waiting in line with every Tom, Dick, and Harry who wants to catch a bit of the trial."

"Thank you, Mr. Durham. What is the defense position?"

"I am in agreement with Mr. Durham," said Kilrayne. "I believe that the Burger Court is making a fundamental mistake and that if faced with the issue confronting this court, the rights of the press at least to observe the proceedings on a regular basis would somehow emerge intact. But more to the point, Your Honor's concern is no doubt as to whether I as the defendant wish to voice any objection as to your orders. I do not. If I have any rights, which I doubt, I specifically waive them, and I intend that to be a knowing and understanding waiver within the meaning of the law."

Somerville smiled from behind a cloud of blue pipe smoke. "That would seem to settle the point," he said. "If you, Mr. Kilrayne, cannot make a knowing and understanding waiver, then I guess no one can. Let's get to the next matter. Neither side has moved for a change of venue. Do I take that, too, to be a waiver?"

"The prosecution," said Durham, "will be content to draw a petit jury from the good citizens of Essex County."

"And the defense?" asked Somerville.

"I am mindful, Your Honor," said Kilrayne, "that a motion for a change of venue never really ripens until an examination of prospective jurors has disclosed a community prejudice on the eve of trial—that is, before I am called upon to make a waiver, a good part of the *voire dire* examination should at least be attempted."

"I think, Mr. Kilrayne, that I appreciate your position more than you know. I do not by this ruling mean to be presumptuous. I will ask counsel for both sides to submit written questions to me and to suggest any questions they would like me to ask as the *voire dire* goes along.

"Now then, I estimate that this trial will run between two and three weeks. I will lock up the jury, as is nearly always done in cases charging murder, and will seat two alternates unless there is objection."

"I do not object," said Durham, thinking to himself

that a jury under close confinement could not help but resent a defendant who was free to move about on bail.

"Nor do I," said Kilrayne, who thought to himself that a jury noticing that the defendant was not in shackles would infer that some judge or other had thought him to be less than a murderer, else he would have been in irons.

"Thank you, then, gentlemen, all of you," said Somerville, tapping his pipe against the edge of the ashtray before him. "Have your proposed questions to me no later than eight-thirty tomorrow morning. We have a special venire of 200 jurors to draw from. We will begin at nine-thirty in the forenoon. And I should mention that I am a bit of a stickler for starting on time. If we are to impose upon this jury to surrender their freedom, we will attempt to compensate their inconvenience by starting exactly on schedule. We will also work Saturdays if I deem it appropriate. I will see all of you tomorrow."

At ten o'clock that evening, Anthony Everard drained off the last of a nightcap snifter of brandy and resolved not to think about the fact that he hadn't the faintest idea what his defense was to be, or what he should say in his opening statement. His client had shrugged aside such matters, simply asserting that no defense would be necessary and that all concentration should be given to assaulting the prosecution at its every turn. He was about to take that notion to bed with him when the telephone jangled.

"Yes?"

"Is this Mr. Everard?"

"Yes. Who is calling?"

"My name is Ephraim Kanter. I know it's late, but I think I ought to see you, for the good of your client."

Everard paused. He had been duly warned that during highly publicized trials in America, every nut and his brother would use each possible artifice to get next to one of the principals. Nonetheless, his caller sounded calm, well-educated, perhaps even a trifle aristocratic.

"Would you like to see me now?" he asked.

"Yes, I would. I'm in the lobby. Where might we meet?"

"If it is convenient," said Everard, "you may come to my rooms. Do you know the number?"

"I'll be there in a few minutes." There was a click.

Three minutes later there was a light tap on the door, and Everard opened it to admit a tall, handsome man with gray hair and brown eyes, impeccably attired in a conservative three-piece suit.

"Good evening," said the stranger, "I'm Ephraim Martin Kanter," said the visitor. "May I sit down?"

"Certainly," said Everard. This, he said to himself, is no nut.

"I won't take much of your time. There has been something gnawing at me for some weeks now, and I'd like to get it off my chest. It could be important to your trial."

"By all means, sir," said Everard. "May I offer you a drink?"

Kanter shook his head. "No thank you," he said. "If I ever have to be cross-questioned about our meeting tonight, I'd rather that I be able to say we were not drinking, particularly me."

"All right, then, what is it?" asked Everard.

"Your client," said Kanter, "is from what I read in the papers, about to be tried for the murder of Sarah Hansen. I knew her."

Everard looked at him with an unblinking gaze. "Yes?"

"I know," Kanter went on, "that the authorities must have searched her apartment. If they did so, they probably found a silver table lighter that I gave her some years ago. It bears the inscription 'Love, M.K.' Sarah couldn't get used to the name 'Ephraim' attached to a Jewish man, so she always called me 'Martin.' It has

occurred to me over and over again that 'M.K.' might
be used to point at your client."

"Everard was puzzled. "A table lighter? You mean for
cigarettes? We've been shown no such object."

"Then perhaps they're holding it back. I know they
must have found it because I was with Sarah two nights
before she disappeared, and it was on her coffee table. I
simply wanted you to know that should it crop up during the trial, I will be willing to come forward and identify it."

"That's very good of you," said Everard. "Quite no-
ble, I should say. We haven't seen it yet or been told of
it. May I, without intruding upon your courtesy in coming forward, ask how you knew the Hansen woman?"

"Sure," said Kanter. "I was in love with her. So were
several other people. I don't know who they were, because Sarah was as complete as she was lovely—inside
and out—and wouldn't dream of passing names about.
I was one of her suitors who would have married her in
a minute, but she wouldn't hear of it. She said that as
wild and wooly as she was, freedom was a base line
upon which each of her days had to begin. I think she
was carrying the torch for someone—indeed, I think it
was for your client—but that is pure speculation to
which I could never swear. If you get hit with the table
lighter, that I can testify to."

"Ah, what do you do, Mr. Kanter?"

"I'm a stock broker," said Kanter. "And a good one,
with a large firm here in Boston. If I come forward, I'm
sure it will cost me a goodly number of dowager clients
who love to entertain the notion that my attention to
them is somewhat more than professional. I can risk
that. I would hate to see Kilrayne convicted with a piece
of evidence that I could have explained."

"You have my admiration, Mr. Kanter," said Everard. "I shall file this evidence away, and call upon you
only if I have to. If I may ask, do you think that Ms.
Hansen is dead."

Kanter shook his head sadly. "I hate to think it. But yes, I'm convinced she's dead. If she were not, she would have called me by now. It's been three months."

"So it has," mused Everard. "Do you think that Mike Kilrayne killed her?"

"No," said Kanter, "I'm rather sure that he did not. I believe that Kilrayne loved her, and that she loved him. Sarah was a completely open and vivacious woman. She had several lovers and intended to keep them. I think she would have given them all up—including me—if the man of her dreams were available. She loved to love, and loved to be loved, physically and emotionally. Perhaps she deliberately set her sights on someone she couldn't have: Women do that sometimes. I do know that she thought the world of Mr. Kilrayne, from various little things that she said. He might have been one of her lovers—perhaps *the* lover—but I don't know that. I've told you what I do know."

Everard nodded. "I thank you for taking this trouble," he said. "If you'll leave me your card, I will call you if necessary, vitally necessary. Otherwise, perhaps should you come to London, you will ring me up at the Inns of Court. I should like to buy you that drink, someday."

"You're on," said Kanter. "Good night."

23

TWELVE MEN GOOD AND TRUE, PLUS TWO
Thursday, September 7

By nine-thirty the following morning, the courtroom was packed with nearly all of the two hundred people who had been summoned for the special venire. They had been shoehorned into every available seat and standing space and in unison turned their full attention to the bench as the bailiff opened court and Judge Somerville took his seat behind the bench. He nodded to the lawyers.

"I would invite all of you to be seated, ladies and gentlemen, except for the inadequacy of our facilities, for which I apologize. I note that those seats which are available have been afforded to the ladies of your group, which is gratifying." He nodded at the clusters of men who were standing. "First, I shall ask the clerk to give all of you an oath that you speak the truth in answer to questions which I shall put to you individually as you are called."

The clerk swore the panel.

"Now then," Judge Somerville went on, "we must confront the difficult task of finding a jury in a community which has been inundated by the news media with stories concerning this case, as is usual whenever a serious charge is brought against a prominent citizen such as Mr. Kilrayne, who is the accused in this lawsuit.

"All of you have heard of the so-called collision between the rights of a free press and the rights of an accused to a fair trial. We are at the point where it is my job to avoid that collision, or at least to minimize its effect so that it does not become a factor in the verdict.

"The only method available to me to accomplish this duty on my part, with the assistance of able counsel, is to put questions to you. There are two things I wish carefully understood by all of you. First, you are under no circumstances to discuss this case with anyone until you have been excused from service and sent home. As to those who are selected as we go along, that same rule will apply unless and until I authorize you to deliberate upon a verdict at the end of the trial.

"Second, I think you will find that counsel are looking not for people who have never heard of this case, or talked about it, but for men and women who can totally lay aside any thoughts or feelings they may have had before this morning, and thus deliver a true verdict based upon the evidence to be produced in this courtroom and my instructions as to the law."

Some prospective jurors nodded in agreement. "More important," the judge continued, "counsel often make background inquiries of jurors after they have been selected, and are apt to learn whether your answers have been completely candid. Should I be shown at any point in the trial that a juror has failed to disclose everything that he knows about this case, I might be forced to order a mistrial, aborting the proceedings at great expense to the parties and to all of us. Should such an occasion arise, the juror involved will be dealt with summarily and severely. I am confident that by reason of the total candor each of you will exhibit when questioned, such a calamitous event will not occur.

"The bailiff will now lead you to the rooms we have

set aside to try to make you comfortable while you wait to be called."

While the hordes slowly shuffled out of the room, Somerville called counsel to the bench. "Gentlemen," he said in a low voice, "based on the estimates of counsel that this will be a fairly short trial, I am inclined as I mentioned yesterday, to seat two alternate jurors. Does either side feel that more would be advisable?"

Everard and Durham shook their heads in the negative.

"Good," said Somerville. "By the way, Mr. Everard, has it been explained to you that under our system here in Massachusetts the alternates are not designated as such until the end of the trial, and then by a lot. That is to say, during the proceedings every juror is in a position where he will *probably* be on the final panel and, hopefully, pays attention as if he were going to have to decide the case?"

"Mr. Kilrayne has explained your jury system to me in quite some detail, Your Honor, including that aspect of it. I must say that I applaud that feature, as opposed to telling jurors from the very beginning that they are spares."

"Yes," said Somerville. "Now, when I have finished the interrogation of a particular juror, I will solicit from counsel any questions you may wish to add to those I have put. When that is complete as to both sides, any challenges for cause may be asserted and heard. If there are none, or if they are denied, peremptory challenges must be exercised, first by the Commonwealth, then by the defense. Any juror who survives all challenges and is not otherwise excused will be sworn then and there, and will become a permanent member of the jury. Neither side may go back at some later time and use a peremptory challenge against a juror already sworn, barring the most extraordinary circumstances."

Everard was beginning to like this American judge. "One other piece of advice to counsel. Do not hesitate to make challenges for cause. I do not subscribe to the theory that we are bound by what a juror says, any more than we are bound by what a witness says. I must still judge the credibility of any answers given, and I may well have doubts as to their veracity, no matter how self-serving they may be. I will, for instance, be very suspicious of any person who claims to have read or heard little or nothing about this case. That would take a Rip Van Winkle or a total illiterate in my opinion, since I will take judicial notice of the fact that the pretrial publicity has been pervasive, including Essex County. Therefore, do not be hesitant in attacking any answers which lack the clear ring of truth. I expect to be quite liberal in considering such challenges. Do I make myself clear?

"Quite," said Everard.

"You do, Your Honor," said Durham.

"Very well. Mr. Clerk, call the first juror."

The clerk spun a small walnut keg on the desk before him in which had been placed slips with the names of all of the venire of tales jurors who had reported that morning. When the keg stopped turning, he opened a small hinged door in its side and withdrew a slip. "Miss Marcia Kittredge," he called out.

A bailiff left the room and returned in a few moments with a slight, pretty brunette in her early twenties. She was wearing a thin cotton dress that revealed a trim figure. She wore large, horn-rimmed glasses.

Judge Somerville invited her to be seated in the witness chair.

"Before we begin to interview Miss Kittredge, Mr. Clerk, please call a second name. Mr. Bailiff, you will bring the person called to a place near the door to the courtroom and see that he or she is comfortably seated. In that way we will minimize the time lost between interviews."

The clerk spun the keg once again. "Mrs. Edna Wilkinson," he said. The bailiff again left the room.

"Now, Miss Kittredge," said Somerville pleasantly, "the jury roster indicates that you live at twenty-three Forest Lane in Magnolia, is that correct?"

"Yes, Your Honor."

"What is your occupation?"

"I'm an accountant with the Cape Ann Fisheries Company in Gloucester. I go to school nights at Northern University, studying to be a C.P.A."

"If you are selected as a juror, Miss Kittredge, you will be sequestered with the other jurors. That means that your employer will have to do without your services and that you will miss a few classes. Will these circumstances in any way work a hardship on you which might interfere with your ability to concentrate on the evidence and the instructions of the court?"

"No, Your Honor. I've thought about that. I could miss several weeks of school if I'm allowed to have my books and notes as well as the notes that one of my classmates has agreed to make available to me covering the lectures and workshops I will miss."

"Do you mean that classroom notes taken by another will be delivered to you from time to time during the trial?"

"Those are the arrangements I made, Your Honor."

"Hmmm," said Somerville thoughtfully. "A rather unusual situation, but reasonable. Would you object to having those notes screened by one of the bailiffs to ensure that no reference whatever to this case is mentioned in them?"

Miss Kittredge blinked. "Oh, Sandy would never. . . . Of course not, Your Honor, that would be all right."

"Good. With that condition, if you are selected as a juror I will permit you your books and papers unless I have an objection from counsel. Gentlemen?"

Durham and Everard nodded their assent.

"All right. Now, Miss Kittredge, do you live alone?"

"In a way. I live in an apartment which my parents built for me over our garage. It's next to their home."

"I see. What does your father do?"

"He's an electrician."

"And your mother?"

"She's a housewife."

"Do you have any sisters or brothers?"

"I have one older brother. He's a flight engineer for Eastern Airlines." There was a note of conspicuous pride in her voice.

"Have you ever served as a juror before?"

"No sir, this is my first time."

"Are any of your family members or close friends employed in the field of law enforcement or any related field?"

Marcia Kittredge thought for a moment. "I have a cousin who's with the Shore Patrol in the Navy. Is that what you mean?"

"Yes," said Somerville. "Have you discussed this case in any way with your cousin?"

"No," she said. "I haven't seen or talked to him in more than two years."

"Are you related to, or do you know, any of the parties in this case—that would be Mr. Kilrayne—or any of the lawyers?" Somerville introduced all of the lawyers and Lieutenant Gilardi.

"I've heard of Mr. Kilrayne," she said. "I don't know any of these others."

"Very well. Now, please tell us in as much detail as you can everything that you have read or heard about this case since the indictment was returned last July."

"Well," she replied slowly, "I read in the newspaper that Mr. Kilrayne had been charged with murdering a woman who may have been blackmailing him. I saw it on television too. Then I read somewhere that a famous lawyer was coming from England to defend Mr. Kilrayne, and another one from California was going to help him."

"Yes," said Somerville with a smile at the defense table. "There have been stories to that effect. Please go on."

"Well, I remember my parents talking about Mr. Kilrayne, but neither one had an opinion as to whether he had done it or not. One of the men at work pointed out that a criminal lawyer as smart as he was would probably beat the case, especially with such high-powered legal talent."

"What did you say when you heard that remark?" asked Somerville.

"I didn't say anything. It wasn't addressed to me."

"Did you hear anyone make a response?"

"Yes, one of the truck drivers agreed with him."

"Did these remarks provoke any internal response within yourself? In other words, did you think that you agreed or disagreed with them?"

"Well, I thought they might be right, in a way, at first. But then I thought, 'Gee, if I were in trouble, I'd want the best I could get, so if Mr. Kilrayne can afford to bring in the best, even from a long way away, he must be doing the right thing.' I mean, he ought to know."

"Very well. Have there been any other opinions that you have either heard, or expressed yourself, vocally or silently?"

"Just my boyfriend."

"What did he say?"

"He said 'They can't prove a murder without a body, and they don't have one.' "

"And what did you say to that?"

"Well, I told him that it was funny she should just disappear like that and not show up. She *could* be dead, and hidden away somewhere."

"That is true," said Somerville. "As I will instruct you later, if you are selected to serve in this case, it *is* possible to prove the fact of death by circumstantial evidence, even though no corpse is produced. It has been done before in other jurisdictions. Do you think that if you were convinced beyond a reasonable doubt that the alleged victim, Ms. Hansen, is dead that you would be unable to vote to that effect because there was no body?"

"Not if Your Honor explained what the rules were."

"Fine. Now, are you aware of any bias or prejudice for or against the defendant as you sit here today?"

"No, Your Honor, I am not."

"Are you aware that the entire burden of proof to show guilt beyond a reasonable doubt is on the Commonwealth and that there is no burden whatsoever to show anything on the side of the defense?"

"Yes, Sir."

"Are you also aware that if at the end of the case you believe that the defendant *probably* committed the offense—but only probably—that you would be required to vote for an acquittal?"

"No," said Marcia, "I hadn't thought about that. I'm not sure I understand."

"All right. Many laymen are confused by that. Let me explain. In criminal cases we require proof beyond a reasonable doubt before there can be a conviction, to assure that all mistakes made by juries benefit, rather than harm, the citizen on trial. In civil cases we allow the side that can show it is *probably* right to win. I want to make sure that you woud not be tempted to convict if the Commonwealth were to show a probability of guilt and nothing more. Do you see?"

"Oh, yes, I think so. Yes, I could follow that rule."

"That's fine, then. I have one final question, and I want to have you consider it carefully before you answer, Miss Kittredge. As you sit here this morning as a prospective juror called upon to judge Mr. Kilrayne, is your mind in that state of impartiality and fairness which you would hope to find in a juror if you were the defendant in this case. In other words, would you be happy to have someone like yourself as a juror?"

"You mean if the shoe was on the other foot?" She

chewed thoughtfully on a knuckle for a moment. "Yes," she said quietly. "I would accept myself if I were on trial. I think I can be fair to both sides."

"Can you absolutely ignore all that you have read and heard and decide this case strictly on the evidence which I permit you to hear, under the instructions I will give you at the end of the case?"

"Yes," she said firmly.

"The juror stands indifferent," announced Somerville. "Do counsel wish to suggest additional questions?"

There was no response.

"Does either side make a challenge for cause?"

Again no response.

"Does the Commonwealth wish to exercise a peremptory challenge?"

"May we have a moment, Your Honor?" asked Durham.

"Certainly. Take your time."

"I'm pretty sure," said Durham in whispered conference with Barrett and Gilardi, "that they'll grab her. I'd like to take her out because we agreed that the less brains on the jury, the better off we would be. But I think we should be reluctant to use up a challenge this early in the game. She's pretty young, and we might get stuck with some tough, take-charge genius later on if we run out. What's the consensus?"

"I agree," said Barrett. Gilardi nodded. "The Commonwealth is content with this juror," said Durham.

Everard huddled with Kilrayne, Shaw, and Stacy Barton, who had come in during the middle of the interview. "This young lady would seem to very much fill the criteria we agreed upon," he said quietly. "Bright, fairly independent, and disciplined on the scientific side of things. Won't accept two and two as adding up to five." All three nodded vigorously.

"If," said Shaw, "we ever get stuck in California with the judge doing all of the *voir dire*, I hope they send this guy out to train our bench. I haven't seen a lot of criminal cases, but he's damned impressive."

"Far above average," said Kilrayne. "And a lot more than I expected. I think he's going to give us a good trial."

"Judge Somerville," said Everard, "could almost qualify for the British bench. Almost, that is."

Everard rose. "The defense is content with Miss Kittredge," he said, smiling warmly in her direction.

"Thank you, counsel. Miss Kittredge, you are about to be sworn as a juror in this case. You will then be taken to the jury room where a bailiff will keep you company until the next juror is sworn and joins you. You may write out a list of the personal articles and clothing you will need for the next few weeks, and the bailiff will arrange for them to be picked up and brought to you. Thank you for your cooperation with the court."

The clerk administered the oath, and Marcia Kittredge was led from the room as Mrs. Edna Wilkinson was brought forward.

For the balance of the morning, and, after a short break for lunch, throughout the long afternoon the endless litany repeated itself. By four-fifteen, fourteen good and true citizens, including the undesignated alternates, had been sworn. Besides Miss Kittredge there were three housewives, one female social worker, two school teachers, a plumber's apprentice, a retired shipbuilder, a bus driver, a postal worker, an auto mechanic, an elderly spinster, and the young president of a small construction company. Durham and his team had watched with some horror as the latter was sworn—he was exactly what they did not want—but their challenges were exhausted, and his answers gave not the slightest ground to go after him for cause.

Their discomfort was aggravated somewhat when Judge Somerville appointed him—his name was James Sutter—as foreman of the jury.

"Good," said Kilrayne. "The foreman is the only one whose name doesn't go into the hat when the alternates are drawn by lot. On balance, despite the fact that our friends have planted some real dummies in the box, I think we have the better end of it."

"You hope," said Everard.

24

THE EYE
Thursday, September 7

Late in July, Sal had a reason to be concerned about his older sister Angela. That she had been gone for over a week in itself was not alarming since Eddie Tomasello, Angela's boyfriend, owned a piece of an apartment on Nantucket Island and would take Angela there from time to time. What bothered Sal was some loose talk—vague at first—that Eddie had offended the regime and just might be among the missing. Sal didn't like Eddie Tomasello and wouldn't have cared one whit if he were taken down hard by the boys—unless some harm should come to Angela in the process. That Sal couldn't take. He loved his only sister more than any creature on earth.

As August wore on, and neither Eddie nor Angela was seen or heard from, Sal became increasingly agitated and apprehensive. On Labor Day weekend, Sal attempted to distract himself by going to a motel on the Cape with two promiscuous seniors from East Boston High School.

Normally a two-on-one scene gave Sal great sexual excitement and stamina. This time he had trouble achieving a half-decent erection and could not produce a single orgasm despite the patient and prolonged ministrations of his two voluptuous companions.

He finally faced the fact that his difficulties stemmed

from a recurring association of sex with Angela and now of Angela with possible harm or death. He just had to step up his quest for information about his sister.

On the day that jury selection began in the Kilrayne trial, Sal came by some startling news. A bookie from Revere, for whom Sal had occasionally done some minor collection work, told him of a rumor that Eddie Tomasello had gotten into "some serious trouble" over the Kilrayne case. Sal knew that Kilrayne had represented Eddie in the past and concluded that perhaps Eddie had been planning to assist the defense in some way that had gotten him jammed up with the wrong people. Maybe, Sal thought, Kilrayne was going to blame the old broad's death on the organization to get himself off the hook, and Eddie was to help. If true, that would explain things.

Sal waited until that evening when he knew his high school classmate, Peter Saleme, would be off duty. Peter was a patrolman with the Boston Police Department, assigned to Station One near the North End. Sal admired Peter and had since the pair had made the All-Scholastic Football Team during their senior year in high school: Peter as a plunging fullback and Sal as the offensive tackle who repeatedly opened gaping holes in the defensive line.

Sal found Peter in a booth at Monte's Tavern across from the old Custom House building on State Street, early that same evening. He introduced Peter to the girl he had brought along as they seated themselves across from him. She was a scrawny, dishwater blonde of nineteen.

"Hey, Pete, say hello to Rita Mason here, old friend of mine. Great kid. What I mean is, she's a little light in the tits and ass, but the best blowjob in the city, really loves it. Pull the wax outta your ears from the inside, is what she can do. She already knows who you are, even though she was just a kid back when we were makin' it big." Sal gave Rita a solid slap on the thigh as she smiled, showing dull silver braces on her teeth.

Peter perked up a bit at the prospect of a little quick and dirty sex, which Sal seemed to be offering him on a platter. This sudden generosity had to have a *quid pro quo* somewhere, he thought.

"Nice to meetcha," he said pleasantly, nodding at Rita. "Always good to sit with an old fan. How's it with you, Sal?"

"Good, Pete, good. Never better. There's just one thing got me a little uptight. . . ."

"You mean Angie?"

"Yeah. How'd you know?"

"There's talk around," said Pete, studying the end of his small brown cigar, "that she and Eddie Tomasello got in trouble with some people."

"Yeah, that's right," said Sal sadly, "I know about the talk. Guy told me today it might be sump'n about that lawyer, Kilrayne, who got that murder case up on the north shore. Like maybe Eddie was tryin' to help him, and pissed off some people. You hear anythin' like that, Pete?"

"Nope," said Pete, his interest in the new rumor quite apparent. "Nothin' like that."

"Look," said Sal, "you got the connections and all, Pete. Maybe you could ask around?"

"Sure," said Pete, puffing expansively on his cigar, "sure, I can do that. Matter of fact, I can go right to the horse's mouth."

"No shit!" Sal was impressed. "How's that?"

"This Lieutenant Gilardi, the big shot from the state police detectives who's really running the show in that trial up there, me'n him're friends. What happened was, I did him a little favor a while ago. 'Course I can't go into no details or nothin' like that, but me'n him, we hit it off pretty good. I could call him, I know he'd remember me," Pete said proudly.

"Shit, Pete, that'd be great. It might be nothin', you

know, but I sure would like to find out if there's any connection, somethin' to move with, know what I mean?"

"I'll handle it," Pete said with a touch of grandeur, "no problem. You check with me here tomorrow night, I'll tell you some straight skinny, okay?"

"Great, Pete," said Sal enthusiastically. "Appreciate that. Rita here, she can show you some real appreciation for me. I gotta run now. You guys have a ball—maybe two of them." He winked at Pete, who said "Right," and winked at Rita, who flushed at the attention being lavished on her. Sal ordered two beers for the pair, dropped five dollars on the table, and swaggered out of the bar.

The following morning at nine o'clock, Peter Saleme dialed a number in Salem which had been given to him by State Police Headquarters. He wondered whether Gilardi would take his call. He should, thought Pete, after I dropped the charge against that hooker when he asked me to. Must have been a friend of his, thought Pete, who remembered somewhat wistfully that the girl had been young and very attractive. This Gilardi, he thought, as he listened to the ring on the other end, sure knew how to live.

That evening Big Sal was waiting in Monte's Tavern when Pete walked in a little after eight o'clock. "Did you pick up any info?" asked Sal anxiously.

"Sure thing," said Pete. "Like I tole you, me and the big guy talk together pretty good. I got to tell you, he says Kilrayne is a real shit."

25

THE PARADE
Friday, September 8

When the jury had been seated, Judge Somerville bade them all good morning. "Now ladies and gentlemen," he said, "the lawyers for the Commonwealth, or prosecution, are given an opportunity to address you, and tell you in narrative form what evidence they expect to present to you. This privilege is not available to the defense attorneys, under Massachusetts rules, until the prosecution has completed its case and the defense is prepared to go forward should it elect to do so.

"I must advise you that statements by the lawyers, now and again at the close of the case, are not evidence. An opening statement by counsel is merely a hopeful indication of what the future may hold. Mr. Barrett, you may proceed."

Walter Barrett rose with all of the solemnity and dignity he could muster. It had been agreed that he would take the lead for this one ceremonial step in the trial and yield to Durham's greater experience and quicker instinct for the handling of the evidence. Walter had hoped to make a detailed, colorful, moving opening statement that would be favorably described in the media, especially in Essex County where the electorate was presumably watching. After being hammered heavily by both Durham and Gilardi—with a tap or two along the way from Uncle Carl—about the perils of announcing

things in opening statement that didn't turn up in the
proof, he had finally and grudgingly agreed to keep it
short and tight and suitably vague. His speech was
printed in speech-maker's type—a large, bold-faced let-
tering that was easy to read from a distance—on sheets
of plain white paper. He placed them gingerly on the
lectern, faced the jury, and began. The words were not
his, and he read them with discomfort.

"May it please the court, counsel, and Mr. Foreman
and ladies and gentlemen of the jury. As His Honor, the
distinguished Judge Somerville, has told you, what I am
about to say is not evidence." Walter adjusted his
glasses nervously and continued.

"The indictment in this case charges the defendant,
Michael Kilrayne, with murder in the first degree of a
single lady named Sarah Hansen, a resident of the
County of Essex. Each of you, in qualifying to sit as a
juror in this case, has sworn that under proper circumstances you could convict on circumstantial evidence as
juries have been doing for centuries.

"I think you will be pleased to hear I will refrain in
this opening statement from going into details as to
what each of the witnesses will say, for indeed there
might be many of them: each short in his testimony, but
each an important link in an inexorable chain. What we
will prove to you is the following:

"First, we will prove that Sarah Hansen is dead, by
showing that she was a creature of reasonably regular
habits"—Walter's throat suffered a lump at this point, as
the sumptuous sexual images of the tape flashed into his
mind and threatened to halt his oratory—"and that in
the course of her day-to-day life, she was in contact
with numerous people on a regular basis. None of these
have seen her since June the seventh, nor have they
heard from her, as they will tell you. Her absence is
utter, total, and absolute, and from this evidence you
will easily arrive at the inescapable conclusion that she
is dead.

"Second, we will show—again by circumstantial evidence—that this death was not from natural causes. She had no illness, was involved in no accidents, and has not been found. When she was killed, she was secreted. The fact that she was secreted will be one of the elements which will persuade you that her death was planned and premeditated—that this was murder in the first degree and nothing less.

"Third, we will show that she had a relationship with the defendant, Michael Kilrayne.

"Fourth, you will be told by one Frank LaPere—under oath—that in April of this year this defendant solicited and urged him to find and procure an assassin to kill a woman who was a problem to him.

"Fifth, and finally, our evidence will show beyond any reasonable doubt that the problem woman could only have been, and in fact was, Sarah Hansen. And although Mr. LaPere took no part in the killing, Mr. Kilrayne found other means and other confederates, as yet unknown but surely to be tracked down and brought to justice by this office, who accomplished the deed, on or about the date set forth in the indictment.

"That will be our case, ladies and gentlemen. I have summarized in order that you, who have made the sacrifice of being separated from your homes, your jobs, and your loved ones, will be able to hear evidence at once, rather than mere lawyer talk."

At Everard's request, counsel met at the side of the bench with the stenographer. "I move, if it please the Court," said Everard, "that Your Honor direct a verdict of not guilty at this juncture on the ground that Mr. Barrett has failed to state a case in his opening. He has leaned heavily on rhetoric and conclusory remarks, described almost no hard evidence, and failed to meet his mark which, as I understand the law of this Commonwealth, requires that at least a *prima facie* showing of some guilt be stated."

Barrett started to respond, but Somerville waved him

to silence. "No, Mr. Everard," he said with a grim smile. "I listened quite carefully. Mr. Barrett was very much like a limbo dancer trying to squeak under a pole eight inches off the floor. It was close, but in my judgment he made it. If the proofs do not match his eloquence, then I shall hear from you again when the Commonwealth has rested. Call your first witness, Mr. Barrett."

When counsel had resumed their places, Durham stood and in ringing tones said, "The Commonwealth calls Mrs. Ingrid Svenson."

Mrs. Svenson was a quick and effective, if somewhat halting, witness. She had come twice a week to Sarah Hansen's home to clean. The days of her labor were not fixed but somewhat at her convenience. Ms. Hansen was a considerate woman. Mrs. Svenson had last cleaned on June fifth, and Ms. Hansen was present. When she returned on June eighth, Ms. Hansen was not present. When she returned on June twelfth, there was nothing to clean. She did some minor dusting, but basically the house was in exactly the same condition as when she had finished on June eighth.

"Your witness," said Durham.

"No questions," said Everard.

Walter Barrett called the next witness, June Hopkins. June was a personal friend of Sarah Hansen. They belonged to the Boston Yacht Club together and had coffee at least one morning a week. They had last had coffee on June fifth. She had not seen or heard from Sarah since.

Durham called Dr. Jeremy Finch. Dr. Finch was Sarah Hansen's dentist and had been for only three months. Sarah had been suffering a possible separation of the gums from the teeth and was very concerned because Dr. Finch had told her that if she did not have immediate treatment, her teeth would loosen and might begin to separate from her jawbone, necessitating first a bridge or two, then plates of false teeth.

"I object," said Everard, rather forcefully.

"Yes," said Somerville, "I understand. A question of law is presented. Mr. Bailiff, take the jury to their room, and order coffee for those who wish some respite. This matter may take some little while."

When the jury had been removed, Somerville eyed the lawyers from both sides rather balefully.

"I anticipated, gentlemen, and Miss Barton, that we would swiftly come to the point that declarations to the deceased and by the deceased—if she is—would become a central issue. That point is now before us. I have done some research on this matter and have arrived at a view. My view is strictly preliminary. I learned long before I took the bench that the touchstone of legal wisdom can only follow the best arguments that able advocates can put forth. I now seek such help. Mr. Everard, you made the objection. May I hear your position?"

"My position, M'Lord, is that the law of this Commonwealth is quite clear: The statement of a deceased person who does not then and there believe that he or she is in the throes of death is hearsay and subject to no exception to the hearsay rule. As such, anything that Ms. Hansen has said to anyone is inadmissible unless it may be shown that she made such a statement in contemplation of death."

"Thank you, Mr. Everard. Mr. Durham?"

"Your Honor," said Durham with ceremony, "while Mr. Everard may have brushed lightly across the surface rule of evidence applicable in most cases, I submit that we have an extraordinary if not unique case here. What we seek to elicit from these witnesses is not accusatory material, putting the finger on the defendant. We seek simply the ordinary and day-to-day remarks of the victim—part of the *res gestae*, in a sense—which might explicate her regularity in human affairs. If a witness were to say 'Sarah told me that Mike wanted to kill her' a different rule might apply. In such circumstances, it would be my obligation to come to the bench and advise the court as to what was expected. But all we seek to now establish is that Ms. Hansen said and did things in a regular way, and the absence of that regularity is a point which this jury ought to learn."

Somerville looked to Everard for response. There was none.

"Thank you, gentlemen, for your views. On existing law, Mr. Everard is entirely correct. My temptation as a judge is to tread that proven route and to insulate myself against reversal by my superiors in the Appellate Division or the Supreme Judicial Court. That would be the way to go, and perhaps the prudent way.

"On the other hand, the Commonwealth has no right of appeal. If I should admit these statements and do not, my ruling will die with an acquittal, should there be one. Mr. Durham, do you agree that should I rule in your favor it would be a departure from any law now in the yearbooks of our courts?"

"I do, Your Honor, but it would nonetheless be a correct ruling," said Durham, smacking his lips in anticipation of a victory he had hardly expected. He confided to himself, and himself only, that had he been in Somerville's position, he would have taken the safe route.

"Mr. Barrett," said Somerville blandly, "you are the District Attorney and chief law enforcement officer of this county. Do you share Mr. Durham's view?"

Aided by a quick shin kick from Durham, Barrett bounced to his feet like an overheated jack-in-the-box. "I do, Your Honor, completely."

"Very well," said Somerville. "I am inclined to be persuaded by Mr. Durham's position. I believe that statements made by the deceased, if she is, to fellow human beings in the ordinary discharge of their routine affairs should be admitted. My ruling has two conditions. If both are accepted by the Commonwealth, that ruling will be the law of the case. If either is rejected, then I must carefully reconsider the position I have decided to take."

"May we know of your conditions, Your Honor," said Durham.

"Of course," said Somerville. "Before you seek to elicit any hearsay from any witness about a statement Ms. Hansen has made which *might* implicate Mr. Kilrayne, you will approach the bench and make a proffer. Should you fail to do so under circumstances which I consider to be culpable, I will declare a mistrial and discharge the defendant."

Durham swallowed hard, and ignored a tap to his shin by Walter. "Agreed," he said.

"Second," said Somerville, "because I am making a ruling without benefit of the precedental wisdom of our Supreme Judicial Court, should there be a conviction in this case I will grant bail to Mr. Kilrayne unless and until that court shall direct otherwise. Unless you can now say that you will not oppose that bail, I must consider the rights of Mr. Kilrayne, and should I do that I have no right to make him a test case in a new theory. You may confer, gentlemen, but understand me well."

"Thank you, Your Honor," said Durham.

"What about that bail thing?" said Barrett.

"Shut up," said Durham hoarsely. "If we hook this poor bastard, it will never stick. Having him out on bail will simply relieve the pressures. Get one thing straight in your head, Walter, or I'm going to pull out tomorrow, and screw your fat-ass uncle. We as prosecutors care only about jury verdicts of guilty. That's all we want in this case. If an appeal goes sour a year or so from now, who gives a shit. The news people are whores just like we are. That's page nine stuff. Either you agree with me here and now to grab for every handy brass ring, or I'm pulling out."

"Okay," said Walter, overwhelmed by what obviously was too much opposition for his shaky ego to contemplate, let alone oppose. "I just asked a question. Let's go along with the judge."

"You tell him," said Durham fiercely.

"If it please the court," said Walter, failing miserably in his attempt to be less than ostentatious, "we accept and agree with the conditions you have set forth. We are ready to proceed, consistent with Your Honor's ruling."

"Let us continue with the witness," said Somerville.

At nine o'clock that evening, as they sat in Everard's suite sipping cognac, Kilrayne stared hard at his glass.

"It seems to me," he said slowly but in harsh tones, "that on this the first day of trial they have killed us. But if my judgment were sound, I would have defended myself. What's your view, Tony?"

"Quite positive," said Everard.

"How in god's name can you think that!" spluttered Kilrayne. "First this insurance genius lets a nothing opening statement pass the mark, and second he makes new law about a dead person's statements and screws me to the wall. What the hell is positive about that?"

"Michael," said Shaw, "I don't like to interrupt, but who in your experience last got bail during an appeal from a murder case?"

Kilrayne drained his snifter. "It has never happened," he said.

"Well, then, don't break your ass knocking the judge who just guaranteed that you'd be the first," said Shaw. "I think you got the best end of it."

"You must pardon Daniel," said Everard soothingly. "He's a terribly talented chap but also terribly young. Three years my junior, at last count." Everard sipped lightly at his glass. As he saw Kilrayne's features begin to relax a bit, Everard added in a dull but very clear voice, "He's also dead right."

Kilrayne snapped to attention like a sailor who has

just met the captain of his ship unexpectedly. "I beg your pardon?"

"I said 'he's dead right,' " said Everard, "and despite your contrary view, that's exactly what I mean."

"Would you mind explaining that," said Kilrayne, his eyes full of daggers for all who might disagree with him.

"Certainly," said Everard. "There are several points I have in mind. First, I had no hope that Somerville would grant a directed verdict on the opening statement, no matter how bad it was—and it wasn't all that bad, in the circumstances. Second, ruling that ordinary and routine statements by Ms. Hansen are admissable is not a very harmful development, in my judgment. I haven't the slightest doubt that a pattern will emerge from all this evidence which will be persuasive of the fact that Ms. Hansen has left with no preparation and no warning, and is not coming back. That pattern would develop with or without her statements.

"But I see something else," Everard went on, "that to me seems very, very helpful. I see in this judge a somewhat remarkable creature who is thoughtful, forceful and innovative—the kind of man who just might have the courage and personal strength to throw this case out on the street and into the gutter, where it most surely belongs. That we need very badly, Michael, because I do not look for him to make any serious errors which would leave you with a good appeal. You have what Daniel calls 'the curse of a good judge,' which may benefit us now but leaves little for insurance."

Kilrayne rubbed his eyes. "I guess," he said, "I'm a little too much on edge. He is, I must admit, a lot more judge than I expected. How long do you think this parade of witnesses is going to go on?"

"For several days, I'm afraid," said Everard with a sigh. "I have been toying with the notion of trying to formulate some sort of stipulation admitting that she is among the missing. But I think that perhaps a little too dangerous. Some juror or other is going to get the idea that we know something, should we make such an agreement, and I am fearful where such an idea might lead."

"It would appear," said Shaw wistfully, "that we are just going to have to sit there and take it."

And take it they did. For most of the following week everyone who had enjoyed any kind of contact with Sarah Hansen was summoned to the Superior Court. There were ninety-seven such witnesses, the butcher, the baker, the candlestick maker—one by one, as either Barrett or Durham brought them forth, they told how often they had seen Sarah, where, when, why and in what circumstances. Always, one clear fact remained: no one had seen her, heard from her, or known of anyone claiming to have been in contact with her since the seventh of June.

26

SURPRISE, SURPRISE
Saturday, September 9

Judge Somerville excused the jury at one o'clock, explaining to them that enough ground had been covered so that an afternoon session would not be necessary. When they had left, Durham approached the bench as Somerville was preparing to step down.

"An important matter has arisen, Your Honor. Might counsel visit with you for a few moments in chambers?"

"Certainly, Mr. Durham. We can do that at once."

When the lawyers had seated themselves before Somerville's desk, Durham dropped a bomb.

"Late yesterday afternoon," he said, "I was personally contacted by a Calvin Whiting, who said that he was a prison chaplain at the federal prison in Danbury, Connecticut. He told me that one of the inmates—a man named John McKiver—had come to him for advice. McKiver said that he had some very damaging information about Mr. Kilrayne and wondered whether he should come forward with it, where he was a prisoner and perhaps not very believeable. Mr. Whiting said he would communicate the circumstances to me.

"After checking to see that Mr. Whiting was in fact the Danbury Chaplain, I sent Lieutenant Gilardi down early this morning to interview McKiver. As a result of that interview, the Commonwealth believes that it has a critical witness which it intends to use in its case-in-chief. Having reached that decision, I recognize my duty to notify the defense so that they may interview McKiver at once if they wish to do so. I should say that I have had Gilardi advise Mr. McKiver that he has every right to talk to a defense representative, and no obligation to do so."

"I see," said Somerville, somewhat suspiciously. "A pity this McKiver didn't see fit to come forward sooner. Do you think this will cause you a delay in the trial, Mr. Everard? I shall grant a continuance if you require one."

Everard whispered a moment to Shaw. "We will try to avoid a delay, Your Honor. Perhaps I could address that subject on Monday."

"You may," said Somerville. "I assume that this development leaves all counsel with their hands full for the next day or so. If there is nothing further, you are excused. Have a pleasant weekend."

On Sunday, Kilrayne met with Shaw at his office. "I am told by Tony," he said, "that you didn't have much luck with McKiver."

Shaw shook his head. "Not a bit. Wouldn't even come to the visiting room. I'm afraid Gilardi's got him in his pocket. I did learn that he intends to testify about something that happened last January sixteenth. Durham told me that, and only after I threatened to go to the judge's home to complain. That's all I can tell you."

Kilrayne reached for his lawyer's diary, and opened it to the page representing his activities on January sixteen. "Not much here," he said. "I had four appointments here that day, but none with a McKiver."

Kilrayne opened his desk drawer, and drew out a slip of paper. "However," he said with a twinkle in his eye, "perhaps all is not lost. I got a phone tip that may help us. This is the name of a hospital in Cleveland. A search of the records last January might shed some light on our friend McKiver, I'm told. Why don't you check it out."

"Hell yes, I will," said Shaw, puzzled. "Who the hell gave you that info?"

"That, Daniel my boy," said Kilrayne good-naturedly, will, for the time being at least, have to remain a secret."

27

AN X-RATED HEARING
Monday, September 11

Having been forewarned about what he would be seeing, Judge Somerville had decided to hold a hearing on the admissability of the intimate videotapes in his chambers. As the images on the television screen disappeared when the tape ran out, he looked grim, and a little embarrassed.

"All right, Mr. Barrett," he sighed, "I've seen your evidence. Please state the ground upon which you believe it to be admissable."

"Yes, Your Honor," said Barrett. "I should point out that as a predicate for the use of these tapes, we will have the testimony of Dr. Tarbell, who will say that although positive identification is not possible, his physical examination of the defendant Kilrayne discloses that the legs and torso of the first dark-haired male—the one *without* a scar on his rump—are consistent with the legs and torso of Mr. Kilrayne."

"And you contend that on the basis you have described, this court ought to allow the jury to view the first tape?"

"Yes, Your Honor. It would be proof that the defendant was engaged in an adulterous affair with the victim, from which the jury could infer that she may have been blackmailing him," Barrett pleaded.

"And what about the other two?" asked Somerville.

"I don't understand, Your Honor?"

"The other two men who were being intimate with her," said Somerville. "Wouldn't the same inference as to motive apply to them, *assuming* that the first adult male on the tapes is in fact Mr. Kilrayne?"

"But Your Honor," protested Barrett, "we don't even know who those other two men are."

"I am far from persuaded that you know who the first man is. No, Mr. Barrett, I'm afraid that this is clearly a case where the prejudicial potential of the proposed evidence far outweighs any probative value it might have, which I find to be slight. If a trial is, as some famous trial lawyers have said, a show for a jury, this particular show is going to have to do without that act. The defense objection to the videotape evidence is sustained, and the tapes will be placed under seal until this trial is ended. At that point, should there be an acquittal, I will entertain the notion of ordering them erased. Are there any copies, Mr. Barrett?"

"No, Your Honor," Barrett lied. Gilardi had made two copies—one for himself and one for Barrett—claiming that one as versatile as Sarah Hansen ought to continue to be appreciated by *someone*.

"Very well," said Somerville, "I will take your word for that, as an officer of this court. Now, as long as we are here, Mr. Barrett, I want you to know that I am still very disturbed about the lack of a corpse in this case. I must admit, I am beginning to have nightmares about this woman walking back into circulation after the defendant has been convicted and been in jail for a couple of years."

"But Your Honor," said Barrett, "the Scott case. . . ."

"The Scott case notwithstanding," said Somerville firmly. "In *Scott*, there was abundant evidence that the defendant's conduct and statements to others that *he knew* his wife was never coming back. I find not one scintilla of that kind of evidence of that nature with re-

spect to Mr. Kilrayne—at least not in your evidence so
far."

"I believe that when *all* the facts and circumstances
are before Your Honor, it will become clear. . . ."

"Perhaps, perhaps," Somerville interrupted. "In any
event there is nothing before me at the moment. I simply want you to know that when you have rested the
Commonwealth's case, you will have a weighty burden of
persuasion before the court in order to convince me that
there is something for the jury to decide."

Big Sal Corso went into the church with trepidation.
He hadn't been to confession since he first had Angela
nearly a decade ago. He didn't want no priest telling
him Angela was his sister and all that. He knew she was
his sister. That's why he loved her.

He crossed himself and headed partway down the
aisle of the empty church. Sliding into a pew, he knelt,
and crossing himself again, lowered his head. He
prayed. He started rocking, banging his head against the
back of the pew in front of him. Tears started coming,
and he let them come. Then he glanced to his left and
noticed the feet under the black cassock in the aisle.

"Can I help you, son?" said the priest.

Big Sal rubbed his eyes with the back of his hand,
getting up. "Nah," he said, brushing by the priest. He
strode up the aisle, the priest coming after him. If Angela was dead—and in his heart he now knew she
was—it was that shithead Eddie Tomasello's fault and
Kilrayne's fault, and if Eddie was dead and Kilrayne
was still alive, neither the priest nor God was going to
avenge her.

28

THE LINKS
Tuesday, September 12

Quietly and methodically, Philip Durham began to establish the points of nexus between Kilrayne and his supposed victim.

First, he offered court records showing that in 1966 Kilrayne had represented a Sarah Hansen in the Lynn District Court on a charge of driving while under the influence of intoxicating beverages. She had been found not guilty of that charge, but guilty of driving to endanger.

The case had been appealed and tried again in the Essex Superior Court. This time Ms. Hansen was acquitted. Everard entered a stipulation that the client in question was the same Sarah Hansen who was the alleged victim in the case at hand.

Durham then introduced a series of telephone bills—Sarah's and Kilrayne's—which showed rather frequent calls between them, most initiated by her. Again by stipulation, the charges were translated into minutes, and several of the calls were of more than thirty minutes' duration. Durham sought a stipulation that Ms. Hansen had had no legal business with Kilrayne since the traffic charge, but the defense refused.

"Call Charles Davidson-Houston," said Durham to the bailiff. A tall, erect, balding man in his fifties strode down the aisle to the witness stand, clad in a dark suit somewhat shiny with age, but immaculately pressed. He was sworn.

"Your name please?"

"I am Charles Davidson-Houston."

"Where do you live, sir?"

"My home is at Seven Fearing Road, Swampscott."

"And your occupation?"

"I am in charge of the dining room at the Boston Yacht Club in Marblehead."

"Do you know a Sarah Hansen?"

"Oh, yes, indeed, sir. For a number of years, now."

"Was she a member of your club?"

"Yes, sir."

"When did you last see her?"

"I'm quite sure it was in the middle of May since the yard boys were setting moorings in the harbor at the time. She came in for dinner."

"Was anyone with her?"

"Yes, sir, that gentleman seated over there." He pointed at Kilrayne.

"May the record show that the witness has identified the defendant, Michael Kilrayne, Your Honor?" asked Durham.

"It may," said Judge Somerville.

"Is Mr. Kilrayne a member of your club?"

Davidson-Houston appeared to shudder slightly at the notion that a mere Irishman might be among the elite. "No sir," he said, "he is *not*."

"On this occasion, how long did they stay?"

"I should think about two hours, sir. They lingered a while over a second bottle of wine."

"Did they appear to have an intimate relationship?"

"Objection!" said Everard sharply.

"Mr. Durham," said Somerville impatiently, "I'm sure it was not your purpose to ask if these people were openly lewd in a public place. Please rephrase your question."

"Very well," said Durham, nodding pleasantly toward the bench. He had made his point, he thought. "Mr. Davidson-Houston, can you tell us whether they appeared to be friendly toward one another?"

"Yes, sir," said the witness. "Quite."

"Your witness."

"I have only one or two questions," said Everard looking at the clock. "Mr. Davidson-Houston, I take it from your accent that your origins lie somewhere to the east of us—say, three thousand miles or so?"

"Exactly, sir," beamed the witness. "Bolton, Lancashire, November ninth, 1922."

"Thank you," said Everard elegantly. "Now then, before coming to court today, you have gone over your testimony with the prosecution, have you not?"

"Yes sir."

"And in the course of doing so, you were asked to identify Mr. Kilrayne?"

"That is correct, sir."

"How were you able to do that?"

"They showed me his photograph."

"In other words, Mr. Davidson-Houston, you did not know the gentleman by name?"

"No, sir. I have never seen him before or since."

"I see. And I gather from your testimony that during the period that these two were under your observation, you detected not the slightest hint of any hostility between them?"

"No, sir, none at all."

"Thank you. I have nothing further."

"No redirect," said Durham.

"You may be excused," said Somerville to the witness.

"Call Anthony Christi," said Durham. A young man in his twenties, dark-haired, dark-eyed and handsome, took the stand. He did not look comfortable.

He gave his name, address, and said that he was a waiter at Felicia's Restaurant on Richmond Street, Boston's North End. He knew Michael Kilrayne and was

able to identify Sarah Hansen from photographs which
had been published in the newspapers. He had served
them somewhat regularly over the last five years, on an
average of once every three months.

Christi tried to smile obsequiously toward Kilrayne,
as if to apologize for telling another man's business in
public. He was obviously hostile to Durham, answering
reluctantly. Durham elected to use a little applied psychology.

"Where would they usually sit?" he inquired.

"Always in the booth near the kitchen," said Christi.

"And would it be fair to say that they usually acted
as if they were angry at one another?"

"No, no!" exploded Christi. "I never told you that.
They were always smiling, friendly to each other."

"Didn't they scowl across the table?" asked Durham.

"No, they sat together. On the same side. . . ."

With the look of a man who in trying to help has
clumsily gummed up the works, Christi looked at Kilrayne helplessly.

"Did I understand you to say, sir, that Ms. Hansen
and the defendant sat *side by side* when they ate at your
restaurant?"

"I, uh, yes they did, I think. I really don't remember
every time they were there." Christi looked quite miserable.

"Thank you," said Durham, sitting down.

"Leave it," murmured Kilrayne to Everard.

"No questions," said Everard.

"Methinks," said Bill Holcomb of the *New Bedford
Standard-Times* to his young assistant sitting next to
him, "that brother Kilrayne will have a little explaining
to do."

29

MADAM JUDAS

Tuesday, September 12

Daniel Shaw hadn't minded the prospect of flying himself and Sam Watkins from Boston to Cleveland. An old girl friend named Jane Whitcomb usually provided him with some happy hours whenever he was in town, and Sam always fended for himself admirably in off hours.

When Shaw phoned Jane's number from the terminal, the operator came on—or was it a recording?—to give him a different number. He tried that one and sure enough the familiar voice answered.

"Jane Whitcomb," Daniel said with relief.

"Wrong," said the voice.

"You sure sound like Jane Whitcomb. This is Dan Shaw. You kidding or something?"

"No way," said the woman. "It's just that I've been called Jane Ladd for the last two months."

"I can't believe it," said Dan, trying to hide his disappointment. "You got married."

"Sort of," said Jane.

"What the hell does that mean?" said Dan.

"Well, I married him, but I'm not too sure he married me. He travels a lot."

"Is he traveling tonight?" asked Dan hopefully.

"No, he's standing right here, wondering who I'm talking to. Would you like to speak to him?"

"Jane, you are one spunky bitch. Thanks no."

"He says he'd like to meet you."

Before Dan could say anything, a man's voice was on the line. "Mr. Shaw? I gather you're an old friend of Jane's. I hope you'll come visit while you're in Cleveland."

"I'd sure like to, Mr. Ladd," Dan lied, "but I'm here checking some facts on an important murder case, and I have to whizz right back to Boston where it's being tried. I was just calling because the old Jane would have been damn mad if she'd heard I'd been in town and hadn't phoned."

"Perhaps some other time," said Mr. Ladd. "Here's Jane."

"Hello, sport."

"If you're accusing me of being chicken by that tone of voice. . . ."

"Yes?"

"You're right. Maybe next time."

"Maybe next time," she said, her voice warm in a way that used to fill Daniel with desire.

When he hung up, a touch of regret gnawing inside him, Daniel thought the finest of them seem to get hitched sooner or later. Soon all of his women will have escaped him. Ah well, there was his new friend Pat Perrin waiting for him in Boston. All he had to do was join Sam in checking the hospital records and hurry back.

It didn't go that quickly. It was after noon the next day before Daniel had the clerk of the court summon Stacy Barton to the phone.

"Stacy, this is Dan. I've got the documents we were looking for. I'm leaving the hospital in a few minutes. If there are no traffic delays because of that lousy weather you're having, I should land at Beverly before four. If Beverly goes down, I'll have to go to Logan and buck the traffic up to the hotel. Tell Mike he's going to like what I'm bringing him."

"Mike isn't going to like anything today, I'm afraid. He's really in the doghouse with the judge."

"*Mike!* What the hell for. He's been a model defendant."

"The judge doesn't think so," said Stacy. "The early edition of the *Chronicle* has an editorial that's got Somerville in a rage."

"What does it say?"

"I'll read it to you. There's a copy of the paper right here. Wait a minute." There was a pause.

The *Chronicle* has learned from a reliable source that Superior Court Judge Gary Somerville is considering throwing the Kilrayne case out of court because the prosecution has been unable to produce the corpse of the murder victim. He reportedly will do that "notwithstanding the Scott Case."

The "Scott" case refers to an established precedent set in California nearly twenty years ago in which a man named Leonard Ewing Scott was convicted of murdering his wife even though no trace of her body was ever found. Scott was obviously guilty, and justice was obviously done.

It's a shame that Judge Somerville doesn't have more respect for the wisdom of the distinguished California courts. Mr. Kilrayne may well be innocent, but that should be determined by the conscience of the community—the jury—and not by a judge who until quite recently was a colleague of the accused. Hopefully, Judge Somerville will reconsider a decision which could be sadly regrettable.

"Jesus Christ," said Shaw, "where the hell did they get that information?"

"The judge is blaming it on Mike. Of all the lawyers who were in the lobby when the judge made that comment, he thinks Mike had the most to gain by leaking a story favorable to him. He's threatening to hold Mike in contempt, or declare a mistrial, or both."

"What does Mike say?"

"He denies it completely, except to say that he discussed the subject with us. He told Tony that Bill Guidetti and Charley O'Shea are mystified as to where their editor—guy named Martin Hanlon—came up with the information. The bad thing is, the quote in the editorial is almost verbatim."

"Damn, that's awful," said Shaw. "Somerville will never direct a verdict now, or they'll call him a crook."

"You're probably right."

"I'll see what I can dig up when I get back. Maybe there's a spy somewhere in the defense camp. See you this evening."

Twenty minutes later, as Shaw watched Sam Watkins open the throttles for takeoff at Cleveland's Burke Lakefront Airport, he was troubled by a nagging thought. He had told his secretary by phone the previous evening about Judge Somerville's inclination. He had been standing in the bedroom at the time while Pat had been in the salon. Still, the door had been open. By the time he touched down at the Beverly Airport in a driving rain, he was visibly upset.

As soon as he reached the suite, he got the number of the editorial offices of *Far West* magazine, dialed direct, and asked to speak to the editor. After a few moments a brisk voice came on the line.

"Severenson speaking."

"Hi, Mr. Severenson, this is Ed Blalock with the *Marin County Register*. I'm trying to get a line on a Boston newspaperman named Martin Hanlon. One of the oldtimers here said you might know him."

"Hell yes," said Severenson heartily, "I used to work for the old bastard. You'll find him at the Boston *Chronicle*. Matter of fact, I talked to him there yesterday."

"Thanks much." Shaw hung up.

When Patricia Perrin arrived at Shaw's suite at ten after five, he was shaving for dinner. She gave him a bubbling account of the day's proceedings but made no mention of the editorial or any problem with the judge. As he was buttoning his shirt, Shaw picked up the bedroom phone, dialed two digits, and whispered "Now" to the party who answered.

Five minutes later there was a messenger at the door. "I'm looking for a Miss Patricia Perrin," he said. He was holding a long, narrow box.

"That's me," said Pat quizzically.

"Hi, ma'am. I have a package for you. I got no answer at your room, so the lady at the desk told me she thought you might be here. Could you sign my delivery slip please?"

Patricia signed, and gave the messenger a dollar tip. Puzzled, she opened the box. Shaw pretended a lack of interest.

Inside were a dozen long-stemmed roses, and an envelope. Out of the corner of his eye Shaw saw her face go agape, and a hand dart to the front of her blouse. She began to look ill.

"Who's the competition?" asked Shaw mildly.

"Oh no one," she replied, blushing. "Just a friend of my boss being nice."

"And who might that be?" he asked.

"Uh, a man named Martin Hanlon. Tom worked for him some years ago."

"I see. What does the note say?"

Patricia was beet red. She made no answer but slowly shook her head. Shaw picked up the note and read from it: "Thanks for a great scoop, honey. Keep that info coming. Marty Hanlon."

"What did you do to earn the roses?"

Patricia was sobbing now, and would not look at Shaw.

"Let me guess," he said. "From the available evidence, it would appear that you passed on to Editor Hanlon a remark you heard me make in confidence to my secretary last night on the telephone."

Patricia nodded, rubbing her eyes and crying.

"I'm not going to tell you how serious are the consequences of what you have done because I don't want to read about it in the *Chronicle*. I am going to tell you to get the hell out of this room and to stay far away from me on a permanent basis. It makes my gut wrench just to look at you."

He put a hand on her elbow and ushered her through the suite to the door.

When he had closed the door, Shaw poured himself a generous Scotch, straight over ice, and took a long, sad swallow. Then he picked up the phone to call Kilrayne.

The following morning Shaw requested a meeting of counsel in chambers before the commencement of the day's proceedings. When all had arrived, Judge Somerville sent for the stenographer, Carole Christiansen. He did not look happy.

"Let the record show," he said, "that Mr. Shaw of the defense team sent word to the court that he had information of vital importance and wished to have a meeting in chambers. All counsel for both sides are present. What is it, Mr. Shaw?"

"Your honor," said Shaw solemnly, "I have a most unpleasant duty to the court which I am about to discharge. It is my understanding that yesterday there appeared in a local newspaper an editorial which purported to reveal an expression made by Your Honor here in chambers."

"You may be a greater master of understatement than your British colleague," said Somerville grimly. "Go on."

"It would appear that through negligence on my part I am responsible for that editorial, or at least for any quotations attributed to the court. For what little it may be worth, I tender my most humble apology for my carelessness."

Somerville began to color. "Perhaps, Mr. Shaw," he

said evenly, "you would be good enough to elaborate further."

"Very well, Your Honor. Prior to the commencement of trial, I applied for a rather large insurance policy, and was given a very thorough physical examination. Some of the results were viewed unfavorably by the insurance carrier, and I am being pressed to submit to further testing. In speaking to my secretary last evening—she has been trying to schedule the reexamination—I mentioned to her that I had learned that Your Honor indicated that this case might terminate when the Commonwealth rested."

"Your secretary? Surely she didn't notify the media . . . ?"

"No, Your Honor. I'm afraid that's where my negligence comes in. In another room in my suite there was a young lady who is doing a feature article for the *Far West* magazine in Los Angeles. She overheard the conversation and apparently passed the information to her boss who passed it to a Mr. Martin Hanlon of the *Chronicle*."

The Judge, obviously angry, paused a moment to compose himself.

"Mr. Shaw," he said, "what you have charitably described as negligence is in my view verging on recklessness and a poor return on the privilege granted you to practice in this court. I would be tempted to revoke that privilege, except that Mr. Kilrayne would be punished in the process since you have obviously made a substantial contribution to Mr. Everard's handling of the defense. I will, however, deal with this matter as soon as we have a verdict. Until recently, I would have been inclined to cite Mr. Hanlon and his paper for contempt, but the current trend of our United States Supreme Court would seem to be that the media can publish any damned thing they get their hands on, no matter how that is accomplished."

"Very well, Your Honor," said Shaw softly.

"Ah, excuse me, M'Lord—I'm sorry, I meant Your Honor," said Everard, "but I believe you just said that you would speak to Mr. Shaw's unfortunate transgression after a *verdict*? I am hopeful that this affair hasn't caused Your Honor to alter your views about the sufficiency of the prosecution's case?"

"You are quite right, Mr. Everard, that was a slip of the tongue on my part—a bit of carelessness I should perhaps bear in mind when determining what if any disciplinary action is to be taken against Mr. Shaw. I should have used the word 'termination' rather than 'verdict,'" the judge said with a wry smile. "But since you have raised the subject, let me say for the record that since the editorial which is the subject of this meeting came to my attention yesterday morning, I have given long and prayerful thought to what effect it might have on my willingness to discharge my duty to direct a verdict should I feel that such action is warranted. I am still prepared to take that step should it be appropriate. I regret that a probable consequence will be, should I so act, that the public will no doubt be told by Mr. Hanlon and others that Mr. Kilrayne is the beneficiary of some sort of cronyism and that there remains a cloud over his culpability."

Everard nodded. "Regrettable, I must say. 'Tis a pity that Americans do not seem to have the same respect for their courts and counsel that the British do. Even so," he went on with a faint smile, "I might say, respectfully, that Your Honor's conduct of this case would do honor to an English Justice, and we unabashedly assert that they are the best in the world."

Somerville smiled warmly for the first time that morning. "Thank you, Mr. Everard," he said. "I consider that to be very high praise. Perhaps you had better stick around after the trial and represent Mr. Shaw."

30

THE ZINGER
Wednesday, September 13

When court reconvened following the lunch hour, the air was crackling with the current of an important climax in the offing. A sharp murmur went through the spectators as Durham stood up and said with exaggerated solemnity, "The Commonwealth calls Francis La-Pere."

"May we approach the bench, please," said Everard sharply.

"Certainly," said Somerville.

When the lawyers had clustered at the end of the bench away from the jury box, with the stenographer nestled between them, Everard said, "Your Honor, the witness who is about to testify has been kept since the indictment in some secret place by the prosecution. He was produced in this courthouse several weeks ago, but refused to speak even his name to Mr. Shaw and Miss Barton, who sought to question him. I am fearful that he may attempt to blurt out, on direct or cross-examination, some notion that he has been in protective custody because he fears for his safety and that he refused to be interviewed by the defense for some sort of similar reason.

"I wish to put Mr. Durham on notice that I do not intend to go into either of these areas. If Mr. LaPere should volunteer claims of the sort I have described, the prejudice to Mr. Kilrayne would in my judgment surpass the point where a curative instruction from the bench would be a sufficient remedy. I should like to inquire whether Mr. Durham has cautioned his witness in this respect?"

Somerville nodded. "Mr. Durham?"

"I have told LaPere not to volunteer anything," said Durham, "but I have not specifically addressed myself to any fear he has from someone who tries to procure an assassination, such as the defendant did in this case."

Judge Somerville looked stern.

"I do not share your view, Mr. Durham. I would be very much inclined to grant a mistrial if LaPere gives such testimony unless Mr. Everard is foolish enough to open the door. Nothing I have seen in this trial leads me to expect Mr. Everard to be foolish in any respect.

"Ladies and gentlemen," he said to the jury, "a question of law has arisen which requires a proceeding outside the presence of the jury. Since it will only take a few minutes, I will adjourn with the lawyers to my chambers rather than have you suffer the inconvenience of marching downstairs to the jury room. We will take a five minute recess, but you may remain in your seats. Mr. Bailiff, please bring the witness to my chambers."

When counsel and LaPere had gathered in Somerville's office and found seats Somerville fastened LaPere's eyes with a firm and solemn stare.

"Mr. LaPere," he said, "I have brought you in here prior to your testimony to resolve a matter of deep concern to the court. I understand that you are not unfamiliar with trial procedure, am I correct?"

LaPere grinned sheepishly. "Sure, Judge, I been in an' out a few times."

"All right. Now, I am given to understand first, that you are in protective custody, and second, that you have declined to be interviewed by representatives of the defense."

"That's right," said LaPere with a smirk. "I was told

I didn't have to talk to them if I didn't want to, and I could if I felt like it. I didn't feel like it."

"It is the concern of counsel, Mr. LaPere, that you might wish to explain, somewhere in your testimony, that your statements or conduct are in some way the product of fear of Mr. Kilrayne."

LaPere nodded solemnly. "That's true, Judge," he said.

"I see," said Somerville. "In that case, I am going to instruct you very carefully that unless you hear me specifically rule that you may give such testimony because defense counsel has deliberately invited you to do so, you will refrain absolutely from even hinting of your claimed fear of Mr. Kilrayne. Do you clearly understand my order?"

LaPere nodded.

"Should such testimony creep into the trial, I will be very much inclined to declare a mistrial and discharge the defendant. That would fairly necessitate a proceeding against you for criminal contempt. I do not wish you to feel threatened by the court's remarks but only to understand the urgency of my order to protect the trial.

"Mr. Everard," Somerville went on, "might I assume that somewhere in your cross-examination you will explore the question of what, if anything, has been promised to this witness in exchange for his cooperation?"

"Indeed," said Everard.

"Very well," said Somerville. "Mr. LaPere, should you be asked such a question by either counsel, and if part of what has been promised you includes protection for you and your family, or a change of identity under the federal witness program, you are authorized and directed to eliminate those portions of your answer."

"But Your Honor," sputtered Durham, "in all the years I've been trying cases, such testimony has been commonplace in these circumstances. I don't think. . . ."

"I'm sure it has," snapped Somerville. "Some judges

have allowed witnesses to go on at length with that sort of evidence. I will not. I view it as an outrage and a reckless disregard of the duty to conduct a fair trial, and when these minutes are eventually unsealed, my colleagues will learn of my stance. Meanwhile, I wish to caution everyone in this room that any violation of these orders will not be tolerated and that contempt penalties will be distributed liberally to those who wish to test my sincerity. Miss Reporter, seal these minutes until they are unsealed either by myself or by a higher court. Now let us get on with the trial."

They returned to the courtroom.

"State your name please," said Durham.

"Francis Bonaventure LaPere."

"You are presently in the custody of the Department of Corrections of the Commonwealth of Massachusetts serving a sentence of seven to ten years for burglary, are you not?"

"That is correct."

"Have you been convicted of any other crimes?"

"Yes."

"What were they?"

"Once was for burglary, and once was for breaking and entering in the daytime."

"Do you know the defendant in this case, Michael Kilrayne?"

"Sure, I know him."

"How did you come to meet him?"

"Three years ago he defended me for bank robbery."

"Were you satisfied with his services?"

"Oh, sure," beamed LaPere. "He got me off!"

A spontaneous chuckle went through the courtroom. Somerville rapped his gavel, but not very enthusiastically, since he found himself smiling broadly.

"Then you have no animosity of any kind toward Mr. Kilrayne?"

"No, I don't," said LaPere.

"When did you last see the defendant?" asked Durham.

"Last April twelfth."

"How are you certain of the date?"

"Because I went to trial the next day in Suffolk Superior Court on this burglary rap."

"Where did your meeting with the defendant take place?"

"In his office."

"How long did it last?"

"About twenty minutes."

"What was discussed?"

"Well, I wanted him to take my case."

"What did he say?"

"He wouldn't do it."

"Did he give any reasons?"

"Yeah," said LaPere, glancing somewhat bitterly at Kilrayne. "I didn't have enough dough."

"I see," said Durham, sympathetically. "After you had finished the discussion, did you have occasion to talk about something other than your case?"

"Yes, we did," said LaPere.

"What was that?"

"He—Mr. Kilrayne, that is—he wanted me to help him find someone to knock off some broad."

"Objection," said Everard.

"Yes," said Somerville. "Mr. LaPere, you may not testify to what you think Mr. Kilrayne wanted. You may recite what he said, what you said, or what a third person said in his presence. You may also, in response to an appropriate question, describe what you saw him do."

LaPere nodded as if brimming with sincerity.

"Tell us what the conversation was," said Durham.

"Well," replied LaPere, "he told me that he had a small problem that was annoying him. He said a woman that he knew was making noises like she was going to cause him some trouble, and he would be grateful if she could be made to disappear without a trace, he put it. He asked if I knew anyone in the business who might take a contract."

"What did you say?"

"I told him I would talk to some people, try and line someone up for him."

"And did you make some efforts of that kind?"

"Nah," said LaPere with disdain. "I don't mess with those kind of people. I was just agreeing so that he might take my case."

"Have you seen or talked to Mr. Kilrayne since that day?"

"No."

"Thank you, Mr. LaPere." Durham turned to Everard with a smile of satisfaction on his face.

Everard rose lightly to his feet, and stood next to his chair. "Mr. LaPere," he said in clear, clipped tones, "how old are you?"

"Thirty-four," said LaPere.

"You have admitted to the commission of several crimes, felonies I believe?"

"Yes, I have."

"Why did you commit them?"

"Why did I . . . ?" LaPere was off balance. "Whaddaya mean by a question like that?"

Everard surveyed LaPere as if he were examining a maggot in a garbage can. "Did you understand my question?"

"I dunno. I guess so."

"Then will you be kind enough to make answer to it?"

"Well, I guess I wanted the bread, that's all."

"Are you generally in good health?"

"Sure," said LaPere, very much confused by Everard's approach.

"Have you been in good health throughout your adult life?"

"Yeah, pretty much."

"Why did you not seek your bread then, by obtaining honest employment?"

LaPere looked hopelessly confused. The many hours he had spent with Durham and Barrett prepping for his ordeal had not even touched upon questions such as were being hurled at him. He looked at the prosecution table for rescue, but Durham averted his gaze.

"Did you understand my question?" Everard said coldly.

"Uh, sort of. You want to know why I didn't get a job instead of rippin' people off?"

"Precisely."

"Well, I guess I wanted a quick buck."

"You were willing to break the law and steal from others in order to improve your own lot?"

"Yeah, I guess you could say that."

"Did you feel any regret at having taken property belonging to others?"

"Well, yeah," said LaPere hesitantly, "I mighta felt like that."

"But not enough to return that property?"

LaPere stared at Everard with exasperation.

"Yeah, yeah, I didn't take the stuff back."

"Very well. Now, when you were apprehended for these several crimes, did you still at that time feel some regret for the victims whose property you had taken?"

"You mean when I was arrested?"

"Yes."

"Well, I wasn't thinking about regret at that time. I was thinking about getting a lawyer."

"In each of the cases where you have been convicted, you have gone to trial and lost a jury verdict, correct?"

"Yes."

"You never offered to plead guilty, even though in each case you were guilty?"

"I got a right to make them prove it!" said LaPere indignantly.

"Of course. Now answer my question. In any of the cases did you ever offer to plead guilty?"

"Nah, I never tried to cop out."

"Thank you. Now, with respect to the bank robbery trial in which Mr. Kilrayne defended you, you had a favorable verdict in that case?"

"Yeah, we won."

"Did you discuss with Mr. Kilrayne, during that trial, your giving evidence in your own behalf?"

"Yeah, we talked about it."

"You wanted to testify that at the time of the robbery you were at the beach with a lady friend, did you not?"

"Mmm, I may have."

"That lady friend was a Miss Pamela Rosen?"

"Yeah, I think that was her."

"You brought her to Mr. Kilrayne's office in order that he might learn of, and later use, her story to help your case?"

LaPere's eyebrows knotted defensively. "Yeah, I brought her in to see him."

"Yes. And after less than an hour with Mr. Kilrayne, Miss Rosen came out of his office crying and left without speaking to you, is that correct?"

"She walked out," said LaPere, grudgingly. Durham was at this point half out of his seat, trying to frame a plausible objection.

"After that," Everard went on in a casual but inexorable monotone, "Mr. Kilrayne told you that he had gotten Miss Rosen to admit that she was lying, that you had asked her to lie, and he told you that under no circumstances would he use her as a witness. Do you recall that?"

"Objection, Your Honor," shouted Durham, flushing beet red. "This is a clear violation of the attorney-client privilege."

"The privilege," said Somerville evenly, "belongs to the witness, not to the prosecution. Mr. LaPere, do you claim that the answer to the question just put to you would contain privileged information?"

LaPere looked at the judge, not exactly sure of what was happening. "Sure, Judge," he said, beginning to perspire around the upper bridge of the nose. "Whatever Mr. Durham says, that's what I claim."

"Very well," said Somerville. "I will rule that as a result of your answer on direct examination that Mr. Kilrayne 'got you off' in this bank robbery case, his counsel has every right to explore what you meant by that. There is an inherent inference that you were guilty and that Mr. Kilrayne somehow manipulated the legal processes to cheat the law. That deserves a searching cross-examination, and for purposes of this case at least you have waived your attorney-client privilege. Even if you had not waived it, I would rule that Mr. Kilrayne had the right to invade it to protect himself from your attack. You will answer the question."

"May the stenographer read the question," asked Everard, politely.

"She may and will," said Somerville. The question was read.

"He said he wouldn't call her," said LaPere, grudgingly.

"And since you couldn't testify without exposing your own criminal past, the case was sent to the jury on Mr. Kilrayne's cross-examination of the prosecution's witnesses, and that alone. Is that not true?"

LaPere nodded. "You must speak your answer, so that the stenographer can record it," said Somerville.

"Yes, that's true," said LaPere.

"In other words," said Everard, drawing out the moment, "Mr. Kilrayne rejected your offer of false evidence and then went on to win the case by the rules, isn't that so?"

"I can explain that," said LaPere angrily.

"Mr. LaPere," interjected Somerville, "you must answer the question as put. If an explanation is proper, it will be asked of you by Mr. Durham when he has an opportunity to question you on redirect examination."

"If it please the court," said Everard with just the right tinge of humility, "while I of course agree with Your Honor's ruling as correct in law, I invite the witness to answer. It may save time in the long run."

Somerville was taken aback. He had hardly expected to have a favorable defense ruling undermined by the defendant's chief counsel, but he could scarcely ignore Everard's apparent desire to flirt with a dangerous situation.

"Very well," he said. "In view of Mr. Everard's wish that you be allowed to explain at this time, you may do so."

"What happened was," said Frankie LaPere, somehow thinking that the judge had ruled in *his* favor for a change, "Mike and I knew that the witnesses were phony. What I mean, they were placing me *inside* the bank, and they said they could recognize me as one of the robbers even though all the people robbing the bank were masked. The prosecutor had gotten them to say that, and it was a lie."

"Of course it was a lie," soothed Everard gently, "you weren't in the bank at all, were you, Mr. LaPere?"

"Damned right I wasn't," said LaPere triumphantly, "and Mike knew that. That's why I got off."

"Precisely. While your colleagues were in the bank you were sitting at the wheel of the getaway car, as you chaps call it, with the engine running. True?"

As LaPere began to bluster, Somerville scowled. "Perhaps," he said slowly, "we are getting close to an area of privilege which ought to be determined outside the presence of the jury."

"If Your Honor will permit me," said Everard, "I think the next question might obviate that problem."

"Proceed," said Somerville.

"Mr. LaPere," said Everard coolly, acting as though his pockets were full of witnesses and documents literally bursting to leap out at Frankie, "did you not in late May of this year tell a Jamaican cell-mate named Waldo Kingston that you had in fact been the driver of the getaway car in that robbery?"

LaPere glowered, but did not respond.

"Perhaps," said Everard softly, "you would know him better by the name you always call him, 'Nigger' Kingston. Does that refresh your memory?"

"That black sonofabitch," muttered LaPere.

"Yes," said Everard, "he is black. Now then, I should like to call your attention to your claim that you bear no hostility toward Mr. Kilrayne. Do you recall telling us that when Mr. Durham was questioning you?"

Frankie LaPere had finally come to understand that the chill, brown-haired Englishman, for all his manners, was a mortal enemy. He squared to face his attacker.

"Yes. I said that, and it's true."

"What was your first thought last April twelfth when Mr. Kilrayne would not take your case. Your very first thought?"

"Well, I didn't blame him too much where I had no bread and all. . . ."

"Mr. LaPere," Everard said harshly, "is it not a fact that while you sat before Mr. Kilrayne's desk he called prosecutor Arthur Mulvaney and asked that your trial date be postponed so that he could consider representing you?"

"Yeah, but that was so that I could raise some dough. . . ."

"Did he make such a call in your presence?"

"Yes, he did."

"When the call was complete, did he not tell you that other court commitments prevented him from starting your trial the next day?"

"Yes."

"Did he not also tell you that any lawyer who would start trial in a serious case on one day's notice ought to have his license snapped away?"

"Yes."

"Thank you," said Everard, softening his tone and gradually backing away from the witness stand. "Now then, sir, you claim it was in this atmosphere of rejection of your application that Mr. Kilrayne entrusted you with the knowledge that he required the murder of a lady friend. Is that what you say?"

"He asked me," said LaPere doggedly. "I remember it like it was yesterday."

"Indeed. Were you told why you, a nonviolent person, were being approached to arrange an assassination?"

"That wasn't discussed," said LaPere.

"Had you ever told Mr. Kilrayne anything about your beliefs and practices which would indicate that you knew those who would take a 'contract' to murder?"

"No," said LaPere.

"When he made his request of you, did you not very much want him to defend you in your burglary case the next day?"

"Sure I wanted him, that's why I was there."

"I see. Since you have told us that you lied to him and indicated that you would try to locate an assassin, when in fact knew no people of that type, why did you not try to trade off your efforts in exchange for his services in your case?"

LaPere was silent for a moment. "I guess I didn't think of putting a lawyer as big as him in the squeeze," he said.

"Have you thought of doing so since?"

LaPere looked puzzled. "I don't understand what you mean. . . ."

"You seem to be putting him in a 'squeeze' today. I'm asking if you have thought about that, just yes or no."

"Yes. I thought about testifying, and I'm telling the truth."

"In exchange for what," barked Everard, raising his voice.

"I got no promises," said LaPere. "I didn't ask for none, and I got none."

"You are then," said Everard in a voice that was pure silk, "testifying out of a civic duty to the public to come forward with the truth. Is that it?"

"That's it," said LaPere sullenly. "You got it right there, mister." Everard's manner and his articulation had LaPere taut with an effort to somehow cope.

"Yes," said Everard in a voice that had a tinge of derision. "Would you be good enough to tell the jury of each prior occasion where you have acted in the public good out of a civic interest?"

"Objection," said Durham.

"Please state your grounds," said Somerville.

"An unfair question," said Durham.

"Overruled," said Somerville. "You may answer, Mr. LaPere."

LaPere, coloring, sat silent.

"I take it, Mr. LaPere, that you are able to recite no such prior occasions. If so, I shall move on."

LaPere continued his silence. Everard approached the witness stand, and exhibited a small photograph to the witness.

"Do you recognize this woman?" he asked innocently.

LaPere's eyebrows shot up. "Sure," he said, "that's my older sister, Antoinette."

"Did you, early in July of this year, ask her to suggest to Mr. Kilrayne that he ought to take the appeal in your case for no fee if he knew what was good for him?"

"That isn't so," roared Frankie like an indignant bull. "I didn't put it that way at all, and if she said that she was just being a dumb broad."

"But you did send a message to Mr. Kilrayne through her that had to do with your appeal?"

"Goddam it," said Durham in a whisper to Gilardi, "why the Christ am I learning *this* for the first time while this asshole's on the stand."

"Your witness," said Gilardi with a sigh, "just got bluffed out. Kilrayne had no way of knowing that the lady who called him on the phone was really Frankie's sister and could never have testified as to who called him. The Englishman flashed her picture at him, and Frankie probably thinks she went to the office in person. So Everard nailed him. I never told you Frankie was a genius."

"No," muttered Durham, "and you never told me about the sister either, Joe. I warned you, you keep secrets from the guy trying the case, you might as well hang your ass in a kettle of boiling oil."

"Mr. LaPere, did you hear my question?" insisted Everard. "Did you ask your sister Antoinette early in July to ask Mr. Kilrayne to take your appeal? Yes or no."

"We talked about it," said LaPere. "She might have, she's always worrying about me."

"When did you learn that he had refused?"

"Improper," shouted Durham, visibly upset with the way things were going. "Assuming a fact not in evidence."

"Sustained," said Somerville. "Mr. Everard, once you have established that Mr. Kilrayne did in fact refuse, it will be appropriate to ask when this witness learned of the refusal."

"Thank you, Your Honor," said Everard. "Mr. LaPere, did you speak with your sister in the month of July?"

"Yes."

"Did you speak with her, as the records of the Walpole State Prison reflect, the day before you testified before the grand jury in this case?"

"I think so."

"Did she report to you at that time that Mr. Kilrayne had denied your request in rather explicit terms?"

"She told me he wouldn't do it."

"I see. One final question, Mr. LaPere. In testifying here today, knowing how important are the things at stake, have you used that same degree of social conscience which has guided you throughout your adult years?"

"Objection," said Durham tiredly. "Improper."

"No," said Somerville with mild amusement, "if the witness understands the question, I will allow him to answer."

Frankie LaPere thought he had been handed an out. "I don't understand, Judge," he said.

"I rather thought he might not," said Everard agreeably. "Hopefully the jury did. I have nothing further. Thank you, Mr. LaPere."

Durham rose wearily but spoke forcefully. "Mr. La-Pere," he said, "is there any doubt in your mind—any whatsoever—that Mr. Kilrayne asked your aid in having a woman killed."

Frankie, buoyed at seeing a friendly face once more in control of the floor, looked almost cheerful.

"None whatsoever," he said loudly.

"Are you positive of that?" asked Durham.

"Absolutely," said LaPere.

"That's all," said Durham.

Just before midnight that same evening, Ellen Somerville lay panting on their king-sized bed next to her husband. Realizing as she had long ago that her spouse was an impressive and attractive man, she had resolved to keep his attention and fidelity by her own personal excellence, rather than by trying to police his life in demand of her wifely rights. In a balanced match, they had matured together and were each convinced so thoroughly of the worth of the other that neither strayed.

Following the evening news they had meandered into a sexual overture that had ripened into a frolicsome romp. Both were exhausted and swimming in warm and satisfied feelings.

"You know," said Ellen, "I've listened to all three TV stations tonight and read two newspapers. I still can't figure who won today, and the reporters certainly don't agree. How did your English friend do?"

"I am sorry, almost ashamed, that I didn't get you a seat," said Somerville. "If I had, of course, we'd have been crucified by those who camp outside the courthouse and sometimes wait as much as a day and a half to see a small part of the trial. But you should have been there. You would have enjoyed it."

"You still haven't told me who won," she said, with mock petulance.

"Ellen," said Somerville, sitting up and taking a sip of a now much diluted Grand Marnier on the rocks that was languishing on his night table, "you will hear two things—as a matter of fact, you already have. One group will say that LaPere was unshaken. The other will say that he was destroyed. The former group will be youngsters who understand little if anything of cross-examination, the latter will be veterans who see what is yet to come."

"You mean the final arguments? You always told me that a trial among good lawyers was no more than a scenario jockeying for position to give the best final argument, which was the only point at which a case could be won or lost."

"Exactly. To put it mildly, our barrister gutted LaPere, bolstered Kilrayne's integrity along the way, and did it all so swiftly and so smoothly that half the people in the courtroom didn't know what was going on. Even Durham was struggling to keep abreast, and he's been in court most of his life. I was pretty good at cross-examination, I thought. I now find that I lacked subtlely, timing, and the startling unpredictability that every trial lawyer ought to have. Next summer, when the Superior Court gives us a full month's vacation, we might go to London and let your favorite husband salivate a little further over barristers in action."

"Sounds good," said Ellen dreamily.

31

SO HELP ME GOD
Thursday, September 14

Philip Durham had a quiet but confident air about him
as he rose while the court was gaveled into session.
"You may call your next witness, Mr. Durham."

"The Commonwealth calls John McKiver," said Durham, somewhat more loudly than usual. McKiver, a
stocky balding man in his mid-thirties, was sworn in and
took the stand.

"Tell us your name," said Durham.

"John Edward McKiver."

"Where do you reside?"

"In Danbury, Connecticut, in federal prison."

"Have you been convicted of a crime?"

"Yes. I was convicted in federal court in Manhattan
of selling unregistered securities, and sentenced to serve
four years."

"Have any threats or promises been made affecting
your testimony here today?"

"No, sir."

"Can you tell us where you were on January sixteenth of this year?"

"Yes. I was in Boston, staying with a friend named
Harold Baumbach at his apartment on Beacon Street."

"Did you see the defendant, Michael Kilrayne, on that
date?"

"I did. He came to the apartment at about seven

o'clock in the evening to see Mr. Baumbach. They asked me to leave the room."

"Did you do so?"

"Yes and no," said McKiver a bit sheepishly. "I went into the kitchen, but I didn't close the door all the way. I was curious as to why. . . ."

"I object," said Everard.

"Sustained," said the judge.

"Mr. McKiver," said Durham, with patient deference. "You are not allowed to tell us your thoughts or what motivated you. Just what you heard said while Mr. Kilrayne was present. Did you hear any conversation between Mr. Baumbach and Mr. Kilrayne?"

"Yes I did. Part of what they said, anyway."

"Tell us what you heard."

"Well, Mr. Kilrayne told Baumbach that he was having a lot of trouble with some woman. He needed her to be taken care of, he said. Baumbach said, 'You mean twepped?' Mr. Kilrayne said 'You got it, my friend.' That's about all I heard, because one of them—I couldn't see who—came and closed the door. About five minutes later Mr. Kilrayne left."

"Do you know what is meant by the term 'twepped'?"

"Yes. Baumbach and I were in the Green Berets together about ten years ago. 'Twep' means 'terminate with extreme prejudice.' You know, kill someone."

"I see," said Durham. "Tell us, had you ever met Mr. Kilrayne before?"

"I had seen him, but we weren't introduced."

"Where and when?"

"In Saigon in 1969," said McKiver. "Baumbach tied a prisoner to a tree and fired three shots just above his head to make him talk. They gave him a General Court-Martial. Mr. Kilrayne came to Viet Nam and got him off."

Durham paused. "Will the defense stipulate to that?"

Everard looked at Kilrayne, who nodded. "The defense," said Everard, "will agree that Mr. Kilrayne did in fact defend Mr. Baumbach successfully in 1969 in Saigon," he said.

"Thank you," said Durham. "Now, Mr. McKiver, are you positive that it was Mr. Kilrayne who came to the apartment last January?"

"Oh, very positive," said McKiver cheerfully. "I recognized him then, and I recognize him now. He was wearing a blue suit that night."

"One last thing," said Durham. "Do you have any means of being certain of the date—January sixteenth of this year?"

"Oh yes, very certain. Baumbach was shot by the cops during an armored truck robbery two days later. I heard about it on the radio and got out of the apartment before somebody tried to get me involved."

"Thank you," said Durham. "Your Honor, I have here the death certificate of Harold I. Baumbach, the same individual Mr. Kilrayne defended in Viet Nam, showing that he died of gunshot wounds in Brockton, Massachusetts, on January eighteenth, 1978, at two-fifteen in the afternoon. I offer it."

"No objection," said Everard.

"You may examine," said Durham.

Everard walked slowly over to the jury rail, riveting McKiver with his eyes.

"Mr. McKiver," he said, "are you quite sure that this alleged encounter with Mr. Kilrayne took place two days before the death of Mr. Baumbach?"

"Yes sir."

"Might it have been, perhaps, *three* days before?"

"No. It was two days before."

"Could it have been the *day* before Mr. Baumbach was shot?"

"No, it could not."

"Then you are positive of the date."

"Yes sir. Absolutely."

"Very well. Now, how long were you in Boston last January?"

"I came on the fifteenth—the day before Mr. Kilrayne came to the apartment."

"And while you were in Boston, did you see anyone other than Mr. Baumbach?"

"No," said McKiver, "other than Mr. Kilrayne."

"You didn't leave the apartment at all?"

"No, I didn't. I knew the feds in New York were looking for me—on the securities thing—I was staying off the street."

"Where had you come from when you arrived on the fifteenth?"

"I drove up from New York."

"Were you alone?"

"Yes, I was."

"And when you left following the shooting of Mr. Baumbach, where did you go?"

"I drove back to New York."

"I see. Now once again, Mr. McKiver, are you absolutely positive that you were in Mr. Baumbach's apartment on January sixteenth?"

"Yes, I am."

"And that you saw Mr. Kilrayne there?"

"Yes, no question about it."

"Is there any possibility that you might be mistaken about that?"

"I object," said Durham. "This question has been asked and answered—several times."

Somerville looked quizzically at Everard. "I will allow the answer," he said, "but really, Mr. Everard, you seem to have covered the point." Everard nodded pleasantly.

"You may answer, Mr. McKiver," said Somerville.

"There is," said McKiver with evident exasperation, "no possibility whatever that I am mistaken. I saw Mr. Kilrayne with Harold Baumbach on last January sixteenth, and heard them discussing killing a woman. That's it. Period!"

"All right, Mr. McKiver. Now, I wonder if you would be good enough to remove your jacket and roll up your left sleeve. With the court's permission, of course."

"I object," bellowed Durham.

"Mr. Durham," said Somerville. "You of course have the right to object, but I must ask you to do so somewhat more temperately. Mr. Everard, what is the purpose of this somewhat extraordinary request?"

"I give the court my solemn word that it is a matter of the highest relevance," said Everard.

Somerville studied him for a moment. "Very well. Mr. McKiver, please do as you were asked. You may remove your jacket."

As McKiver rolled up his shirtsleeve, Everard picked up a white envelope from the defense table and walked to the witness stand. "Would you show the jury your left forearm, please."

McKiver held out his arm. There was a scar about one inch long, slightly redder than the surrounding skin, plainly visible.

"This scar," said Everard coldly, "is I believe a consequence of some minor surgery you had a few months ago?"

McKiver nodded his head. "Yes, that's right."

"You had a growth removed by a Dr. A. E. Samuels at the Selfridge Hospital in Cleveland, did you not?"

"Yes, I think that was his name."

"And the growth turned out to be benign, did it not?"

"Mmm-hmm. That's what they said."

"Yes. And you were in the hospital for three days, were you not?"

"About that."

"And when was this surgery performed?"

"Last winter. I don't remember the exact date."

"I see." Everard opened the envelope, and handed a

sheaf of photostatic records to the witness. "I wonder," he said, "if these might help you to remember. Look at them please."

McKiver looked at the top sheet, and a red flush began to creep up from his collar. "These must be mistaken," he said weakly, going rapidly through the stack.

"Do those records not indicate that you were admitted on January thirteenth at noon and discharged on January seventeenth in the evening, Mr. McKiver?"

McKiver nodded.

"Does it not appear from the surgeon's report, all of the nurses' notes, and the administrator's admission and discharge forms that you were confined at Selfridge during that entire period, Mr. McKiver?" Everard's voice crackled with disdain.

"Let me see those please," said Judge Somerville. After examining them, he turned to McKiver, scowling darkly.

"Mr. McKiver, I believe that based on what is before me, I have a duty to advise you that whatever you say might be used against you in a future proceeding. You may have time to retain and consult with counsel if you wish."

McKiver sat still for a moment. "No, Judge, I'll just take fifth. I won't answer any more questions."

"You refuse to testify further?"

"That's right."

Somerville looked at Durham and Barrett. Both looked sick.

"Very well. Mr. Bailiff, please return Mr. McKiver to the custody of the United States Marshal who brought him to this court. Ladies and gentlemen, when a witness refuses to submit to cross-examination, there are several remedies available to the court. In these circumstances, I am going to strike the testimony of Mr. McKiver. You are to disregard it utterly and completely. Is that clearly understood?"

The stunned jurors nodded in unison. It was plain that they had been jolted.

"That little experience," said Theo Wilson to Wallace Turner, "has got to have them thinking about LaPere in a new light."

"The court," said Somerville, "is going to be in recess for twenty minutes. The District Attorney," he said slowly, looking directly at Walter Barrett, "may wish to use some part of that time to consider whether he ought to bring this matter to the attention of the grand jury."

That evening, shortly before midnight, Shaw and Kilrayne were having a nightcap in the cocktail lounge. "I wonder," said Shaw, "if Walter's going to prosecute brother McKiver?"

Kilrayne laughed. "Don't hang by your thumbs," he said. "Our friend McKiver turns out to be an informant for the FBI in New York. Doing a little undercover work for them on drug traffic at Danbury. If Barrett makes one move in his direction, McKiver will get immunity from the United States Attorney in the Southern District of New York and testify that Gilardi promised to get him out if he testified and also told him to lie about that to the jury. McKiver's safe."

"Christ," said Shaw, "when did you learn that?"

Kilrayne chuckled. "Some phone calls tonight," he said. "The who, I'm afraid . . ."

"I know, I know," said Shaw. "It's another damn secret."

Shaw finished his drink, said goodnight to Kilrayne and headed for his room. He was puzzled, even troubled, by the fact that Kilrayne had twice kept the source of vital information about McKiver from his defense counsel. Shaw wondered whether or not it just might be possible that McKiver had been a plant: a programmed witness, set up for destruction before the jury, as a counterpoint to Frankie LaPere. If so, it was a bold and brilliant tactic of questionable legality.

32

THE FLOATER
Friday, September 15

Holding his helicopter no more than thirty feet above the shore, Grady Benson skimmed along the sands of Wingaersheek Beach, then Crane's Beach. He was on his way from the airport in Beverly, Massachusetts, to his home base in Portland, Maine. Benson liked to buzz the beaches along the route, whenever the weather was decent, to relieve the monotony of cross-country flying. The clear, white sands of the Northern Massachusetts shore were beautiful and serene, and occasionally Benson would surprise one or more pairs of lovers copulating in the sand dumes

Dusk was gathering as he passed the mouth of the Merrimack River and zoomed along Salisbury Beach. He moved his flight path to parallel the shore about fifty yards out over the ocean; the kids in the Salisbury area were great for flying kites along the beach, and in the fading light Benson did not want to chance an encounter with a kite string. More than one helicopter had been snagged out of the sky by kites, and with an offshore wind blowing, Benson wanted to keep the risk to a minimum.

As he approached Seabrook Beach, the southernmost coastal spot in New Hampshire, he spotted something odd-looking out of the corner of his right eye. He banked the helicopter sharply to the right and circled back. Again he saw it, something floating in the swells. His curiosity was sufficiently aroused to take a closer look. He lowered the collective control and eased the cyclic stick back, gradually bringing the ship to a hover. The blast from the rotors whipped the tops off the waves below him.

As Benson drew closer, he felt his stomach begin to sour. The object of his curiosity looked like what had once been a human being with long blond hair. The body, partially clothed, was horribly bloated and discolored. Benson, sick to his stomach, had to fight to keep control of his ship. He added power and wheeled toward the beach, not certain of what to do next. While his mind was reeling from the ghastly sight he had just seen, he noticed the whirling blue light of a Massachusetts State Police cruiser. He set the ship down no more than a hundred feet from the cruiser, blowing the cap off the trooper who was in the process of giving a stern lecture to some errant teenagers in a hopped-up Ford.

The trooper marched angrily toward the cockpit of Benson's helicopter, crouching slightly as he walked to avoid the spinning blades of the main rotor. He was about to blow a gasket in Benson's direction when he got a look at Benson's face. He sensed that something was very wrong.

"What's the problem, buddy?" he asked cautiously.

Benson did not answer, but pointed his finger at the ocean. "Out there," he finally managed to warble.

"What's out there?"

"A body," said Benson. "Looks like a blond woman. It's horrible!"

"Floaters usually are," said the trooper. "Mind taking me out for a look?" Without waiting for an answer, he climbed in next to Benson, who minded very much the prospect of going back to what he had just seen. Afraid to refuse the request, he lifted off and grudgingly returned to the scene. He did not look down as he hovered near the body while the trooper made a few grim notes.

"Car ninety-one to headquarters," said the trooper into his squad car microphone.

"Headquarters bye."

"Car ninety-one on patrol at Salisbury Beach, Trooper Smith reporting a floater in the water just off the beach. Been in the water a long time. May be an adult female. Located very close to the line between Salisbury and Seabrook."

"Roger ninety-one, stand by."

There was silence for a few minutes. Smith stood outside his cruiser, microphone in hand, waiting for instructions. "Ninety-one," crackled a voice, "this is Captain O'Reilly, Detective Division. Understand you have an adult female floater. How close a look did you get?"

"Real close," said Smith. "The party was spotted by a helicopter pilot. He landed to report to me, and took me out for a look."

"Roger, ninety-one. Did you get a look at the hair?"

"Affirmative. It looks blond, kind of long."

"Ten-four. Stand by."

Five minutes elapsed, and then the radio crackled to life again. "Ninety-one, Captain O'Reilly here. I've got Lieutenant Gilardi on the phone. This may have something to do with his case in Salem, I'm going to patch you in. Stand by."

"Smith? This is Gilardi. Is that helicopter pilot still there?"

"Affirmative."

"See if he can pick me up at the Beverly Airport in fifteen minutes. On the Danvers side, North Atlantic Aviation. He can bill the Department for his time."

Smith looked at Benson, who nodded. His revulsion of a few moments before was receding, rapidly being replaced by the excitement at being involved in something important. "Glad to do it, no charge," he said.

"Pilot's on his way, Lieutenant, happy to come and get you as a public service."

"Good. Now look, Smith, get hold of a boat somewhere there, and when you hear us coming back, put your headlights on a good landing spot. It's going to be dark."

"Will do."

"Okay. Have you got a portable searchlight?"

"Affirmative."

"One more thing. We're going to need something to scoop up that floater in. Ask around, and see if you can get a sail or a big sailbag from one of the people in the harbor."

"Ten-four," said Smith.

"See you in half an hour," said Gilardi. "Headquarters is sending two more units your way, pronto."

There was a shift in the sound as the connection broke. "This is Captain O'Reilly, Smith. Stay close to the cruiser so we can reach you."

"Ten-four," said Smith.

At nine o'clock the following morning, Daniel Shaw was roused from a deep sleep by someone thumping on the door of his suite at the King's Grant Motor Inn. He shuffled into a robe and opened the door a crack. Bill Guidetti was standing outside, bristling with excitement. Shaw invited him in, rubbing the sleep from his eyes.

"Sorry to bust in," said Guidetti, sounding for all the world like he had just run the four minute mile, "but all hell's breaking loose. They've found Sarah Hansen's body!"

"They *what*?" said Shaw.

"Found her body, that's the word they're letting out. Pulled her out of the ocean up near the state line, in Salisbury. Bad shape, I guess. Gilardi and the medical examiner have been up all night. They've got her dentist, who makes her with the teeth—and some surgeon, who can identify a pin he put in her leg-bone after she broke it skiing a long time ago. This sure is going to put some punch in the Commonwealth's case."

Shaw slumped down on the divan, his head spinning. He wished silently that the Scotch bottle on the bar were a little more full and that his system were a little more empty.

"Have they got a cause of death?"

"No one's saying," replied Guidetti. "I don't know if they can get one. I guess she's been in the water a long time. Listen, I know this is off the record, but what do you think this does to Mike's case?"

Shaw lit a cigarette, inhaled deeply, and stared at the carpet. "Off the record," he said, "it cuts us from three issues down to two issues. If it is her, then the fact of death is put to rest. That leaves us with how she died, and if someone caused her death, who that someone was. That still gives Durham and his boys a long bridge to cross, but at least now they've got a bridge. All they had until this morning was open water."

"What'll you guys do now?"

Shaw looked at him with a crooked smile. "Bill, I'd love to tell you what I think we should do. But the way I was set up by your boss with that Perrin girl, I think I'd better say a little less than nothing. No offense, I hope. You and Charley are tops in my book."

"No, I understand," said Guidetti with a grin. "If it makes you feel any better, Marty's getting sacked over that little caper. They're going to call it retirement, but it wasn't Marty's idea to retire for a few years yet."

"I would gladly," said Shaw, "shoot him between the eyes myself, that sonofabitch. Thanks for the info, Bill. Once this case is over, I'll buy you and Charley a pop or two."

"You're on," said Guidetti with a wink as he closed the door to the suite behind him.

33

A MATTER OF OPINION
Monday, September 18

Throughout the remainder of the weekend, both sides worked furiously to adjust to the new evidence. At a special session of court called Saturday afternoon, Judge Somerville ordered that the defense and its experts be given full access to the human remains alleged to be Sarah Hansen, as well as the names of Grady Benson and Trooper Smith. In a brief hearing, it was established that the body, when actually recovered, was perilously close to the state line between Massachusetts and New Hampshire. Somerville directed that a panel of three surveyors be appointed to attempt to settle the point, since it might turn out that jurisdiction over the homicide—if there had been one—would lie in the New Hampshire Courts.

Gilardi had spent every spare moment in the company of Dr. Sebastian Olivero, the Essex County Medical Examiner. It was critical, now that the Commonwealth had a body as part of its proof, that there be some evidence of criminal agency in the death. If Ms. Hansen could have died by accident, and there was nothing to prove the contrary, the prosecution was still at risk on the question of a directed verdict. Through a combination of cajolery, veiled threats and arm-twisting, Gilardi finally convinced Dr. Olivero that—no other cause being apparent—Sarah Hansen had suffered a fatal blow to the back of the head.

On Sunday the defense brought in Dr. James Kiernan, the Coroner of Allegheny County in Pittsburgh, Pennsylvania, and a forensic pathologist of national renown. After two hours with Dr. Olivero, he emerged from the morgue with a grim look about him.

"My not very distinguished colleague," he told Kilrayne, Everard, Shaw, and Stacy Barton, "plans to testify that death was caused by a violent blow to the back of the skull. Now, there is a definite fracture at the lower occipital area—the cracks in the bone are quite evident—but there's no way in the world to eliminate drowning because everything is deteriorated so badly that one can't say for certain whether the fracture caused the death or came after it. I can testify to all that and will if you want me to, but you can expect trouble from Dr. Olivero."

Most of Monday morning was taken up with the testimony of Benson, Smith, Gilardi, and the surveyors. The defense pushed desperately to show that the body had been found in the New Hampshire waters and thus terminate the case on jurisdictional grounds, but in the end Judge Somerville ruled that the question was one of fact and that he would submit it to the jury.

There was a rising murmur of sound when Dr. Sebastian Olivero took the stand at two o'clock on Monday afternoon. The judge rapped his gavel once lightly to remind the press and spectators of his views on disruptive noise, and the murmur died away.

Durham went into painful detail in qualifying Olivero as an expert pathologist, drawing out all of his educational background and field experience bit by bit. Everard's offer to stipulate that the witness was qualified in his field was refused. The defense noticed with some discomfort that the jurors seemed absolutely enraptured by Olivero's every word.

"Now, Doctor," said Durham after Judge Somerville

had formally ruled that the witness was qualified, "I should like to turn to the matter at hand. Where were you last Friday evening?"

"Initially, I was at home with my family. Later, I met Lieutenant Gilardi and other officials at my office."

"What if anything did you do at the office?"

"I perfomed an autopsy on the body of a mature female whom I later learned to be a Ms. Sarah Hansen."

"How did you determine the identity of his person?"

"There were two means of positive identification," replied Olivero, "despite the fact that this corpse had suffered a prolonged exposure to sea water. First, I located her dentist, Dr. Norman Irwin. He came to my office with the dental charts of Sarah Hansen, and by comparing these to the teeth of the victim, which were in good condition, Dr. Irwin was able to establish his patient's identity. He did this by comparing fillings, a set of caps, and a fixed bridge, all of which were his work, as well as wax impressions of the teeth themselves which he had made when treating Ms. Hansen. I examined these comparisons personally, and observed that the match was complete and total.

"Second, I discovered in the course of the autopsy that this victim. . . ."

"I object," said Everard, on his feet. "For the second time the Commonwealth's expert has referred to this corpse as a 'victim.' Whether she was a victim of anything or anyone is for the jury, not for the doctor, to decide."

Somerville did not invite Durham to respond. "I think, Doctor," he said, "that counsel has a point. Would you please avoid a repetition of the use of the term 'victim' for the present time at least."

"Very well, Your Honor," said Olivero, a bit ruffled. He thought about pointing out that the word "victim" applied to accidental deaths as well as those which were

inflicted intentionally but decided not to give Everard
the satisfaction of that concession.

"As I was saying," he went on, "in the course of the
autopsy I found a stainless steel pin in the right femur—that's the large bone in the thigh. A check with
Ms. Hansen's personal physician led me to the records
of the Massachusetts General Hospital, which disclosed
that in 1969 she had undergone surgery for a fracture
of the right femur suffered in a skiing accident in North
Conway, New Hampshire. I have those records with
me," he said, tapping his briefcase.

"To be doubly sure, I contacted Dr. Herman Calvin,
the surgeon who performed the operation. He positively
identified the steel pin."

At this point, Judge Somerville called counsel to the
bench. "You may if you wish," he told Everard, "take
the witness on *voire dire* on the question of identity.
Noticing as I have that you did not object to the hearsay
of this witness with respect to the dentist and the surgeon,
and what he says they told him, it occurs to me that perhaps the defense does not intend to dispute the issue of
the identity of the corpse?"

"Quite so, Your Honor," nodded Everard, "and precisely stated. While we do not stipulate or concede that
this body is that of Sarah Hansen, we will not dispute
the fact or present argument to the jury that the issue is
in doubt."

"Very well," said Somerville. "In view of that, Mr.
Durham, why don't you move on to some of the more
vibrant issues affected by this witness's testimony?"

Durham agreed, with mild disappointment. He had
hoped that the defense would challenge the question of
identification since he was certain that he could bury
them on that issue. His respect for Everard's tactical
judgment was, he thought, continuing.

"Now, Doctor," said Durham, "could you describe
for us briefly the autopsy you performed?"

"Yes," said Olivero, producing some notes from his

briefcase, together with a brown envelope. "First, I observed the exterior condition of the body after the remnants of clothing were removed. It had obviously been immersed in water for an extended period of time and in many respects was badly deteriorated. I made a standard 'Y' incision and opened the chest cavity," he said turning to the jury and drawing a large "Y" on his own chest. "I examined the body organs—heart, liver, spleen, kidneys, lungs, and so on, and found nothing remarkable.

"I then made the incisions necessary to conduct a complete examination of the skeletal structure of the body," he said. "Again," he went on, speaking more slowly now, "I found nothing remarkable—with one prominent exception."

"What was that, Doctor?" asked Durham, feigning surprise.

"At the base of the skull, in the area where we all have two bony protuberances," he said, "there was a substantial bone fracture."

"Would a fracture of the severity of the one you discovered on the skull of Ms. Hansen," asked Durham, "be a competent producing cause of death?"

"It would," said Olivero.

"Did the fracture or the surrounding tissue enable you to form an opinion, with reasonable medical certainty, as to the cause of the injury?"

"Yes," said Olivero. "What remained of the tissue adjacent to the wound indicated a stellate, or ragged, condition. That coupled with the severity of the damage to the skull itself caused me to conclude that the head had been struck forcefully with a solid object."

"And can you, Doctor—again with reasonable medical certainty—offer us any opinion as to what caused the death of Sarah Hansen?" Durham was on pins and needles as to precisely how, and in what manner, Olivero would respond.

"I can," he replied. "Based on the history—that is,

when last seen, Ms. Hansen was in good health—and on the physical evidence made available through examination, it is my opinion that she met her death as a result of a violent blow to the back of the head by some blunt instrument."

"Thank you, Doctor," said Durham, affecting a grim and troubled look. "Now, I believe that you have some photographs with you?"

"Yes," said Olivero, picking up the brown envelope.

"And were these photographs taken during the autopsy?"

"Before, during, and after," said Olivero.

"And do they fairly represent the scenes which they purport to depict?"

"Yes," said Olivero. "I took them myself as I do in almost every such case."

"I will offer these, Your Honor," said Durham.

"Have they been shown to the defense?" asked Somerville.

"The defense has copies which were furnished yesterday," said Durham.

"What is your position with respect to these exhibits, Mr. Everard?"

"If it please the court," said Everard, rising, "we do not challenge the authenticity of these photographs. Their relevancy is another matter. The sea, despite her splendor and grace, is a cruel coffin. I should think that quite a number of these exhibits are sufficiently distasteful as to offend the jury without shedding any light on the issues before us. A few—notably those depicting the fractured area of the skull and the surrounding wound—are not objectionable and are decidedly relevant. I respectfully suggest that the court review these photographs, and admit into evidence those which the court feels might be helpful."

Somerville stared at Everard for a moment. He had been neatly boxed. If he sent the gruesome photos to the jury and they resented being required to look at

them, he would get the blame. On the other hand, by
not actually objecting, the defense had indicated a lack
of concern about the consequences of losing the point.

"Very well," he said, as the clerk handed him the
brown envelope. "The court will be in recess for ten minutes."

During the recess, Kilrayne stood in the hall outside
the courtroom, smoking a cigarette and talking with Everard.

"What do you think of Olivero, Tony?"

Everard stroked his jaw. "He's smooth, experienced,
and not far off the mark except as to the cause of death.
There he's reaching unconscionably, I think. Seems as
though our distinguished opponents have exerted a bit
of influence on the old boy, I should say."

"A bit," said Mike in disgust. "Gilardi and Durham
probably held a gun to his head."

"Even so," said Everard, "his direct examination, assuming that it's nearly concluded, was startlingly brief,
didn't you think?"

"It was, which is surprising. That's usually not Durham's style."

They were about to go back into the courtroom when
Stacy Barton came running up the stairs, flushed with
excitement. "Tony," she said in a loud whisper. "I just
talked to Daniel. He says to drag the cross a bit if you
can. He's on his way in with what he describes as a
'super goodie,' and he thinks you'll want it to use on the
doctor."

"Did he say what it's about?" asked Kilrayne.

"No, just that he got a call this morning from a lawyer in Hamilton. He's never met you but wants to help.
Told Daniel to come to his office to look at what he
described as a document that ought to be interesting,
perhaps fascinating, to the defense."

When the jury was seated and Judge Somerville had
resumed the bench, he addressed the laywers.

"Gentlemen," he said, "at the request of Mr. Everard I have considered all of these photographs. For the moment, I am going to receive into evidence only those depicting the relevant area of the skull. In the course of further examination of this witness, I may be persuaded to admit others, depending on the nature of the questions which I permit him to answer. Meanwhile, I am ordering the balance—those that will *not* be received—sealed until further order of the court. It would be no service to this or any other community to foist them on the public through the news media, or in any fashion. You may proceed, Mr. Durham."

"Thank you, Your Honor. I have no more questions of the witness. I ask that the photographs admitted be passed among the jurors."

"Yes, that may be done. Mr. Everard, I shall ask that you hold your cross-examination until the photos have been circulated." A few minutes passed in awkward silence until the last photograph had been passed from juror number fourteen back to the clerk.

"Thank you Mr. Everard," said the judge. "You may cross-examine."

"Doctor Olivero," said Everard sharply, his voice like the crack of a whip, "I notice in your direct examination you made no mention of the possibility that the victim drowned. Did you ever consider drowning as a cause of death?"

"Yes, I did," said Olivero. "I saw no evidence of drowning."

"Indeed. Perhaps we should explore that a bit. But first, Doctor, may I inquire whether or not you are familiar with a text called *Gray's Anatomy*?"

"Yes, of course."

Stacy Barton, rather conspicuously, placed a copy of *Gray's Anatomy* on the counsel table in full view of Dr. Olivero, the binding facing in his direction.

"Are you familiar as well with a book called *Legal*

Medicine—Pathology and Toxicology by Gonzales, Vance, Helpern, and Umberger?"

"Yes."

"How about *Gradwohl's Legal Medicine*, as edited by my countryman, Sir Francis Camps?"

"Yes, that too."

"And finally, Doctor, have you read the three-volume treatise titled *Forensic Medicine* by Tedeschi, Eckert, and Tedeschi?"

"I have heard of that work," replied Olivero guardedly, having noticed that Ms. Barton had placed all of the described books on the defense table. "I have not reviewed it as yet. I believe it is rather recent."

"Somewhat, perhaps," said Everard, as if this were no excuse to be ignorant of a monumental effort in the doctor's chosen field. "Now then, it is true is it not that where drowning in sea water is suspected, it is rather standard practice to perform a Gettler test on the heart?"

"Yes, that's true."

"And in performing such a test, one seeks to measure the amount of chloride found on the left side of the heart as compared to the amount found on the right side, is that so?"

"It is," said Olivero.

"You were unable to perform a Gettler test because the heart was so badly deteriorated. True?"

"That's true."

"What about the epiglottis, Doctor? What was its condition?"

"It was also deteriorated beyond the point where any observations of a meaningful sort could be made."

"And when you removed the calvarium, or top of the skull, did you examine the membrane which surrounds the brain called the dura mater? Specifically, did you examine it for any evidence of staining?"

"Yes. From its condition, I could not tell whether it had been stained or not because of the nearly total hemolysis, or breakdown of the red blood cells. The brain, you see, was of a soupy consistency and did not tell us much."

"But if there had been no staining of the dura mater, that would have been at least one indication that the victim had drowned?"

"It could have been, yes."

"Thank you, sir. Now, would you tell the jury what is meant by the 'petrous portion of the temporal bone'?"

"Yes. The temporal bone is found on the roof of the auditory canal, in the middle ear."

"You examined it, did you not?"

"I did."

"And you examined it a second time in the presence of Dr. Kiernan, a pathologist from Pennsylvania?"

"Yes."

"And you agreed that his observation of a certain amount of blood staining being present in the temporal bone was correct, did you not?"

"Well, I looked and. . . ."

"No, no, Doctor, please answer my question. Did you agree that staining could be seen?"

"I probably did."

"And according to your knowledge of many of the texts on forensic pathology that we have here in court, except the Tedeschi volumes which you haven't read, experience has shown that staining of the temporal bone is a classic symptom of death by drowning, is that not true?"

"Yes, they do say that, I guess."

"And in your own long experience, Doctor, which you described for us earlier, you have found that to be the case, have you not?"

Olivero sighed. "It is often present."

"Thank you. It would appear, then, that of four tests usually made in cases of suspected drowning, three were not possible to conduct and the fourth was positive. Is that a fair statement?"

Olivero paused. Everard reached for one of the books on the defense table, and began to open it. Olivero coughed. "Reasonably fair," he said.

"In view of the fact that our jurors are by definition reasonable men and women," Everard said pleasantly, "I will accept your answer and turn to a different area of inquiry. Doctor, please tell the jury what a contrecoup injury of the brain is."

"It is a term used to describe an injury where force applied to the skull causes damage away from the point of impact, at the opposite side of the brain."

"And that is because the brain literally bounces from the initial impact against the other side of the skull, is it not?"

"Essentially, yes. . . ."

"And with respect to the corpse you examined, the brain was—as you put it—so 'soupy' that it was not possible to determine with any certainty whether the opposite injury phenomenon was present, correct?"

"Yes, that's so."

"And a contrecoup injury, where one is evident, is an indication that the head has fallen against a hard object, rather than having been struck?"

"Generally, yes."

"So, under the circumstances, one could not with any certainty eliminate a fall as the cause of the skull fracture, could one?"

"It would be difficult to eliminate, yes."

"Yes, of course. And now, Doctor, it is a fact that in evaluating an injury such as you have described, and your photographs have shown, one of the first things the forensic pathologist seeks to learn is whether the injury is ante-mortem or post-mortem, is that so?"

"One of the things, yes."

"And this determination is normally made by discovering the presence or absence of hemorrhage in the tissue surrounding the injury, true?"

"That's the primary indicator."

"And in this case, the skin and tissue had been awash in the sea for such an extended period that any hemorrhage which *might* have been present could not be observed, is that right?"

"Yes, the evidence of hemorrhage was long gone."

"What evidence, Doctor?" Everard pounced like a leopard. "What evidence is it that disappeared?"

"Well, I was assuming. . . ."

"Please don't assume, Doctor Olivero. For all you know, there never was any hemorrhage present in the first place. Is that not true?"

Olivero flushed. "There is no way of telling."

"So if Ms. Hansen did drown, as we've agreed she might have, this injury to the skull could well have occurred after she was dead, could it not?"

"It could have."

The door at the rear of the courtroom opened, and Daniel Shaw entered, walking casually down the aisle toward the bar enclosure. He gave a slight nod toward Everard.

"Your Honor, might I have a moment to confer with my colleague?"

"Certainly," said Somerville, who had been enjoying the cross-examination immensely. "Take your time." There was a hurried and hushed conference at the defense table.

"I thank the court, and I am ready to resume," said Everard. "Doctor Olivero, I want to suggest a proposition to you. I suggest that whenever a body has been immersed in water for sixty days or more, and no matter what injuries may be found, short of severance of the head, it is medically and pathologically impossible to eliminate drowning as the primary cause of death. Do you agree with that?"

Olivero cocked his head suspiciously. "No. I cannot agree with that statement."

"I see. Would your position change if I told you that

the author of that remark was an experienced pathologist?"

"Not necessarily," growled Olivero. "It is not uncom-
mon that my various colleagues have differing opinions
in certain areas, in fact. . . ."

"Excuse me, Doctor," Everard interrupted. "Would
your position change if I told you that the experienced
pathologist who took that stance was Dr. Sebastian
Olivero, testifying in the Supreme Court of Queens
County, New York, Fourth Trial Part, in a case entitled
Thomas Bonin vs. *The Paragon Insurance Company*,
on December fifth, 1969, at page two-oh-four, according to the transcript of evidence which I am holding?"
As he spoke, Everard held out his hand and Shaw
placed a thick white envelope in it.

Olivero looked for all the world like a child who had
been caught with his hand in a cookie jar.

"I, ah, I may have given such testimony, I do seem to
remember such a case. . . ."

"It was a case where drowning as the cause of death
was a primary issue, in which you testified as an expert
for the plaintiff, Doctor. Is that your memory of the
event?"

"Ah, yes, I would think so."

"You took that position firmly and unequivocally
while on your oath to the Supreme Court of the State of
New York?"

"I believe I did."

"And it is true, is it not, that not one single case you
have handled in the past nine years would justify your
changing that rather firm opinion?"

"I cannot think of one at the moment."

"Thank you, Doctor Olivero," said Everard with a
sigh. "I do not believe, Your Honor," he said to Somerville, "that it will be necessary to further cross-examine
this witness."

34

LADY AND GENTLEMAN BELOW

Monday, September 18

With the finding of the body, the trial went national. *Time, Newsweek,* and the wire services were now reporting it as the trial of the year. And in the evening television news there was usually a shot of the scramble of reporters trying to buttonhole the participants and extract something other than a "No comment" from them. Some days all the viewers got was the TV reporter in front of the courthouse, but the people who hated lawyers watched, wives watched the tube because a philanderer's lust had caught up with him, and a lot of lawyers hurried home earlier than usual to catch the evening news perhaps because they secretly identified themselves with Michael Kilrayne's fate.

After Dr. Olivero had been excused, Durham asked Judge Somerville to recess for the day on the grounds that his next witness, an oceanographer, had a flight delay.

Somerville seemed a bit annoyed. "Can't the Commonwealth substitute another witness in the meantime?" he asked.

"Dr. Wurtzman is my last witness, Your Honor," said Durham, apologizing most profusely.

Somerville assented to the recess on Durham's assur-

ance that the evidence for the Commonwealth would
end the next day.

As the participants left the courthouse, Stacy managed to catch up with Shaw and walked alongside of
him.

"Daniel," she said, "Tony just said that since I've
done most of the research, I should examine this expert
tomorrow. Mike doesn't mind. What do you think?"

Shaw looked at her eager face. "Capital idea," he
said, "especially since I'm its originator."

"You suggested it to Tony?"

"I'm the guilty party."

Stacy's impulse was to hug him with joy, but there
were all those people milling around. And so she said,
"I did work at Woods Hole as a research assistant one
summer. Still, I don't want to do anything to screw up
Mike's case. . . ."

"Don't worry, my love, you'll do just fine."

"I hope so. Listen, Dan, I had an idea this morning.
This Dr. Wurtzman, whoever he is—and he isn't much,
from what I can find out—is without doubt going to
claim that the body was killed close to shore somewhere
south of the state line and drifted north for more than
three months before it was discovered last Friday. I'm
willing to bet he's done damned little on-site investigation."

"Perhaps so."

"Well, whether he has or hasn't, I had better know
the area—say from Cape Ann north—pretty damned
well. I can get a lot of it from the marine charts, but I
thought a cruise along the coast might be helpful.
There's a couple who keep a Grand Banks 48 at the
Eastern Point Yacht Club in Gloucester. I thought I
might shoot up there this afternoon and borrow it—I
have its use while they're in Europe this month. Want to
go along? I'd just like to browse a bit."

"That's a lot of boat for one lady to handle," said

Shaw, teasing. "As a Lieutenant Commander in the world's best Navy, I think I'd better come along and afford you a little guidance in matters marine."

"That's exactly what I had in mind," said Stacy. "I'll meet you there in forty minutes, at the dock. It's easy to find, and they have a launch service."

"I'll be there," said Shaw, "with bells on."

When Stacy arrived at the dock, there was no sign of Shaw. "Oh," said the dock boy, "I took him out and opened her up. He said it would be all right." He did not mention the twenty-dollar bill nestled snugly in his watch pocket.

Stacy handed a bag of groceries and a small totebag to Shaw as the launch pulled alongside the *Empress*. She was surprised to find the generator humming and both diesels rumbling quietly.

"Jesus, Daniel," she said, a little annoyed. "You could have really screwed me up. If you don't start these things the right way, you can damage them."

"Do tell," said Shaw, with a wicked grin. "Matter of fact, perhaps I should have told you, I've had an identical twin to this beast parked in San Francisco Bay for three years now. Great boat."

Stacy smiled sheepishly. "I should have known. Here, since you're so smart, you can put these things in the fridge. I assume you turned it on?"

"Right after I turned on the generator," said Shaw. "How else was I to keep the champagne cold?"

Shaw cast off the mooring line, and Stacy, from the control station on the flybridge, turned the ship in its own length by throwing one engine in forward, the other in reverse. When they had rounded the breakwater, she synchronized the twin diesels at eighteen hundred revolutions per minute, set the autopilot, and told Shaw to watch out for lobster pots while she went below. Five minutes later she was back in a skimpy pale blue bikini.

"On a gorgeous day like this," she said, "it would be

criminal not to get a little afternoon sun. Where are your trunks, Daniel?"

Shaw responded by slipping off his trousers to reveal a pair of white swim trunks. "Ah yes, a little sun," he said, removing his shirt, shoes, and socks. "Now captain, lead on," he grinned.

Stacy smiled and changed heading to take them just outside Thatcher's Island. The *Empress* plodded along at her hull speed of nine knots, the diesels barely audible on the flying bridge. As they were passing Dry Salvages—a small group of rough islets off of Rockport Harbor—she pointed out that these were the subject of T. S. Eliot's "Quartet."

"I read Eliot in college," mused Shaw. "Had to, like every English major. I couldn't turn on to him too well, though. Too dried-up, despairing, depressed. Give me a Yeats or a D. H. Lawrence—those were lusty, hopeful, vibrant men."

"Is that what you are, Daniel? Lusty, hopeful, and vibrant?"

Shaw smiled sheepishly. "I don't know. I guess I try to be, for whatever that's worth. You might be a better judge than I as to whether I'm successful in that aim."

Stacy stared out over the bow at the gentle waves shimmering in the sunlight. "Oh, I think you are, Daniel," she said. "Good lord, every time you walk into the courtroom that little Marcia Kittredge goes all a-flutter. Women can read the signs."

"Wonderful. So I turn on Marcia Kittredge. Seducing jurors in the middle of a trial is probably not a smart idea, especially for counsel who is already facing some ominous punishment from a good but damned unhappy judge."

"Now that you mention it," said Stacy, as casually as she was able, "I had a little conversation with the source of your grief last Friday night while Gilardi and friends were fetching bodies out of the water."

"Pat? Why were you with her?"

"She called me at my apartment, about nine o'clock. I didn't have the heart to hang up on her. I invited her up for a cup of tea. It turned out to be several brandies, but she needed them."

"Tell me about it," he said, the tautness of annoyance in his voice.

"Well," she said, "Pat sort of poured it out to me. Basically, she said that after she had been assigned to do a profile on you, her editor—Tom something or other—called her in and informed her that an old friend of his was the editor of the Boston *Chronicle*. He explained that this man—Marty Hanlon, of course—had a couple of crack reporters assigned to the case, but that both were pretty friendly with Mike—which is true, by the way.

"Anyway, her editor said that she was to keep her eye on things and report to Marty Hanlon anything adverse to Mike that wasn't hitting the *Chronicle*. Marty thought his boys might be too subjective.

"She didn't want to do it. Tom said he would assign someone else to the job. She wanted to meet you and get to know you, she admits, so she agreed.

"Then you hit her with the conditions of the interview: no leaks. She decided to ignore her marching orders and to keep her mouth shut. After all, her boss would have no way of knowing what she might have heard.

"By the time you had damned near killed her in that Lear Jet of yours, she was pretty well hooked. She considered abandoning the article for fear that she was becoming as subjective about the case as Hanlon thought Bill and Charley were. But she decided to continue, partly because she thought she could still do a decent job, and partly because she didn't want to leave you.

"A week ago tonight, she called her editor in California while the two of you were having dinner. It was a routine call. She asked him what a 'directed verdict' would do to the case. He asked her why she wanted to know. Without thinking, she told him that you had heard Judge Somerville threaten the prosecution with a directed verdict—which you hadn't, but I know Mike told you about it—and that he used the words '. . . notwithstanding the Scott case.' She never talked to Martin Hanlon in her life and didn't dream that this information would be what he wanted anyway. Her editor, however, must have phoned Hanlon. At least that's her story. Maybe you know differently."

Shaw rubbed the bridge of his nose with his thumb and forefinger. Severenson's words—"I spoke with him there yesterday . . ."—rang in his inner ear. "No," he said, "it checks out."

"Perhaps," said Stacy, "you have ignored one of the principles of our profession. Perhaps you acted on emotion and instinct before carefully learning the facts."

"Perhaps," said Daniel, "you are right."

"For what it's worth," said Stacy, "I bet that she was telling me the truth."

"She probably was," said Shaw sadly.

"I'm glad you agree," Stacy said briskly. "And now, I am going to entrust this gorgeous yacht to you while I cook us a couple of sumptuous steaks and a salad with my own internationally renowned dressing. Well, it would be if we were in international waters, because you're going to love it. Keep a sharp eye, mate, and give me your glass. I'll hand you up a fresh drink. Then we can watch the currents until dinnertime, or isn't that what this expedition was organized for?"

Stacy had made a lot of notes before they got around to dinner, which was delicious as only salt air can make food taste. Stacy cleaned up the dishes quickly, and they returned to the flybridge.

"Get what you came for?" Daniel asked.

"Half," she said.

The sun was beginning to sink into the horizon when Stacy flipped off the autopilot, reversed the course, and engaged it again. They were seated together, on the starboard side of the flybridge settee, when the bases of the clouds to the west began to turn a brilliant vermillion, and the sea beneath them began to follow suit. It was a scene that would have driven the most stoic monk to fits of romance. Its effect was not lost on Shaw, who slipped his arm around Stacy's shoulders.

"Daniel," she said, "there's one other thing I ought to tell you. I don't have any hangups. I love life, and every day that I live it. I used to feel fortunate that I worked for the very best. Working for three very best is pure ecstasy. As I remember," she said, sliding her hand slowly across his chest, "there was talk of a rain check at your hotel suite last July."

"I remember," said Shaw. "Shall we drop the hook and go below?"

"No need," said Stacy softly. "This radar has a collision avoidance interconnect. Any target comes within two miles, an alarm goes off. Can you move quickly in an emergency?"

"You don't know the half of it," said Shaw.

"I don't want to know the half of it," said Stacy, rising and taking him by the hand. "I want to know the whole of it."

Two hours later, she jostled Shaw on the queen-sized bed in the master stateroom. "Daniel," she said quietly into his ear.

"Huh?" Shaw unceremoniously struggled to emerge from his reverie.

"Daniel, I have to work tomorrow. Big cross-examination, remember?"

"Right," said Shaw, sitting upright and rubbing his eyes. "That's true."

"Perhaps, then, you should get up and drive this boat back to Gloucester Harbor while I catch another forty."

"Perhaps," said Shaw appreciatively, nuzzling her neck, "I should do just that."

35

ARE YOU VERY SURE?
Tuesday, September 19

The witness on the stand, peering with difficulty through his thick glasses, gave his name as Dr. Weldon Wurtzman, and his occupation as that of a physical oceanographer.

He had been educated, he said, at the University of North Carolina, where he received his Ph.D. in oceanography. He had served on the staff of the Skidaway Institute at Sapelo Island, Georgia, involved in numerous research projects studying ocean currents. He had never testified in court before and was an unemployed "consultant" at the moment.

"Now Doctor," said Durham, "since being retained by the Commonwealth in this case last weekend, have you made certain studies of the local currents."

"Oh yes," said Wurtzman agreeably, "yes indeed."

"Has there been pointed out to you the place on the coast where the body was found?"

"Yes. Very close to the northern state line and a few feet offshore."

"Have you made a study of the weather patterns that have prevailed in this general area from June seventh until last Friday?"

"I have. I spent Sunday night and all of Monday here in Massachusetts. Monday night I returned to my home in North Carolina to consult some texts, and Tuesday

morning I started back here, but our airport was fogged
in and the airliner overflew. I arrived late last night."

"Have you reviewed the facts in this case with other
experts in the field?"

"I have."

"As a result of your education, your experience, and
the study you have made of the circumstances surrounding the disappearance and reappearance of Sarah
Hansen, are you able to come to any conclusion as to
where that body first contacted the sea and how it pro-
gressed to its point of discovery?"

"Yes, I am."

"Do you have an opinion, based on reasonable scientific certainty, as to where Ms. Hansen was killed?"

The doctor was nodding his head in the affirmative
when Stacy shot to her feet. "Objection," she said.

"Yes," said Somerville. "Mr. Durham, this witness
could not possibly know whether Ms. Hansen was killed
or whether she died by accident. That will be for the
jury. Miss Barton, do you wish to take the witness on
voir dire?"

"Please, Your Honor."

"Very well." He turned to the jury. "Ladies and gentlemen, before an expert is permitted to offer an opinion, the opposite side is entitled to cross-examine him
with respect to his qualifications, and the basis for that
opinion. Until this hurdle is past, there is no evidence
before you. Sometimes this is done in the absence of the
jury. In this instance, I shall permit you to remain, to
save Ms. Barton the need to repeat her questions a second time for your benefit."

"Dr. Wurtzman," said Stacy, "have you ever before
this case done any oceanographic work in the Gulf of
Maine?"

"Ah, no, I have not."

"Is it fair to say that two of the best oceanographic
institutes in the world are located in the Gulf of
Maine?"

Wurtzman hesitated.

"I am referring, Doctor," Stacy went on, "to the Woods Hole Oceanographic Institute in Massachusetts and to the Bigelow Laboratory for Ocean Sciences at McKown Point in West Boothbay Harbor, Maine. Surely you are familiar with them?"

"Oh, yes, of course."

"If experts from one of those institutions were making a study on the southeastern coast of the United States, you would expect them to contact people from Skidaway in order to have the benefit of local knowledge of the waters, would you not."

"Yes, I guess they would."

"Did you, consistent with that practice, contact either of the two institutions I have described?"

"Ah, I talked to some people at Woods Hole. I didn't contact the other one."

"Did you speak with Mr. Alfred C. Redfield at Woods Hole?"

"He was one of the gentlemen, yes."

"Who was the other one?"

"A Mr. Miller, Arthur R. Miller, I believe."

"Did they tell you that I had consulted with both of them on Monday?"

Wurtzman looked troubled. "No, they didn't mention that."

"I see. Did both of them not tell you, based on their long experience with the shores and currents in the Gulf of Maine, that due to the length of time the body was in the water it would be impossible to even guess where it had started out?"

"Well, they didn't use those words."

"But did they not both express that opinion, in substance?"

Wurtzman looked grim. "Something like that."

"And that is the sum total of the local knowledge that is embraced in your opinion?"

"They're the only ones I talked to, if that's what you mean."

"Thank you. Now, Doctor, the currents on the surface of the ocean are likely to be quite different than deeper currents because of the effect of the wind, is that true?"

"Generally yes."

"During the three months and seven days that the body was in the water, how many days was it near the surface and how many days was it in the deeper currents?"

"Well, really, Ms. er. . . ."

"Barton."

"Ah, yes, Barton, thank you, really, I have no way of knowing that."

"Then you can't be sure on how many of those days the body was affected by the surface wind, can you?"

"Not exactly."

"From your study of the weather reports, you learned that in the spring and summer in New England weather systems move very rapidly out into the Gulf of Maine from the west, northwest, and southwest, did you not?"

"Yes."

"And that as these systems move, the surface wind is likely to change direction and velocity as much as four times in a single twenty-four hour period?"

"Ah, yes, on some days that happens."

"Very well. I take it that somewhere in your study you have developed a theory that the body entered the water somewhere to the south of where it was found and drifted in a northerly current until it was discovered?"

Wurtzman brightened. "Yes, that's what happened, you've got it right."

"Thank you, Doctor, but the question now is whether you have got it right. Did you find evidence that the coastal current is generally one which moves to the north?"

"That was my finding."

"But if the body spent many days on the surface—*where it was found*, Doctor—then its movement would have been governed by the surface winds, not by the prevailing current. True?"

"Ah, that could be so, yes."

"Doctor, ignoring the effect of the wind for a moment, are you assuming that if a current were moving to the north the body would move along with it?"

"Yes, I am."

"Then you have not taken into account the effect known as the Ekman Spiral, have you?"

"Well, I think . . . that is. . . ."

"Doctor, the Ekman Spiral is a phenomenon based on coriolis force, is it not?"

"Basically, ah, that is correct."

"And in the northern hemisphere, that would tend to deflect water and anything in it *to the right* of the direction of the current, is that true?"

"Ah, yes, there can be that effect."

"So, if the current were in fact one of pure northerly movement, it would have pushed the body out to sea."

Wurtzman searched for an answer. Stacy felt a light touch at her elbow. She glanced down at the counsel table and saw a note which Kilrayne had written in large block letters: "YOU GOT HIM—GO FOR THE JUGULAR!"

"Doctor," she said patiently, as if talking to a small boy, "based on all that you have just told us, is it not true that any deduction as to where this body came from must be defined in *possibilities* rather than scientific certainty?"

"Well," said Wurtzman, "that may be correct—but," he went on, his voice becoming shrill, "they are distinct possibilities, madam, I wanted to make that very clear. What we have here is a possibility that is *very distinct!*"

Durham covered his brow with his hand, and Somerville sighed, nodding as Stacy glanced up at him.

"Dr. Wurtzman," the judge said, "it is unfortunate that no one has explained to you that we in the law cannot countenance possibilities in any form in our evidence. They are simply not admissible. You are excused. Ladies and gentlemen, I am going to strike this witness's testimony as inadmissible, and you are to totally disregard it. We will take a ten minute recess."

Durham leaned over to Barrett. "Walter, I don't know where you found this clown," he said, jerking his thumb at Wurtzman, who was still on the witness stand trying to understand what had gone wrong, "but I suggest that you tell him to go jump in his ocean and come back in three months to tell us where he's been." He got up and strode out of the courtroom, flushed with anger.

"Really, Stacy," said Everard with a grin, "I don't know how Michael or Daniel or I can teach you much about the art of cross-examination if you insist on starting at the very top. I mean, knocking the witness clean out of the box is the very last lesson, not the first."

"I'm awfully sorry," she smiled. "I'll try to do better next time."

36

TO BE OR NOT TO BE
Tuesday, September 19

Everard, Shaw, and Stacy Barton were sitting at the long rosewood table in the conference room in Kilrayne's offices when he walked in, shaking the drizzle off his raincoat before draping it across one of the empty chairs.

"What's the general thought here?" Kilrayne asked, sitting down at the head of the table. "Have they got enough?"

Shaw shook his head. "No way," he said. "They haven't got two sticks to rub together. Even finding the body doesn't give them a case, after what Tony did with Dr. Olivero. What they have is, a woman died and you, if they believe Frankie LaPere, talked about having some woman killed. Nothing to say it's even the same woman."

"Tony?"

"I quite agree with Daniel," said Everard. "A British justice would make short work of this case, I'm sure."

Stacy nodded in agreement.

"We seem to be in accord," said Kilrayne slowly, looking from one to the other, "which fortifies a suggestion I have come to. How would you all feel if we put up no defense?"

Stacy's jaw dropped, Everard's eyes narrowed, and Shaw was stunned. "Christ, Mike, I know they're awfully weak, but do you think the jury will forgive you for not testifying?"

"That's a risk I—and I alone—am prepared to take. I don't underestimate that risk. But I have some very definite reasons for reaching this most difficult decision. Would you care to hear them?"

All three nodded emphatically.

"Very well. I do not think it will be helpful for me to be cross-examined about my relationship with Ms. Hansen, even though nothing I could say will disclose any motive—any possible motive—which would prompt me to want her killed. Still, I have visited her at her home, and some of the women on the jury might resent a married man doing that. That's a minor reason.

"The principal factor in my decision is a long experience with what I consider to be the cowardice of our appellate courts, and sometimes our trial judges in deciding motions for a new trial.

"Over and over again, where the prosecution's evidence was patently insufficient, and where the defendant absolutely and unequivocally testified as to his innocence, judges have said: 'The fact that the jury saw and heard the defendant, *and chose to disbelieve him*, coupled with the evidence adduced by the prosecution is sufficient to allow the conviction to stand.' In other words the defendant cuts his own throat by laying his credibility on the line, even if he is totally unscathed on cross. It's a damnable tactic, and judges who do it ought to be impeached, but it happens all the time. I don't propose to let it happen to me."

"You've got me," said Shaw. "This is strange ground as far as I'm concerned. Although come to think of it I have occasionally seen something like that in civil appeals."

"Extraordinary," mused Everard. "Our judges don't use crutches of that sort—at least not that blatantly. I often think," he sighed, "that we may have been better off back in the days when the accused was not permitted to give evidence. There was nothing to argue about then."

"Mike is right," said Stacy. "Our Supreme Judicial Court has pulled that more than once in appeals that I have handled for Mike. The old bootstraps trick, we call it. And Mike is not the most popular guy in that court. If he should be convicted, the appeal goes straight to them, without going through the Court of Appeals, because the charge is murder."

"It's your neck, my friend," said Everard. "It's a daring decision, but it is of course yours to make. Let's hope it's the right one." He did not sound terribly convinced.

"Okay," said Kilrayne. "I will leave you denizens of the bar to work out a thumping argument for a directed verdict. I will see you in court in the morning." He picked up his raincoat and left.

"I wonder," said Shaw, "if he is to any degree trying to protect his wife Lucy from the publicity. He certainly has kept her out of the picture throughout this thing. Christ, Tony and I haven't even been introduced to her, and she hasn't been near the courtroom. I hope the jury doesn't think she's staying away because she knows or believes that he's guilty."

Stacy stared at a small turquoise ring on her right hand. "Perhaps I should have told you guys," she said, "that Lucy Kilrayne suffered a rather severe stroke seven years ago. She speaks with difficulty and would not remember meeting either of you for more than twenty-four hours. Mike won't let her near the court because some might think he was using her for sympathy. She doesn't think he's guilty. At times I doubt that she knows he's on trial."

"Shit," said Shaw, remonstrating with himself. "I'm sorry I said anything. Mike's sure got more than his share of crosses to carry on his back."

Everard shook his head sadly. "Amen," he said.

The following morning, when the jury had been seated, Somerville looked politely down at Everard. "You may make your opening statement, now," he said.

"That will not be necessary M'Lord—I'm sorry, Your Honor." A titter went through the courtroom, including the jury box. "The defense," said Everard, pausing for dramatic effect, "rests its case. We see no need to offer evidence."

Kilrayne glanced at the prosecution table. Durham, Barrett, and Gilardi were sitting in abject horror. Judge Somerville himself was taken aback. "The monkey," he thought to himself, "is on my back sooner than I expected."

"Very well," he said. "Ladies and gentlemen, I am going to excuse you for the day. I will have a number of legal matters to cover with counsel, and then I am going to adjourn for the day to permit counsel to devote their full attention to their final arguments, and to permit the court to put the finishing touches on its charge. We will convene at nine o'clock in the morning, and I shall have the case in your hands sometime in the afternoon. Please remember the admonitions I have given you throughout this trial. You must withhold any judgment until I have authorized you to deliberate. Mr. Bailiff, please take the jury to the hotel at this time."

When the jury had filed out, and the press were streaking for telephones to report the shocking news, Walter Barrett was all over Durham in a frenzy. "We *have* to get that lighter in!" he insisted. "That's one of our best pieces of evidence."

"No, Walter, we can't. We didn't turn it over, remember? The lieutenant was sure Kilrayne would testify—talk to him about it."

Durham cast a bitter glance at Gilardi.

"We've got to try, at least!" said Walter.

"Walter," said a furious Durham, "take that goddam lighter and shove it up your ass!"

"Maybe they'll agree to let us reopen," said Walter,

in panicky desperation. He turned to Everard, who had heard the whole exchange. "Tony," he whined, "we seem to have forgotten a piece of evidence. I wonder if you'd consider. . . ."

"You have forgotten nothing," said Everard coldly. "You have *withheld* evidence to which we were entitled. I will oppose any motion on your part to have received the silver table lighter initialed 'M.K.' that you are concerned about. Should you persuade Judge Somerville to let you use it, I will produce immediately the gentlemen who bought it and gave it to Ms. Hansen. He has come forward willingly. Perhaps you should consider disposing of this evidence exactly as your distinguished colleague recommended."

Everard walked away, leaving Walter open-mouthed.

During the balance of the morning Somerville heard arguments from both sides on the question of a directed verdict of acquittal, and reserved judgment, promising a decision the following morning. He discussed with all counsel the instructions he was planning to give, and the ground rules for final argument. By eleven-thirty, court was in recess, with everyone's nerves beginning to tingle for the finale.

37

HANGING BACK
Wednesday, September 20

Ellen Somerville, dressed in a thin negligee, moved softly and smoothly around her kitchen as she fixed a margarita for her husband. She took it to his study where he was sitting in a large leather chair, his feet on an ottoman, staring blankly at the wall.

"You look troubled, my love," she said, as she handed him his drink. "Is it the case?"

Somerville sighed. "I'm afraid so," he said. "For the first time since I took the bench, I am very uncertain as to what my judgment should be on a very important question."

"The directed verdict?"

"Yes. I'm afraid so."

"What does your gut tell you to do? It's been pretty dependable in the past."

He smiled. "My gut, sweetheart, tells me to throw the thing out. They haven't even proved that she was murdered, as far as I'm concerned, much less that Kilrayne was involved."

"Then why don't you end it all tomorrow morning?"

Somerville tugged at his jaw. "I'm not sure that that would be the best disposition," he said. "One great problem with the justice system in this country is that when one is released from a criminal charge, friends and neighbors are prone to suspect that the defendant 'beat the rap.' But if a judge dismisses a case on any ground, it is generally thought that the defendant is the beneficiary of some technicality. In this case, the problem is compounded by Mike's being a member of the profession. I don't think the press will take kindly to a directed verdict, and I *know* I'd get reamed by the *Chronicle*."

"Your appointment is for life," said Ellen softly. "Screw the *Chronicle*."

"Perhaps you're right, my sweet. I'd better sleep on it."

"You do that," she said, stepping out of her negligee. "Later."

The following morning, the courtroom was literally vibrating with excitement as Somerville took the bench. When everyone was seated, he looked at Everard.

"Before we bring the jury in," he said, "it is my duty to rule upon the defendant's motion for a directed verdict in this case. I am going to deny the motion," he said evenly, "but without prejudice for the defense to renew it after verdict should the defense be so inclined." Everard felt a prickly feeling along his spine. Was the judge telling him something that offered a bit of insurance? He could not be sure.

"You may proceed to sum up for the defense, Mr. Everard."

38

THE SHOUTING
Thursday, September 21

Anthony Everard woke from a deep sleep in the early morning hours with an urgent desire to get to the bathroom to throw up or die. He, who hated to lose control of a case for a moment, felt as out of control of himself as a new sailor in his first tempest at sea.

Feverish, he got to the wash basin in time and, gripping its sides, could not return to his bed for nearly twenty minutes, upset within and afraid that this damned intestinal flu or whatever it was had robbed him of the essence of his professional life: the ability to stand up straight in front of judge and jury and do his best.

When he got to the courtroom, Shaw and Stacy both asked him if anything was wrong. There were uncustomary beads of sweat across his forehead.

"Sick to the stomach," he said. "Awfully sorry." The last remark was to Kilrayne.

"Will you be all right?" asked Stacy.

But the court was being called to order, the judge was taking his place, and in minutes Everard was being summoned to the lectern to deliver his summation.

Judge Somerville noticed how uncertain Everard's walk seemed. He couldn't imagine that the barrister would have taken more than a single brandy to fortify

himself for the occasion. Even that would have aston-
ished him. Then he noticed Everard's pallor. A greenish
cast had come over his face.

Everard turned toward the bench. "Your Honor," he
said, taking a deep breath.

"Would someone bring Mr. Everard a glass of water," said the judge.

Everard shook his head and started walking toward
the nearest door, which led to the Judge's chambers.
Suddenly, his hand shot out for support, missed, and he
crumpled to the floor, his chest heaving, his entire body
now covered in sweat.

"Mr. Bailiff," said the judge sharply, "Call the emergency room at the hospital and have them send a physician and ambulance at once!"

Turning to another bailiff, he said, "Take the jurors
to their rooms immediately. And clear the courtroom of
all but counsel, the defendant, and court personnel. Mr.
Shaw, if you feel that it is safe to move Mr. Everard, I
suggest you bring him to the couch in my chambers. We
will be in recess."

Shaw and Kilrayne lifted Everard up and slung each
of his arms behind their necks, and literally dragged
him into Somerville's chambers. He looked terrible.
Perspiration was popping out all over his face. When he
had been laid out on the couch, Shaw took his pulse. It
was weak and uneven.

In less than ten minutes the emergency vehicle arrived, with a squadron of white-jacketed doctors,
nurses, and attendants. Somerville and the others left
the room while Everard was given a preliminary examination.

After a short while, a doctor wearing horn-rimmed
glasses stepped out and walked up to Somerville, who
was standing, still in his robe.

"I'm Ralph Perkins, Your Honor. The gentleman
will be all right, but not today or tomorrow. I'm afraid
it's a bad case of the intestinal flu traveling around Bos-

ton, maybe worse than that. We need to get him to the hospital."

"Of course," said Somerville. "Do whatever you can for him. He is one very fine human being." Somerville rubbed his jaw. "As soon as Mr. Everard has been removed from my chambers, I will see counsel—including Mr. Kilrayne."

When they had gathered, fifteen minutes later, Somerville was staring out the window, his back to them. "It would seem," he said, slowly turning around, "that we are confronted with a very nasty situation. I have just spoken once again with Dr. Perkins after the ambulance left. I am satisfied that we have lost Mr. Everard for at least two or three days, perhaps longer. Dr. Perkins said that, depending on the toxin, a swift recovery might be possible, but he can't guarantee that. With that prognosis I can't in good conscience keep this jury locked up day after day."

He looked thoughtfully at Kilrayne. "Mr. Kilrayne, you are in essence the victim here. I see three possible choices. I can declare a mistrial, in which case you may have to suffer this entire ordeal a second time. I can permit you, or Mr. Shaw, or Miss Barton to sum up for the defense, and continue the trial. Or, I can reconsider Mr. Everard's motion for directed verdict, which was denied with leave to renew."

"We would object to the latter, Your Honor. As District Attorney, I feel that. . . ." Walter Barrett was stammering. Durham rolled his eyes toward the ceiling in exasperation.

"Be quiet, Mr. Barrett. You will be heard when I have finished addressing Mr. Kilrayne."

"I suppose, Your Honor," said Kilrayne grimly, "that I would be a fool not to say that I prefer alternative number three."

"I'm quite sure you would, and in your position I would feel the same way. Let me explain my view, and perhaps that will assist you in reaching a decision.

"I believe the final arguments of counsel to be a critical, if not *the* critical, point in a trial. It is the focus where counsel glue together all of the jumbled pieces which arise in the evidence, and test the coherence of what they have put in order against human logic and reasoning. Before deciding a question as weighty as the sufficiency of the evidence in this case, *I* should like the benefit of the detailed thinking of two excellent lawyers. I was very much looking forward to hearing Mr. Everard, as I gather many were. But I am not ignorant of the fact that there remain in this case two very experienced trial lawyers, and in Ms. Barton a third who is described as very competent by my colleagues who have watched her work.

"I would still like to have the benefit of a jury's thinking before I ultimately decide. I realize that you may be fearful that an adverse verdict would be very difficult for me to take away. I want to assure you that if I see my duty in that fashion, I will do it, despite predictable howls of outrage from the press and possibly the public. Finally, I believe that a jury verdict would best dispose of this matter. I'm going to suggest that the defense team confer privately for a short time, and then report back to me with your positions and arguments."

When Stacy, Shaw, and Kilrayne arrived in the attorneys' conference room, Kilrayne said, "Daniel, I'm inclined to go on with the show. What's your view?"

"I was looking forward to hearing Tony's summation," said Shaw.

"Of course," said Kilrayne. "So were we all. He can't. One alternative is for me to do it, but I don't want a fool for a client."

Stacy and Shaw managed a smile.

"Listen," Kilrayne said, "you went over Tony's outline with him last night, didn't you?"

"Yes," said Shaw. "I've gone over the argument in this case a dozen times or more."

"Well," said Kilrayne, "I'm ready to put my chips on your square."

"I'd consider it a privilege to sum up your defense."

"Then what are you waiting for, for Christ's sake?" said Kilrayne raising his voice.

"Mike," said Shaw, "I'm ready to blow Durham and his crew out of the water, as we say in the Navy."

"Then let's go get them," said Kilrayne, slapping Shaw on the back.

The jurors were sitting in their box, expectantly. The reporters, poised on the edge of their seats, were ready to streak for the courthouse telephones. What had happened to Everard? What was going on?

As Somerville took the bench, there was absolute silence. He smiled at the jury.

"Ladies and gentlemen," he said, "an hour and ten minutes has passed since we were suddenly forced to recess. I am pleased to report that while Mr. Everard cannot be with us for a few days, he will recover from the attack which felled him so suddenly this morning. This situation has created a serious—and in my experience unprecedented—situation. I was not happy at the prospect of keeping you sequestered for another few days in the hope that Mr. Everard would recover. On the other hand, I could not fairly ask Mr. Kilrayne to proceed without the services of his most skillful and delightful chief counsel.

"Fortunately for all of us, a second member of the defense team has stepped into the breach. Mr. Kilrayne has very kindly consented to permit Mr. Daniel Shaw, whom all of you met at the outset of this trial, to fulfill the responsibilities of Mr. Everard until he is well again.

"Having Mr. Shaw take over at this juncture would ordinarily be a horrendous transition. Based on his background, which is known to the court much better than it may be to you ladies and gentlemen, I am satisfied that he can well shoulder the duties suddenly imposed upon him. Nonetheless, the court expresses its gratitude, as well as yours, ladies and gentlemen, as I'm sure you would want to do, to Mr. Kilrayne for his willingness to accept the loss of his chief counsel so graciously, and in a spirit so considerate of the sacrifice you have made in serving in this case."

The smiling nods of the jurors told Kilrayne at once that he had made the right choice.

"Jesus," said Barrett under his breath to Durham, "he's practically telling this crowd that Kilrayne's a prince of a fellow. He's screwing us to the wall."

"Shut up," said Durham, "before *I* begin thinking he's a nice guy. The judge may be right. I'd have gone for the mistrial, rather than lose that Englishman."

When Daniel Shaw had positioned himself before the jury, a seasoned advocate could have described his visceral function in detail just by watching him. His systems were in high tune and high gear. His blood pressure was up just a touch, as was his heartbeat. His brain was the beneficiary of the increased flow of blood, and stood poised at the top of its potential, ready to swoop down as in a skier's rush over fast new white powder. There was a calm about him, a total comfort and control of his circumstances, that had the jury's attention before he ever opened his mouth.

"If it please Your Honor," he said in a measured cadence, glancing at the judge, "counsel, Mr. Foreman, and ladies and gentlemen of the jury. For the defense, this is the end of the trial. When I have finished, and must seat myself next to Mr. Kilrayne and my lovely colleague, we will be silenced as surely and completely as a man struck dumb. Mr. Durham will be given leave to retort to every word and thought that I utter, and I shall have no chance to offer rebuttal. Judge Somerville will instruct you in the law, and then you will discover—to your probable surprise and possible horror—

that all who have served you are through, and that you are on your own to find your way through, the tangled thicket of what we call 'evidence' to that elusive pinnacle of human ambition which we call 'truth.'

"Had I any choice in the matter, I would be sitting at counsel table listening to my senior colleague, Tony Everard, perform this most critical function. I cannot and do not hope to match the eloquence, the grace, and the skill which he could have brought to this moment. But that is not a plea for your sympathy. If I did not feel that I could discharge this high function in the manner which this case demands, I would not have agreed to venture forth at the eleventh hour.

"The fact is, I suggest to you any half-decent law student could argue this case and show it for what it really is: A shambles, a cruel joke, and a rank insult to due process."

Shaw paused, and let his gaze wander over the jury box with a slow and deliberate shift. He had boldly stuck his knife to its hilt in the prosecution's gut, and the messages he expected to see were there. Marcia Kittredge was practically orgasmic. James Sutter showed him a restrained nod of approval, and several of the others bordered on a smile.

"Consistent with that view," he went on, the vibrance of his voice deepening, "I shall spend but very little time with you. You have suffered the isolation that only a sequestered jury can know, and you have listened patiently to the evidence. You know more than I, in a sense, for while I have had to read what some of the witnesses have said in a printed transcript, you have sat through every word.

"It is not my function to tell you what you heard, and any lawyer who tries to do that for you insults your intelligence. Nor is it my function to review in tiresome detail all of the evidence, for you have listened to it. And you will find as your deliberations progress that

collectively you have retained all of it that struck your
minds as significant."

As he spoke, the sweep of his gaze continued to sur-
vey the fourteen faces before him for signs. Unlike the
multitudes of his colleagues at the trial bar who had
condemned themselves to be less than great by bringing
to the lectern reams of notes or prepared speeches to
sum up a lawsuit, Shaw worked only with his memory
and his wit, keeping his eyes ever on his audience. The
slightest quizzical brow, a mere change of expression
from a single juror, these would be a sign from which
he could shift and bear down on a point, paraphrase it
if he thought the first shot hadn't gotten through, or
shift his topic if he caught attention starting to drift.
The fascination evident on the countenances of the
small but nearly omnipotent group facing him indicated
that so far, he had them.

He leaned heavily on the definition of a reasonable
doubt and reminded the jurors sternly that each had
sworn in the process of qualifying that if he or she
found only a probability of guilt, the vote must be not
guilty. He ranged over the reasons that Kilrayne's testimony had not been necessary to the trial, so poorly had
the Commonwealth gone about the discharge of its burden of proof.

"This case," he said harshly, "has wasted invaluable
hours of the precious time of many, including yourselves. It has caused the deep anguish and personal hurt
that only Mr. Kilrayne and his loved ones can really
know. We have spent these many days, in the atmosphere of what was supposed to have been a murder
trial, hearing evidence of what must surely have been a
boating accident. From what you know of Sarah Hansen—and you know a great deal because of the nearly
endless string of friends and acquaintances who were
paraded to this witness stand before her body was
found—it must be very clear to all of you that no per-

son on the face of this earth would have cause to wish
that lovely creature physical harm."

He next turned to the subject of Frankie LaPere.
From Frankie's own lips there had been drawn—albeit
reluctantly—the best evidence of Michael Kilrayne's integrity. Kilrayne had, Shaw said, the one thing that
Frankie would never understand: a deep and unyielding
respect for an oath.

"Each of you," he said slowly and solemnly, "would
turn aside the word of Frankie LaPere if he merely
claimed that an honest citizen had stolen ten dollars. To
vouch for his story about talk of an assassination—as
Mr. Durham must do when I am through—is an insult
to your intelligence."

At the end of forty-five minutes of evenly paced and
brightly articulated speech, Shaw thought that he had
carried the ball well past the goal posts. A glance at
Kilrayne endorsed that feeling. There was a calm and a
confidence about his face that Shaw had not seen at any
prior time during the trial.

"You will listen carefully, I'm sure, to the words of
Mr. Durham. He is an accomplished lawyer, and will
no doubt make the most of what he has, little though it
be. But as he goes through his evidence, I am confident
you will detect two things: first, he has very little to say
and second, he is having great difficulty believing his
own words.

"When we have done, and Judge Somerville has
given you your instructions, our trust in your fairness
and your judgment will be total and absolute. As men
and women of the quality which rendered you acceptable to this monumental responsibility, I am confident
that you will review the evidence, discover together that
it is grossly lacking, and swiftly and thumpingly publish
that pearl of wisdom for which justice cries: that Michael Kilrayne be restored to his good name, and his
freedom."

Shaw thanked them and sat down.

Stacy saw that the ladies on the jury were as moved as she was. "They are in no mood," she whispered to Kilrayne, "to open their trust in Philip Durham."

Durham started from strength, pounding on the fact that the prosecution was worthy of deep trust; after all, he virtually shouted, they had proven circumstantially that Sarah was dead, and the truth of that claim had thereafter appeared beyond the point of dispute.

As to Frankie LaPere, sure he was a crook. "But," said Durham, "you don't invite the same people to a conspiracy to kill that you do to a wedding. If it were not for the LaPeres of this world, murder and other crimes would more often than not go unpunished."

For slightly more than an hour, Durham pounded away, using innuendo where he had little fact, nearly urging that Kilrayne had failed to prove his own innocence. When he came dangerously close to the point of saying that Frankie LaPere's story was "uncontradicted"—an argument that would in essence be a wrongful comment on Kilrayne's silence since on the evidence he alone could have rebutted Frankie's story—Judge Somerville barked suddenly, "Mr. Durham!"

"Ah yes, Your Honor, I was just turning to my next point."

After that, his momentum noticeably dwindled, and his rhetoric lost some of its steam. He was repeating himself, for he had run out of things to say. When he had finished, Shaw scanned the jury box. "I don't think," he said quietly to Kilrayne, "he even made a dent."

After recessing for a box lunch, which he ordered brought in for the jury, the lawyers, and himself, Somerville delivered his charge. By long tradition, he and the jury remained standing for the first few paragraphs, then were seated.

He defined the crime of murder, reviewed the concept of the presumption of innocence and the companion burden of proof resting on the prosecution alone. He translated the term "reasonable doubt"—the linchpin of the criminal justice system, into ordinary language that the average citizen might use in describing the degree of his own certainty.

Just short of sixty minutes later, he dropped his prepared text and looked at each juror in silence, building for the moment when he would conclude.

"Let me tell you where you are in blunt terms, Mr. Foreman and ladies and gentlemen. You are on one side of a deep and yawning chasm, called reasonable doubt. You stand next to the presumption of innocence, as you have throughout the trial. A verdict of guilty is on the other side. In order to reach that verdict of guilty, you must cross the chasm three times, something you will attempt only if you find three separate planks, each fashioned of good solid evidence persuading you beyond any reasonable doubt.

"Your first crossing will be in answer to this question: Did Ms. Hansen's death occur in the Commonwealth of Massachusetts? Are you persuaded of that fact to a moral certainty? If you are, your first crossing will be complete.

"The next question is, did Ms. Hansen die by accident, or was she killed? Was there a homicide here? If you are satisfied from the evidence that she was killed by criminal means—that is deliberately—you may cross a second time.

"The final question, should you get past the first two, is this: Has it been shown from the evidence that Mr. Kilrayne was responsible for the death? Or, if she *was* murdered, might it have been someone else. That will be your final plank.

"Should you cross that chasm three times comfortably and surely, it is your duty to convict. If you fail or even falter in any of these three attempts, then the pit of reasonable doubt is before you, not behind you, and you *must* return a verdict of not guilty."

"We will now draw lots to strike two jurors, who will remain in the custody of the bailiff until released by my order. Mr. Clerk, deliver the forms of verdict to the foreman."

39

THE TOOTH
Friday, September 22

The courtroom was abuzz as the crowd waited for Judge Somerville and the jury to come in. The press were all in their assigned seats, and spectators, including many lawyers and a couple of judges, took up almost every available square foot of floor space. When the bailiff called "All rise," a hush flooded the air.

Judge Somerville seated himself, and eyed the crowd. "Ladies and gentlemen," he said in deliberate and stern tones, "I appreciate the fact that your very attendance at this stage of the proceedings is evidence of the tremendous public interest in the outcome of this case. That is as it should be. Only by operating under the continual critical scrutiny of the public and the press can our judicial system fulfill its aim to serve justice in the broad sense.

"On the other hand, inherent in the job of exercising the awesome power of a trial judge is a duty to apply well-settled legal principles even though that action may not meet with popular approval.

"This court is about to call the jury in, and to learn and publish their verdict. I will tolerate no demonstrations and no outcries of agreement or disagreement with the verdict, whatever it may be. Any person in this room who violates this order will be in contempt of this court and will be summarily arrested and removed by the bailiffs. There are, at my request, seventeen bailiffs present, only five of whom are in uniform.

"I realize that some of you may, by reason of close personal association with the defendant, the deceased, or possibly some witness, be unable to avoid an emotional reaction to the verdict. You are not to be criticized for a human failing, unless having been forewarned you elect to stay in this courtroom despite your knowledge of such a predisposition. I will allow thirty seconds for any persons in the spectator section who fear such a possible loss of control to leave the courtroom."

No one so much as shuffled a shoe as thirty long seconds of uneasy silence ticked by.

"Very well," said Somerville. "The record will show that all of those now in the courtroom have by their presence evinced an understanding of this court's order and an intent to obey it to the letter.

"When the jury has reported," he went on, "I will have a further order to publish." At this point Judge Somerville held up a white number ten envelope, franked with the official address of the Essex County Superior Court.

"In fact," he said, "two orders. The court will require total silence until their publication is complete. Then, and only then, will persons be permitted to leave this room. As a courtesy to the press, who have maintained generally a commendable decorum throughout this trial, during the first sixty seconds after we have recessed only those with press credentials will be permitted through the exits. This special privilege is a recognition of their duty to make a timely report to their respective organizations, and also in recognition of the limited number of telephones in this courthouse. Perhaps," he went on, "this arrangement will provide an informative indicator of the extent to which the women's liberation movement has intruded upon the chivalric principle 'Ladies first.' I say that having taken appropriate notice of the fact that many of our press representatives are ladies."

The tension of the courtroom was broken by a spontaneous outbreak of appreciative laughter, which rose quickly and then faded like a cat's paw breeze on a glassy sea.

"Like all judges," said Somerville, "I will ignore breaches of my order for silence which are the product of a meagre attempt at humor from the bench. But the time for humor is ended. We will take the verdict now. Bring in the jury."

Daniel Shaw felt the tension of the moment. He thought, no one who has ever heard those words spoken in a real courtroom in an important case can possibly appreciate their impact on the human sensibility. The lawyers and parties to the case are full of the fear of losing. The court personnel and press, veterans of the shattering electricity of jury verdicts, are waiting, like gamblers during the critical moments of a horserace, to see whether their bets will be vindicated by the result.

The public spectators, stiffened by conducted rigidity from others, find their loyalties between the underdog defendant and the majesty of the prosecution suddenly swiveling.

And the judge—in this moment, Judge Gary Somerville of the Superior Court—is the most rigid of all in a sense. He hopes with all his heart—if he is worthy of his office—that the verdict of the jury will comport with what he, in his wisdom, believes the result ought to be.

As the jury filed in, the lawyers and the press scrutinized each of them for one of the time-proven signals telegraphing their result: either the suppressed flicker of a smile, a sure sign of an acquittal, or a stony-faced looking-at-the-floor advertisement of a conviction.

The members of the jury were totally inscrutable.

The jury stood in its box.

"Mr. Foreman, has the jury reached a verdict?" intoned the clerk.

"We have," said James Sutter, holding up the verdict sheet.

A bailiff handed the sheet from Sutter to the clerk, who glanced at it briefly and handed it to Somerville. Somerville, straining every fiber of his being to appear as dispassionate as he had required his audience to be, nodded expressionlessly at the clerk and handed the sheet back to him. "You may publish the verdict," he said.

"We the jury," said the clerk, "find the defendant, Michael Kilrayne, not guilty of the charge and the indictment. So say you, Mr. Foreman, and so say you all, ladies and gentlemen of the jury?"

The jurors nodded their heads almost in unison, and several of them mouthed an audible "Yes."

Just as Barrett felt his chest suddenly empty of air, Shaw and Stacy and Kilrayne especially felt the electricity of vindication.

There was a ripple of reaction from the others in the courtroom. It faded abruptly as Somerville loudly unsealed the white envelope containing his orders, with a rip of his thumb.

Somerville smiled at the jury and totally ignored the rest of the courtroom. "Thank you, ladies and gentlemen," he began, "for your patient and faithful service in this case. The accused, Mr. Michael Kilrayne, is discharged and free to go without delay."

Somerville nodded at Kilrayne.

"I think," he went on, "that before you are released to return to your loved ones and your homes, you ought to be advised of an order of this court entered under seal contemporaneously with the commencement of your deliberations. Please be seated. This order indicated that it was signed and sealed, and given to the custody of the clerk, less than an hour after the jury had been given the case. It reads as follows:

At the conclusion of the evidence in this case, counsel for the defense made and persuasively argued a motion asking that this court direct a verdict of not guilty on the ground that the evidence supporting the charge of murder—the only charge in the indictment—was palpably insufficient. Nonetheless, the court denied this motion, notwithstanding its apparent merit, in the belief that both the community and the defendant would be well-served by having the judgment of a jury. I do not retreat from that belief.

When mistakes by juries *do* occur, it becomes the awesome duty of the trial judge to seemingly defy the community voice of the verdict and set it aside.

Sadly, in my years as an advocate, I have more than once seen trial judges backwater in the face of such a duty and allow an improper verdict to stand, even though they knew in their minds and hearts that it should not.

I believe that I should not confront that sort of dilemma in this or any other case. I therefore order, should there be a conviction in this case, that the jury's verdict be set aside and that a judgment of acquittal be entered and recorded.

I have done so on the ground that the evidence in this case is plainly insufficient to show that Miss Hansen's death was criminally caused, or that Mr. Kilrayne had anything to do with such cause, if there was one.

There was a general smile of approval from the jury box and more than one nod.

"Before I release you to leave, ladies and gentlemen," Somerville went on, "I have one more brief order to enter and publish. During the trial a remark made by this court to counsel in chambers was published in a local newspaper. One of counsel in this case voluntarily made known to me that this breach of security was the product of inadvertence on his part. I have carefully considered the imposition of sanctions against him, and have concluded that none are warranted. His overall conduct of his part in this case reflects substantial credit upon the bar.

"This court," said Somerville, "is now adjourned."

When Judge Somerville had left the bench, the press representatives streaked appreciatively for their phones, ahead of the pack. Spectators lunged forward to the bar enclosure to try to shake the hands of any of the defense team they could accost. Durham, Gilardi, and Barrett left through the side door, unheralded and without congratulations. When the sixty-second press advantage had expired, no one hurried to leave the courtroom. They moved, like a school of fish, swarming to be near the defense team, or any of its members. Watching them, Daniel Shaw thought, in America trials resemble a national sport, and the big ones, a World Series of sporting excellence. Those in attendance had just witnessed the annual Super Bowl, and although not all truly applauded the result, while there was still a chance to press the flesh of the victors and then tell the neighbors about it over a boastful beer, applause was everywhere to be had. Vince Lombardi was right, after all: winning is the only thing.

Salvatore Corso had wished, hoped, even prayed that the legal system that he feared and hated would somehow chew up Michael Kilrayne and spit him out ruined for life.That would satisfy him, for his sake, for Angela's sake. Now, parked next to the curb around the corner from the entrance to the courthouse, he had been waiting for nearly an hour. When he learned of the verdict of his car radio, he shook with rage. The announcer himself had hinted that there was the possibility that Kilrayne had beaten the rap. The son of a bitch had gotten off.

For only a moment was Big Sal angry at God. God, he remembered, worked in mysterious ways. That is why he was here. Before this, he had only killed on orders.

He crossed himself.

Michael Kilrayne stepped before the microphones thrust in his face by myriad reporters for an impromptu press conference. He was surprised to find that although he himself had been the defendant, the feelings coursing his sensibilities were very similar to those he had experienced when taking verdicts for a client. The tension had been released as if a guitar string had suddenly snapped, as if he were a drumskin and someone had released the friction wing nuts along the perimeter, allowing the drumhead to sag.

Claudia Coleman, a striving but pimpled and overweight reporter for the *Lynn Register,* beat the others to the starting gate. Her manner reflected the resentment buried deep in her psyche that for all of her twenty-nine years she had been unloved.

"Mr. Kilrayne," she said acrimoniously, "Juror Kittredge had just said that the jury acquitted you on the ground that the Commonwealth had failed to prove jurisdiction. Doesn't that leave you with the impression that they may have thought you murdered Sarah Hansen, but let you off on a technicality?"

"I have not talked to the jurors, . . ." Kilrayne began, when he felt a nudge from Shaw. "May I?" said Shaw under his breath. Kilrayne stepped aside, as Shaw slid in front of the microphone.

"In answering the innuendo of Miss Coleman," he said in slow, deliberate articulation, so that none of the throng of media people could legitimately miss one word, "my client is ill-equipped to give a direct response since he was not present when Miss Kittredge was queried. I was no more than five feet away. First, Miss Coleman offered Miss Kittredge, on behalf of her newspaper, three thousand dollars for an exclusive interview *provided* Miss Kittredge would agree to speak with no other reporters for at least sixty days. Miss Kittredge said that she would like to talk with her parents before making any agreements and that she would not feel right selling a story about a serious public duty which involved many other people whom she respected. Miss Coleman then asked on what ground the jury had voted not guilty. Miss Kittredge said that the jury had agreed to examine first the strongest element of the Commonwealth's case, which was jurisdiction, and that their vote on that issue required an acquittal. The two other issues, she told Miss Coleman, the jury thought were a joke: they were not convinced that Miss Hansen's death was not accidental, and they didn't believe one word that LaPere uttered.

"During this conversation with Miss Kittredge, Miss Coleman repeatedly tried to push her away from other reporters. She did not succeed. I observed Mr. Walter Nyland of the Worcester *Herald* standing nearby and taking notes. He may be able to corroborate what I have just told you." Shaw stared at Nyland, and all eyes swung to follow his stare. Nyland, taken by surprise, cleared his throat as he clutched his notebook.

"That's about right," he said.

"Thank you," said Shaw. "I believe that Mr. Kilrayne has a statement to make, whereafter we will depart."

Kilrayne stepped back in front of the cluster of microphones.

"I have this to say," he said wearily, his eyes flashing dangerously nonetheless, "I have watched this so-called trial unfold with a sinking heart. There was no good faith in that courtroom on the side of the prosecution; there was blasphemy to the good name of justice, over and over again. If I had a grand jury, as the prosecution has in its back pocket, I would indict each lawyer and official involved who perpetrated this disgrace. I would also indict Mr. Carl Barrett, who prodded the entire charade into being. You know, all of you, that this was a phony case. Whether or not you take *your* powers seriously, as I have done. Had I not done so, I would not be before you now. I will answer questions at some later time. I will go now and spend some few moments in prayerful appreciation of the fact that whereas some have sought to rape every principle of justice in this case, they had no measures in hand to overcome the obstacles of a strong and decent judge, and a jury that they didn't dare to try to reach. Good night."

Five minutes later Kilrayne, Shaw, and Stacy Barton were standing on the front steps of the Essex County Courthouse, confronting the downpour of a heavy thunder shower. The skies were a dark gray, and it did not appear that there would be any immediate relief.

Big Sal could feel his anger in his chest, in his arms, in his face, as he watched the defense team on the front steps of the courthouse enjoying their victory.

"I'm the one who's owing," said Kilrayne, "so I'll get the car." With that he turned up the lapels of his suit jacket and began to trot toward his sedan diagonally across the street.

As Kilrayne began to move through the slanting rainfall toward the street, Big Sal saw his opportunity. He shifted the automatic transmission into drive and stepped on the accelerator so hard that his rear wheels spun momentarily on the slick pavement. He turned the corner, then stopped abruptly as he saw Kilrayne halt in midstep to let him pass. He smiled at Kilrayne and motioned him across.

Kilrayne nodded a thank you, put his head down and pulled his coat lapels closer across his chest, and jogged across the street in front of Big Sal's car, which had been stolen only a little over an hour before. As he passed clear of the left front fender, Salvatore stepped on the gas and pointed the sawed-off shotgun, which had been lying next to him on the seat under a towel on the driver's seat. Kilrayne was less than ten feet away when Sal pulled the trigger. The echo of the discharge reverberated through the interior of Sal's car, making it sound like two shots in rapid succession.

Kilrayne felt the terrible thump in his back and heard the sound at the same time. He crossed his arms in front of himself as if to contain the contents of his chest, dropping the keys to his car into the puddled street. His hands were suddenly filled with blood, and he was crumpling forward, everything in his vision turning gray, then nothing. The twelve-gauge buckshot had shredded his heart.

Several people in the rainswept street screamed, but none louder than Stacy Barton from the courthouse steps, whose eyes had been fixed on Kilrayne as, flushed with victory, he had trotted down the stairs and across the street to his doom.

Daniel Shaw was already heading toward the body.

Joe Gilardi, whose cruiser was inching out of the parking lot fifty yards from Big Sal's position, had heard the loud sounds in rapid succession and instinctively was out of the car and running. His car, driverless and still in gear, inched forward behind him.

When Sal floored his accelerator, and four hundred and twenty cubic inches of displacement in the big engine drove the huge vehicle forward again, he saw, too late, the cruiser, still in drive, moving slowly forward directly in his path, no one at the wheel. He smashed into it head on, and slammed forward against the steering wheel, knocking the wind out of his lungs.

When his vision had begun to clear a few seconds later, he looked up to see a heavyset man staring down at him through the driver's window, holding a snubnose .38 detective special only inches from his head.

"I'm a police officer," said Gilardi, "and you're under arrest. Why did you kill him?"

"My sister," gasped Sal, "he killed her."

"You mean Sarah Hansen?" said Gilardi incredulously. "She had no brothers."

"No, I'm Sal Corso," wheezed Salvatore. "He had my sister killed along with Eddie. A friend told me he got it straight from the big man, Gilardi, that's why. . . ."

Gilardi's mind spun like a wheeldex. He remembered a call from a young cop named Pete something, a kid calling a due bill. Gilardi had blamed the death of a young girl on Kilrayne, with absolutely nothing to go on. If that story got out, there would be nothing left for him at all, what with the result in this case. . .

"Hand me that weapon," he said harshly, indicating with the muzzle of his revolver what he took to be a shotgun with two empty chambers.

"Sure," said Big Sal, picking up his shotgun with his right hand. He was about to juggle it so that he could hand it to Gilardi stock first, when Gilardi shouted in a loud voice, "DON'T," and then shot Salvatore Corso in the head.

For a second Sal Corso, who had not fully recovered from the impact of the crash of his automobile, felt confused. A dull feeling spread through the left side of his head, but no pain. He forgot about trying to grasp the shotgun by the barrel, and continued to swing it slowly in Gilardi's direction. Gilardi, who had been sure a moment ago that it was an empty weapon, was stunned for a moment that the man he had just shot in the head was still moving. As the barrels of the shotgun turned toward his face, he panicked and shot once more, this time blowing a hole in Salvatore's face where his left eye had been. He reached in the window to grab the shotgun when suddenly he felt something hard in the middle of his back.

"Freeze!" said a hard, flat voice, "or I'll kill you. John Mellors, FBI."

"What the hell?" asked Gilardi, not comprehending.

"I am arresting you for traveling on interstate commerce and using the interstate wire to procure the prepared testimony of John McKiver in Danbury, Connecticut, on September 9, 1978. I will take the chance that you know your rights without me reading them to you. Why did you kill that man?"

"That shotgun," Gilardi stuttered, "he was swinging it and. . . ."

"Bullshit," said Mellors. "He was handing it to you as you had asked, and his finger was nowhere near the trigger guard. You may persuade a jury that you were defending yourself but not unless they disbelieve me."

For the first time in his life Joseph Gilardi learned the real feeling that accompanies the cold, ratcheting sound of handcuffs being locked into place.

40

FOR THE FILE
Monday, September 25

Shaw had arranged to pick up Everard at the hospital. They arrived together at Stacy Barton's office, at her request. They chatted briefly when told she was on the phone, glad that in the two days that had passed since Kilrayne and Corso had died, Everard, though pale and weak, had recovered and the police had completed enough of their investigation to say that Everard was free to return to England and Shaw to San Francisco.

As soon as Stacy was off the phone, she came out to greet them warmly and invited them in, closing the door behind them.

"What's up?" asked Shaw.

Stacy reached into a drawer and produced three envelopes. "These," she said holding them up, "are the reason I asked to meet with you."

"What are they?" asked Shaw.

Stacy shook her head. "I'm not sure. I'll tell you what little I do know, and then you can advise me what, if anything, we ought to do with them.

"Last June, Mike gave me the first envelope and asked me to put it in a safety deposit box in both our names. After putting it in, I was not to open the box under any circumstances except in the event of his death, in which case I was to deliver it to a man who would identify himself to me by giving me the ten-digit number on the flap." She held it up to show them the number.

"The second envelope was given to me in July and the third one four days ago. Each was placed in a different box in a different bank. Mike said he might need them some day, but he hoped not. He left no instructions as to what I ought to do with them if he were—unavailable." She choked a bit trying to avoid remembering the shotgun blast that still rang in her ears.

"I have a strong feeling that they have something to do with the case. I'm in a quandary as to what should be done."

"Has anyone come forward?" asked Everard.

"No one," said Stacy.

Everard tugged at his ear. "I think I know what one ought to do in England in these circumstances," he said, "but perhaps things are different in American ethics. What do you say, Daniel?"

"I don't know," said Shaw. "I don't think this situation was ever contemplated by those who drew the canons. I think we should open them, in order, with the understanding that we may be bound by any attorney-client secrets they may disclose."

"I agree," said Everard.

"I do too," said Stacy, sliding a silver letter opener under the flap of the first envelope. She looked at the sheets of yellow lined paper that had been folded inside, and said, "It's in Mike's handwriting. Apparently he didn't even want to share this information with one of our typists."

"Please read it to us," suggested Everard.

Stacy nodded. "It is entitled 'Memorandum for File,' and dated June 10, 1978. It says:"

Yesterday I was called at my home by a gentleman whom I shall call X for purposes of this memorandum. He asked me to come as soon as possible to Yarmouth, Nova Scotia, about a matter of life or death. I traveled to Yarmouth aboard his corporate aircraft and met with him in a suite at the Dunsmore Hotel. He had a tragic story to tell.

He stated that on the evening of June seventh, he set sail from Marblehead Harbor in a large sailboat which he had borrowed from a friend. With him was a woman named Sarah Hansen, who was going to accompany him to Yarmouth. I was surprised to learn that this was the same Sarah Hansen I had defended many years ago for driving while intoxicated, and whom I have visited on a social basis since.

He told me that soon after leaving the harbor, he set the autopilot on an easterly course and left Sarah to stand the first watch. She was supposed to wake him at midnight. He awakened at about five A.M., and found her missing. Evidence indicated that there had been a sudden wind shift and that the boom had swung suddenly across the cockpit and struck her, presumably on the head, knocking her overboard. He determined from a weather broadcast that the wind shift had occurred at about midnight and assumed that's why she didn't awaken him. She was not wearing her life jacket although he had instructed her never to leave the cabin without one.

He thought of reversing course to look for her and of calling the Coast Guard to ask for a search helicopter. He did not because the water temperature, which was forty-eight degrees, would have permitted her to have survived no more than two hours, three at the most, since she was not obese.

X is a person of position and wealth and is in the middle of a messy divorce proceeding. He confided to me that his reluctance to report the incident was based at least in part on his desire to protect both his business and his case. He asked me to advise him as to what his rights and obligations were.

I informed X that under these bizarre circumstances, lawyers might disagree as to what he ought to do. I advised him that while he had a duty to report the accident, he had a right under both the Massachusetts and federal constitutions not to incriminate himself. I told him that adultery was still a crime in this hypocritical state and that while people were seldom prosecuted for it, a person of his position might inspire a publicity-seeking prosecutor to charge him. I further advised him that it was possible that he could be charged with negligent homicide, since he had been drinking heavily that afternoon and evening—which he described to me—and had left a relatively inexperienced woman in charge of a rather substantial sailing ship. In all of the circumstances, I advised him that he had no obligation to say anything to anyone except counsel.

He informed me that there was one person who knew that Sarah had left with him and who would be expecting to hear from her. This woman—a close personal friend—I will identify as Y. He asked if I would inform Y of the incident. I explained that to do so would require that he waive the attorney-client privilege, which could be extremely dangerous for him. After discussion, I agreed to phone Y and to simply explain to her that Sarah had been the victim of an accident.

It is the principal purpose of this memorandum to protect X should he be implicated in Sarah's death. If anything should happen to me, he might be hard put to establish that he had remained silent as a result of competent legal advice. I intend to put this document in a secure place. Should he ever need it, I have made arrangements through Stacy to have it furnished to him should I die in the interim. In my judgment it would be perfectly admissible to show his state of mind as a result of the advice I have given him.

"At the bottom," said Stacy, her eyes misting a bit, "is his signature."

"Christ!" said Shaw.

"Extraordinary," said Everard, "most extraordinary. May we learn the contents of the next envelope?"

Stacy nodded, opened it, and again withdrew several folded sheets of yellow foolscap.

"This one," she said, "is entitled 'Commonwealth v. Michael Kilrayne.' It is dated July thirty-first, and reads as follows:"

Incredible as it may seem, this memorandum is being written not to protect my client, but myself. Carl Barrett's nitwit nephew, who is tragically the District Attorney of Essex County, has seen fit to indict me for the alleged murder of Sarah Hansen. The case against me is a joke, and although I am bitterly disappointed at having lost the services of my trusted friend Fred Osborne, he assisted me in engaging two of the sharpest lawyers I have ever had the pleasure to meet. While I take some comfort in this, I know better than most men that having a good lawyer does not guarantee the right result in our court system.

I have naturally discussed this matter with my client X at some length. He is horrified at what has happened, and while he scoffed at my suggestion that he just *might* be accused of criminal conduct as a result of Sarah's death, he now realizes that one who needs publicity to hold elective office will resort to any travesty of justice necessary to his purpose, and Walter Barrett is that person—prodded, no doubt, by his uncle.

I have looked for guidance as to what *my* rights and obligations are in the canons of ethics, and I find very little. The controlling language appears in a *footnote,* no less. It says, generally, that when an attorney is under attack himself, he may for the purposes of his own protection invade the attorney-client privilege to the extent necessary for the protection; he must, however, accomplish this invasion in a manner calculated to inflict minimum damage on the client whose privilege has been so invaded. This is the troublesome part.

There is virtually no jurisprudence on this legal issue. The only case I can find which even touches on the subject is that of *United States* v. *Friend,* in a pretrial ruling made by Judge Kevin Duffy of the Southern District of New York. In that case Judge Duffy ruled that Friend, a lawyer who had been indicted with his clients for mail fraud, had the right to testify concerning his conversation with those clients in order to show his own innocence.

While this decision endorses the footnote, and is reassuring to me, it does not solve my problem. First, X is not under indictment, and of course shouldn't be. Second, any disclosure on my part will harm his pending divorce litigation in a way that I can hardly minimize. Third, Judge Duffy is by reputation a far cut above the average, and since his decision was never appealed, I do not feel that I can necessarily count on similar treatment from the Massachusetts courts.

My dilemma, then, is as to what my duty is to minimize the damage to X. It is clear that I cannot compel him to testify though he is willing to do so, if I ask, and suffer the consequences. Under the circumstances, if I were to attempt to testify about my conversation with X in order to vindicate myself, I would probably be barred from doing so under our archaic rules of evidence in Massachusetts, since the conversation would be hearsay.

I have reached the following agreement with X. Because I believe fervently in the absolute protection of what a client tells his lawyer, I believe that my duty to "minimize" the damage in this case involves at least standing trial, and possibly going through an appeal as well. Before I am ever incarcerated, however, X has agreed to come forward with his evidence. I realize that there are risks involved in taking this stand. If I am convicted and thereafter produce this information, the prosecution may claim that it is a story fabricated in desperation. By placing these memoranda in safe-deposit boxes, I will at least be able to prove the dates on which they were written.

I am disturbed by the fact that this predicament will probably make it impossible for me to testify in my own defense, since accounting for my whereabouts during the days after Sarah disappeared would lead straight to X. Hopefully a directed verdict for lack of evidence will solve the problem. Indeed, it may be my only hope: I doubt that any instruction to the jury, no matter how forcefully given, can truly cause them to ignore the fact that a trained trial lawyer refused to testify in his own behalf.

It is discouraging to realize as I write this that sworn officers of the Commonwealth of Massachusetts have obtained perjured testimony to use against me. Sadly, there is very little that I can do about it.

When she finished reading, tears were running down Stacy's cheeks.

"Poor bastard," muttered Shaw. "What a spot to be in."

Stacy opened the third envelope.

"This one is also entitled '*Commonwealth* v. *Michael Kilrayne*' and is dated the day before the case went to the jury," she said. "It says:"

It was extremely difficult not to be able to tell Tony and Dan the real reason for my not taking the stand. I don't think they bought the grounds that I gave them for my decision, and I am afraid they may suspect that perhaps I am guilty.

My decision that I could not inform my trial counsel of the full details of my predicament turns on several hair-line points of law, for which, again, I can find virtually no precedent or guidance in any canon, statute, or decided case. First, X has not given me permission to divulge his problem to anyone, even other counsel, and I cannot in good conscience encourage that he do so, since I cannot guarantee what the result might be. Second, if I were to make such a disclosure, my counsel might well feel an independent obligation to place *something* on the record to protect my rights should there be a conviction. This might require that the prosecution's counsel be informed—I cannot predict that Judge Somerville, much as he has impressed me, would feel that he had the power to keep such a matter in camera, ex parte and under seal. He might indeed feel that the prosecution had a duty to investigate these new facts, and to exonerate me if they should prove out. This would of course make a shambles of X's life, when his only offense has been to seek and follow my legal advice. If I am condemned by these circumstances to explore new legal ground, it seems clear that my professional obligation is to bend in the client's direction rather than my own, and assume that the jury's verdict will be correct, thus ending the matter.

The jury looks fine from a defense point of view, but that could change rather dramatically when they learn that we will offer no evidence. My reading of Judge Somerville is that he is very close to granting a directed verdict, but is fearful of the consequences in the media should he do so. I suspect that he will not, even though he is troubled by the paucity of the evidence against me.

I have sweated out many verdicts with clients, and it is

never easy. This one will be the toughest of all. For no
logical reason, I have an ugly sense of foreboding about
what the future may hold.

Stacy let the letter drop onto the table.

In the silence that followed, Everard slowly shook his
head. Finally he said, "These three letters prove beyond
anything that our friend Michael was a brilliant lawyer."

"As well as a good guy," added Stacy.

"Yes," said Shaw. "It's a pity Patricia Perrin doesn't
do profiles of good guys."

"Sometimes she does," said Stacy, looking straight at
Shaw.

Everard sensed his responsibility as the senior of the
three. "At first I was tempted that we should consult
Osborne about those letters, but I think that since the
trial was passed to us, this decision is now also. What
do you think, Daniel?"

Shaw felt for a moment as if he were a witness and
Everard were examining him. "My temptation," he
said, "would be to lock up the first one in case X ever
needs to use it."

"We're not jurors," said Everard. "Let's think of the
possibilities."

"Well," said Shaw, "the prosecutors will never indict
X and admit they were dead wrong about Mike. But
they'd have to if they came across these documents by
whatever means. These letters are more dangerous to
X than valuable."

"Good," said Everard. "And so?"

"I would destroy them," said Shaw.

"I'd love to let the world know what the truth really
is," said Stacy, "but we'd feel Mike's fury straight from
heaven if we ever violated a client's confidence."

"And so?" asked Everard again.

Stacy looked at Shaw for support. He nodded.

"I'll burn them," she said.

There were too many pages to fit into an ashtray. The only thing in her metal wastebasket was the morning paper. She removed it, crumpled the pages of the three letters, and dropped them in. Daniel supplied the match. In less than a minute, there were only ashes in the bottom.

Shaw was already on the phone to Sam Watkins, luring him away from the delights of Boston's Combat Zone for the flight back home.

When he hung up, Everard shook hands with each of them in turn. "I hope British Airways has an empty seat from Boston tomorrow," he said. "You have an interesting country," he added. "I'll be back soon."

ABOUT THE AUTHOR

F. LEE BAILEY is the prominent defense attorney known for such celebrated cases as the Boston Strangler, Patty Hearst, Dr. Sam Sheppard, Dr. Carl Coppolino, and Captain Ernest Medina.

He was born on June 10, 1933 in Waltham, Massachusetts, graduated from Kimball Union Academy in New Hampshire in 1950, and attended Harvard College. He left Harvard in 1952 to enter the military as a naval flight trainee. Awarded Naval Aviator Wings in 1954, Bailey served as U.S. Navy fighter pilot and legal officer in the United States Marine Corps until late 1957. Bailey then returned to Harvard and was graduated in 1957. Earning his law degree at Boston University Law School in 1960, he was admitted to the Massachusetts Bar in the same year. He was admitted to the Federal Bar in 1961 and then to the United States Supreme Court in 1964.

Bailey's professional credentials include former chairmanship of the Penal Reform Committee for the Association of Trial Lawyers in America and co-chairmanship of this association's Criminal Law Section. He is now the co-chairman of the Foundation for the Advancement of Inmate Rehabilitation and Recreation and a faculty member of the American Institute of Hypnosis in California.

Bailey is the author of three bestsellers: *The Defense Never Rests, For the Defense* and *Cleared for the Approach*. In addition, he co-authored the eight-volume Criminal Law Library Series with attorney Henry Rothblatt, including: *Fundamentals of Criminal Advocacy; Investigation and Preparation of Criminal Cases, Federal and State; Successful Techniques for Criminal Trials;* and *Crimes of Violence, Homicide and Assault.*

A flying enthusiast, Bailey is the president of Enstrom Helicopter Corporation in Menominee, Michigan. He holds commercial, multi-engine, instrument, rotorcraft, and Lear Jet ratings, with over 12,000 flying hours logged.

Bailey has hosted ABC-TV's "Good Morning America" and has lectured at over 500 Universities and Colleges and to over 1,000 public associations and groups.

Secrets is Bailey's latest book and his first work of fiction.

Bantam Book Catalog

Here's your up-to-the-minute listing of over 1,400 titles by your favorite authors.

This illustrated, large format catalog gives a description of each title. For your convenience, it is divided into categories in fiction and non-fiction—gothics, science fiction, westerns, mysteries, cookbooks, mysticism and occult, biographies, history, family living, health, psychology, art.

So don't delay—take advantage of this special opportunity to increase your reading pleasure.

Just send us your name and address and 50¢ (to help defray postage and handling costs).